NICE AND EASY

BOYS OF THE BIG EASY BOOK THREE

ERIN NICHOLAS

NICE AND EASY

New Orleans firefighter, Caleb Moureu had to trade body shots and hot all-nighters for sippy cups and actual up-all-night fevers when his sister was killed, leaving his niece in his care. But two years in, he's definitely got the hang of this fatherhood thing. Of course, he couldn't do it without nanny-turned-friend and fellow single parent, Lexi. Because of her, things have always been pretty easy.

Getting pregnant and going it alone wasn't in Lexi's plans, but thanks to Caleb, she's doing okay. He's helped her out with everything from diapers to car repairs over the years. So, when she suddenly needs a place to live, of course Caleb steps up. That's just what he does. This is a simple favor, like everything else.

Until a hot kiss, the very first night under the same roof–of course– changes everything...

ISBN: 978-0-9998907-6-9

Editor: Lindsey Faber

Cover design by Angela Waters

Cover photography Wander Aguiar

1

"Hey, I have something of yours here."

Caleb shifted his phone to his other ear and pulled his truck keys from his pocket. "You do?" He hadn't been at Logan's for a few days and hadn't been missing anything that he knew of. "Like what?"

"Well, she's a gorgeous brunette, about five-three, big brown eyes, amazing breasts, and currently drunk off her ass," Logan told him.

Caleb stopped mid-stride. He cleared his throat. "That sounds a little like Lexi, except for the drunk part. And the you havin' her part."

Logan chuckled. "So you do acknowledge the amazing breasts part."

He wasn't stupid. Or blind. "Where are you?" he asked, instead of answering. Though he'd already turned in the direction of Trahan's Tavern.

Logan let Caleb avoid the topic of Lexi's breasts. For now. Caleb knew that wouldn't last. "The Tavern," Logan said, confirming he was at the bar he and his brother Gabe owned in the French Quarter. "And it's definitely her. Including the drunk part."

Caleb scowled. "What's she doing there?" Lexi rarely went out to bars. Not even to the tavern owned by their really good friends. She definitely never got drunk.

"She's with the ER crew from St. Mike's."

Caleb realized he was already partway down Decatur Street. The tavern was about a ten-minute walk. Eight if Lexi was drunk. Six if she was with the guys who worked the ER at St. Michael's Hospital. Caleb knew the ER crew over there well, and there were plenty of guys in that group who would think Lexi was, well, all the things she was—sweet and gorgeous, with a great laugh and a way of making a guy feel like he was about a hundred times smarter, funnier, and more talented than he really was.

Those bastards would think she was amazing.

"What the hell?" Caleb asked, dodging a group of tourists who stopped to look over the novelty tees in the doorway of one of the souvenir shops.

"They're buying her shots," Logan reported. "Apparently she did some amazing thing at work and they're congratulating her."

Caleb rounded the corner and nearly mowed over a group of early-twenty-something girls who were coming out of the praline shop. He sidestepped just in time but was hit by a cloud of perfume. One of the girls gave him an overly friendly, I'm-in-town-for-a-wild-weekend-wanna-be-part-of-it grin. He gave her a wink but kept moving. He didn't do tourist hookups. Unlike a lot of his friends who loved the female visitors who came to New Orleans looking for a good time with southern boys. Besides, those girls were *young*. They had to be barely drinking age. But then his scowl returned as he realized that they were Lexi's age. And, while her age had kept him from acting on his occasionally inappropriate thoughts, it sure hadn't kept him from having them.

"I didn't know she was working tonight," Caleb told Logan,

shoving all of those thoughts firmly to the back of his mind. "She was at my house, last I saw her."

Of course, that had been yesterday morning. On top of his usual twenty-four-hour shift, he'd put in another seven because of a four-alarm warehouse fire that had taken them all way past quitting time. He'd obviously let Lexi know he'd be late and the last he'd heard from her was "no problem."

Thinking about that, he pulled his phone from his pocket.

And sure enough, she'd texted him. Eight hours ago. *Called in to help in the ER. Bea's got the kids.*

It occurred to him, just now, that she might have been called in because of the same fire. There hadn't been any deaths but lots of injuries and smoke inhalation. So it made sense the closest ER might need some extra help. He'd have to get used to that. She'd only been done with nursing school and on the job for three months, but it was causing some need for scheduling adjustments and he suspected there would be more to come.

He turned off of Decatur, hoping to find a thinner crowd on one of the less touristy blocks.

Pretty much whenever he wasn't at his house, Lexi was. They took turns taking care of the kids—his four-year-old niece, Shay, and Lexi's two-and-a-half-year-old son, Jack—while the other worked. Bea was a sixty-something grandmotherly type—if your grandmother swore a lot, and had a terribly sarcastic sense of humor, and had no delusions about her grandchildren being sweet and perfect. She was, in fact, raising her four grandkids and was one of many friends he and Lexi shared from the single parent support group they belonged to. She was also one of their fill-ins when their work schedules overlapped. They had plenty of people able and willing to help out here and there, but Caleb and Lexi were the other's support 99% of the time. They both had crazy shifts with long hours and the chance of being called in almost any time. When they'd found each other and teamed up to help with the childcare issues, it had been a match made in heaven.

"Well, she's a huge hit with these guys," Logan said with a chuckle. "But I thought maybe you'd want to know what was up."

Yeah, he definitely wanted to know where Lexi was. Especially if it involved a bunch of other guys and a lot of liquor. "It's five thirty-seven p.m.," Caleb said.

Though it sure as fuck didn't feel like it. It felt like he'd been working for, oh, about thirty-four hours straight. Which he had. He scrubbed a hand over his face as he waited on the corner for an SUV to turn in front of him. Who was he to judge Lexi and the crew being already past drunk? Long shifts did that to you. The adrenaline of those shifts sometimes made a couple of drinks the perfect way to unwind, and celebrating as a team was an important part of the work they did. You had to trust the people who were working with you and make quick decisions about life or death. Partying and laughing and relaxing together could be a great team-builder. He and the guys at Engine 29 did plenty of it. Or had before Caleb had become a single dad overnight.

He shoved that away. Along with the stupid surge of jealousy he felt over Lexi having a great time with a bunch of other people. That kick-him-in-the-gut jealousy happened sometimes, but it was just a by-product of his strange, should-be-simple-but-really-didn't-feel-simple relationship with the girl who'd been saving his ass for about two years now. *Another* by-product. There were many.

Caleb finally crossed St. Charles and headed for the front door of Trahan's. Gabe, Logan's brother and business partner, spotted him through the wide-open French door and lifted a hand. Gabe didn't seem surprised to see him, so Caleb assumed he knew Logan had called. Gabe pointed toward the bar.

Caleb's gaze followed Gabe's finger. To Lexi. Where she was sitting *on* the bar. Laughing. And tipping back a shot. With three guys gathered around as if they were worshiping at her altar.

Yep, jealousy was definitely one by-product of their relationship.

Lust was another.

And the most complicated one.

Caleb just paused and took her in for a second. She looked fucking gorgeous. She was wearing a pale blue top that hung off of one shoulder, showing the thin strap of the white tank underneath, and her long dark hair fell almost to her ass in soft waves. That alone was enough to make him stop short. She never wore her hair down at home—at *his* home anyway—when she was there for twenty-four-plus hours with two kids under the age of five. She always had it up in a ponytail or a braid, whether he was just getting home from his shift, or she was dropping Jack off on her way to work.

He hadn't realized how long it was. He *had*, however, realized how much he wanted to run his hands through it. And how much he wanted to grab those ponytails so he could tip her head back and kiss her.

Dammit.

That kind of shit made him crazy. He wasn't some dirty old man who could only get it up for sweet, young things. He did just fine...more than fine...with women his own fucking age. A couple who were even older than him, thank you very much.

He started in her direction, but suddenly Gabe and Logan were both in front of him.

"Before you get all pissy and weird with me, you should know that I checked her ID. She's twenty-one, man," Logan said. "She'll be twenty-two in two weeks."

Caleb frowned at him. "No shit."

He should think it was funny that Logan felt the need to reassure Caleb that he wasn't serving Lexi underage. But Caleb's protectiveness of her was a well-known fact. And not really all that funny. It was serious. If someone did something that would potentially harm Lexi, he *would* be pissed. And he'd take it out on that person, no question.

Logan frowned, too. "You knew that she was almost twenty-two?"

Caleb lifted a brow. "Yes. I know how old Lexi is." Young. That was how old she was. Seven years younger than him.

Logan looked at Gabe. "I thought you all thought she was like nineteen, about to turn twenty."

Gabe nodded. "That *is* what I thought."

"You thought she was *nineteen*?" Caleb asked. Gabe had already been a member of the single parent support group when Caleb joined, a month after being named Shay's guardian. Lexi had joined two months later when Jack, her baby, was a month old. He'd always thought it was interesting that they'd both lasted one month before realizing they needed support.

"That's what Addison told me," Gabe said with a shrug. "I'd never really thought about it. I knew she and Ashley were both young."

Addison was Gabe's wife, but first she'd been a part of the support group, too, right after moving to New Orleans. "Ash is nineteen, almost twenty," Caleb confirmed. "Lex is older by a couple of years."

"Thought it was the other way around," Gabe said, scratching his jaw. He looked at Caleb. "So why have you been so adamant about not starting anything with Lexi?"

"You thought I was lusting after a *teenager*?" Caleb asked. He shot a glance around and lowered his voice. She was young, but holy shit. "Jesus, man."

"Well, in Gabe's defense, that's the first time you've admitted to the lusting after her part," Logan said, grinning a grin that often made Caleb want to pop him in the mouth.

Caleb ignored that. He had never admitted it, but his friends knew that he had a soft spot for Lexi that was a weird combination of protectiveness that he only felt for her and Shay and Jack, an addiction to how she saw him as her hero, and yeah, a dash of lust. Or a fucking gallon of lust. The girl was all soft skin and silky hair, with eyes the color of his favorite bourbon, and lush curves. She always smelled like a mix of bubble gum and grilled cheese. Maybe a weird scent to be turned on by—okay, not *maybe*—but here he was.

"So all this time that you've been convinced that I have a thing for her, you thought she was barely legal?" Caleb asked. "For fuck's sake, you guys."

He'd known Lexi for a little over two years. That meant these guys thought she'd been seventeen when they'd met and then eighteen for most of the time she'd been coming to his house and driving him crazy.

"I thought that was why you weren't acting on it," Gabe said, putting his hands up.

"She was my *babysitter*," Caleb ground out. "She *worked* for me."

"She doesn't anymore," Logan pointed out, ever helpful. "You don't pay her anymore."

Caleb sighed. That was true. He hadn't paid her in over a year. He hadn't technically paid her at all, but it had taken him several months to catch onto the fact that Lexi returned all the money he gave her. She'd either put it straight back into his wallet, or she'd leave it around the house in drawers, or put it in random envelopes and stack them with his monthly bills. When he'd figured that out, he'd told her to knock it off, so she'd started buying things. Mostly for Shay—clothes and toys and books— but sometimes for him, too. He'd find a shirt hanging in his closet he didn't remember buying, or a package of steaks in the freezer that he didn't remember grabbing at the store. When he'd figured *that* out and told her to stop, she'd insisted that he did as much for her and Jack as she did for him and Shay. They shared laundry duties, took turns grocery shopping, and obviously shared childcare responsibilities. Caleb also took care of her car and did minor repairs around the house she shared with her mom. She'd insisted they were more than even. So he'd finally stopped paying her. Grudgingly.

But he still knew that he had some...power over her. He'd stepped into her life when she'd been a brand-new, young single mom and had helped her out with her piece-of-shit car. He'd offered her a job and free childcare when she was struggling to make ends meet. He'd offered a girl who had been raised by a single mom and whose baby daddy had bailed, a look at a decent, nice guy who she could count on. No way could he make a move on her. Did he think she'd say no? Definitely not. But any feelings she had for him were mixed up in gratitude and a little bit—or a lot—of hero worship.

He loved being her hero.

"She has me up on this pedestal," he finally said to the guys. "I can't take advantage of that."

Gabe nodded. "I guess." He didn't look convinced.

"That does *seem* easier," Logan agreed.

Caleb didn't appreciate Logan's emphasis on *seem*. It *was* easier to keep his hands to himself where Lexi was concerned. No matter how much he'd love to put his hands on her. All over her. Over and over again. That's not what she needed from him.

He cleared his throat. "Yep. The way it is, taking care of her is easy."

And he really fucking needed something to be easy today. Work had not been. The call from the doctor's office following up on Shay's tests had *not* been. He really needed Lexi to be easy right now.

He heard the laughter coming from Lexi's little group of minions and he straightened. "Thanks for the call. I have a group of jackass ER dudes to disappoint." He started in Lexi's direction.

Lexi saw—or felt—him coming. She lifted her gaze from the guy right in front of her to Caleb's when he was halfway to the bar. And her face lit up.

There. *That.* That was what he wanted. He didn't need anything more from her than that.

Lexi was always happy to see him. He could be an asshole. He could be a hard-ass. He could be less-than-chivalrous. His work often required him to bark commands, physically move people out of his way, and tell people when they'd fucked up. He was the Lieutenant for Engine 29 and that meant he gave orders. Orders that he couldn't soften up or explain in detail. It was "do it and do it *now*" stuff.

And when it came to women, the ones he hung out with didn't need, or expect, romance. They wanted a good time and he gave it to them, without a lot of sweet talk or gallantry required. He was pretty straight-to-the-point with women, too. And the ones who came back for more, liked it.

But he was a different guy with Lexi.

He was kind and patient and generous. He was fucking *sweet* to her. He had a hell of a time saying no to her, and when he was around her, he found himself buying the Caleb-is-amazing stuff that she so clearly believed. For a little over two years now, he'd soaked up her admiration and just how damned happy she always was to see him.

Lexi was unlike any other female he spent time with. She was special. He needed to treat her that way.

And lusting after her did, in fact, make him a dirty old man.

"Caleb!"

He came up behind one of the guys gathered around her, and Lexi hopped off the bar. She wobbled slightly when she hit the floor, but there were three guys *right there* to grab her and keep her upright.

She gave them all a dazzling smile. *His* dazzling smile, as a matter of fact, Caleb thought with a scowl. She gave *him* that smile and he'd, apparently, thought it was just for him.

He moved forward, extricating her from the other men's holds and pulling her away slightly.

"I'm so happy to see you! What are you doing here?"

And suddenly she had her arms wrapped around his waist, her cheek against his sternum, and her breasts pressed against his diaphragm. Which had to have been why he was suddenly struggling to take a deep breath.

They never hugged. In two years of shared childcare, chores, and being in each other's lives, and homes, several times a week, they had never hugged. They were always picking up or dropping off kids and armfuls of supplies. They spoke for a few minutes about the kids, their schedules, anything that had happened. But they didn't linger. They didn't have in-depth conversations. They didn't talk about themselves other than when their next shift was. Until support group night. Thursday nights, they spent two hours together talking about the challenges of parenthood and what was going on in their lives—like finishing nursing school and the loss of one of his fellow firefighters. But they were hardly alone there, either. The support group had several other members who had become not just friends, but family.

So yeah, he and Lexi had never hugged. He'd never felt her breasts against his chest, her hips in his hands. He'd never been close enough to bend and kiss the top of her head.

Which he didn't do now, either. But it was by sheer force of will.

They needed to get back to not hugging really soon.

"You okay?" he asked, hesitating for just another few seconds, because dammit, those breasts felt really good right where they were.

She tipped her head back to look up at him, but she didn't loosen her hold on him.

Her grin was wide and infectious. And a little drunk. "I'm *so* good," she told him.

"What's going—"

"She's a fucking champ," Zach Christy, one of the residents in the ER, and one of the guys who'd been standing around Lexi like he was paying her homage, said.

And that was saying something about Lex, because Zach pretty much thought *he* was a god.

"Oh yeah?" Caleb didn't mind keeping his hands on Lexi, and hers on him, while Zach looked on for a moment. "What happened?"

"She stepped in, no fear and—"

"I pulled a shish kabob skewer out of a guy's cheek!" she said over the top of Zach's explanation.

With another of those bright grins that Caleb had thought were reserved for him.

Her eyes were sparkling and wide and Caleb had to actually hold himself back from kissing her right then and there.

Damn. This happened from time to time. Usually when she was all excited over something one of the kids had done. When Shay got her ABCs right the first time. When Jack had said, "Mama". When Shay had told Lexi she loved her. Every time she was so fucking gorgeous, it made him ache. And when Jack had taken his first steps, Caleb had actually lifted a hand, intending to cup the back of her head and pull her in. He'd stopped himself and scratched his nose instead, but it had been *really* close.

There was something about her unabashed emotions that got to him. And probably the fact that her emotions were almost always happy or excited. She made him smile. Every time he saw her.

She also made him want to push her up against the wall and kiss her senseless, and cup one of her magnificent breasts in his hand.

Caleb took a huge breath and let go of her. As much as he liked the way Zach's eyes narrowed checking out how Caleb held her, he needed space. She wasn't actually his to hold like this. And he didn't want Lexi getting any ideas.

She had a crush on him, but what they had, the relationship

that allowed them to both raise healthy, happy kids while going to school and working demanding-but-amazing jobs, was the most important thing in his life and he could not fuck it up.

He set her back but gave her his full attention. "A shish kabob skewer? Seriously?"

She moved back a few inches and nodded. "Yep. Guy's best friend stabbed him with it at a barbecue and it went right into his *cheek*!"

Caleb nodded. "I could imagine doing that to some of my friends."

She laughed. "Liar. But yeah, it was sticking out of his face and he was yelling—so I knew that he didn't have any nerve damage—but he wouldn't sit still because he's still pissed off at his friend."

"He left the skewer in his cheek? He didn't try to pull it out himself?" Caleb asked.

She nodded, clearly enjoying the story. "Because he wanted "professionals" to see what his friend did. He *drove himself* to the ER."

"No one came with him?" Caleb couldn't help but be caught up in the story. Firefighters, cops, and ER staffs had the most outrageous stories and they loved to sit around and one-up each other with them in social settings. He'd never done this with Lexi, though. It hadn't even occurred to him that they *could* do this.

Lexi shook her head with a little laugh. "He was pissed off and just got into his truck and drove himself down. His friends showed up right behind him, but he didn't want to talk to any of them."

"So somebody had to get him to sit still and let them take the thing out, and Lexi stepped right up," Zach said.

Caleb watched as Lexi gave Zach a pleased, sort-of shy smile. It was clear that she liked Zach's praise, though. Caleb frowned, but smoothed his expression quickly when she looked back to him.

"Yeah, I started telling him about the time I pulled a butcher knife out of a guy's shoulder."

"You pulled a *butcher knife* out of a guy's shoulder?" Caleb interrupted. He'd never heard that story. But come to think of it, he hadn't heard any stories about her work. He knew she loved her new job, but they didn't spend time talking about specifics.

That was too bad. Because this girl? This excited, proud-of-herself, amused, and confident woman standing in front of him? She was the most beautiful thing he'd ever seen.

Lexi laughed. "Yep. Last week. But—" She glanced at Zach. "I might have embellished it a bit."

Zach laughed. "Or a lot."

Caleb shook his head. Okay.

"So anyway," Lexi said, turning back to Caleb. "I was talking to him and making the story really dramatic and gory, which totally shut him up, and then I just leaned in and pulled it out. The guy barely flinched!"

Caleb felt his eyebrows rise. He looked at Zach. "Yeah?"

"Yep." Zach grinned at Lexi. "She leaned in with those big brown eyes, smelling like bubblegum, and the guy was in his happy place."

Caleb frowned. She did smell like bubblegum, but he'd always assumed it was because she'd just given Shay a bath with the bubblegum bubble bath his niece loved. Lexi smelled like that *all the time*?

"You flirted with him to get him to hold still?" Caleb asked her, suddenly wanting his hands back on her.

She tipped her head. "How is telling a guy about cut-up muscle tissue and blood, flirting?"

Because if she leaned close again, *he'd* definitely forget all about blood and other unpleasant things. That was the effect Lexi had on him. Her bright smile and stories about the kids and, yeah, the bubblegum smell, took away any smoke and ash and blood from his night at work. He hadn't realized until that moment just how much he loved going home to her. She made things brighter and happier.

And apparently, *that* wasn't all just for him, either.

"I guess not flirting exactly," Caleb admitted. She didn't do any of it on purpose. She wasn't greeting him at the door with her big smiles and bubbliness because she was trying to make his homecoming pleasant. It was just who she was.

Even when they'd first met, her cheerfulness had been present. There seemed to always be something going on that was making her life harder—her car breaking down, changes to her hours at the bakery where she'd worked before starting nursing school, Jack's colic. The girl hadn't been able to catch a break. And yet, she'd smiled and she'd made everyone in the support group feel like they were smart and impressive and doing an amazing job parenting. They all loved her.

"We were all so grateful she just took the guy on," Zach said. "She was calm, cool, quick-thinking and sweet."

And Lex freaking blushed.

Caleb felt himself scowling. Which was fine, because at the moment, Lexi was looking at Zach with a pleased, almost disbelieving expression. Disbelieving? She acted as if no one had ever given her a compliment before.

"We definitely want her around full-time," Zach said.

Who wouldn't want her around full-time?

"But you have to get her drunk to talk her into it?" Caleb asked.

Lexi looked up at him then and he had to pretend he'd been joking. He gave her a little smile.

"This is my *celebration* party," she said. "They just moved me from the float pool to the ER full-time. I *want* to work in the ER," she told him. "It's so exciting!" She glanced at Zach. "I think I've got quick reflexes because of Jack. You have to learn to move fast with a two-year-old."

Zach laughed. "I'll bet. And you have to be good at thinking fast and being sweet but firm at the same time, right?"

She grinned and nodded. "I guess I did kind of treat that guy like a toddler."

Zach reached out and squeezed her upper arm and Caleb had to hold back from pulling her away.

"I'd say 99% of the guys who come into the ER can quite effectively be treated like toddlers. If they're not drunk, they're in pain or sick and you know men can be huge babies when it comes to that. Especially self-inflicted pain."

Caleb couldn't argue with Zach's assessment. The fire department responded to far more medical calls than fires.

"And," Lexi said, looking up at Caleb. "I can make more money down there and work my way up to the *helicopter*."

He knew St. Mike's had a medical helicopter, but he'd had no idea that Lexi was interested in that. But hell, he hadn't even realized that Lexi wanted to work in the ER. She'd been in the float pool for the past few months, which meant she was assigned to cover whatever unit needed extra help during her shift. He'd thought she was happy with seeing a little bit of everything and getting a lot of varied experience. But, he realized, he hadn't *known* that she was happy there. He'd just assumed.

"Wouldn't that be cool?" she asked him, her eyes bright.

It would be kick-ass. And he was having a hard time picturing Lexi at a mass casualty event, flying in, dealing with the broken bodies and blood. He was having a hard time picturing her yanking a metal skewer out of a guy's face, too. But that was probably because when he saw her dealing with messes, they were of the mac-and-cheese or finger-paints-on-clothes or cupcake-frosting-all-over-the-kitchen variety. The times he saw her messy were colorful and sweet and with the kids. Not out at the site of a multi-car pileup where people were hurt and scared and bloody and dirty.

"Yeah," he forced himself to say. "Of course that would be cool."

And dangerous. And not even a little bubbly.

She grinned at him as if he'd announced she'd won some big contest. That grin. That you-are-the-best grin that she gave him was his fucking weakness.

"I have to have two years of experience first," she said. "But I'm moving to the ER right away."

"We definitely need her," Zach said.

Caleb shot him a look as Lexi glanced at him. *Back off, Zach.* It wasn't just the idea of talking Lexi into harder, more intense, and potentially more dangerous work. It was the tone in his voice that said maybe Zach didn't just like Lexi's nursing skills.

Or Caleb could have been reading all of that into the situation because he felt stupidly possessive of the petite-yet-curvy bundle of happiness.

"Maybe we should talk about blood and helicopters when you're sober," Caleb told her. "Might seem less cool when your brain isn't swimming in schnapps."

She turned back to him quickly and wobbled slightly on the heels she was wearing.

That was something else he never saw, he realized. The whole Lexi package tonight was throwing him off. With her hair down and her legs bare in short shorts and her feet in high heels and her eyes outlined with some kind of black something that was making them look bigger, he was having a hard time concentrating.

It wasn't as if he'd never seen her legs bare before. But, again, *this* skewer-pulling-blood-is-cool-hair-down Lexi was a sharp contrast to the Lexi he knew. That Lexi wore shorts but they were loose cotton. They went perfectly with her loose cotton T-shirts. The kind of thing you wore around the house when you were chasing two little kids and your day consisted of peanut butter and coloring books.

These shorts...they weren't loose. At all. They weren't cotton, either. They were denim. Tight denim.

"Not schnapps," Lexi told him. "Bubblegum shots." Then she looked back at Zach. And wobbled a little again. "Wait, is there schnapps in those?"

Caleb raised an eyebrow at Zach. He held his hands up. "Ask Logan. He mixes 'em. But no schnapps."

"And Logan just handed you a shot?" Caleb asked Lexi, who had turned back to him again.

Lexi shrugged and giggled. "Nope. Logan handed me *three* shots."

Caleb sighed. Three shots. That wasn't nothing, but he had a feeling it was going to hit tiny, never-drinks Lexi hard. "I think three's enough."

"It was actually four," Zach said.

"Four is definitely enough," Caleb decided.

She frowned. "I'm fine."

"Okay. Still, probably time to go get Jack and Shay," he said.

"Oh my God! Caleb!"

A woman's voice from behind him made him turn. It was Ana, one of the women he occasionally...hung out with. He'd met her here at Trahan's, as a matter of fact, and she lived in the Quarter, which made it convenient to...hang out after work once in a while.

"Hey," he greeted her warmly. Ana was a gorgeous redhead. She was sexy, independent, and smart, and he enjoyed spending time with her. Naked time. They had some laughs, but their relationship consisted of a drink or two and then an orgasm or two. It was very simple.

Caleb liked simple.

And now, standing between Ana and Lexi, he was struck by just how perfectly he had his life set up.

On one side, Lexi took care of things at home. They were raising their kids together, doing laundry for one another, sharing groceries, and helping each other with things like car repairs and potty training. It was nice. And easy. Being able to share chores and the run-of-the-mill daily tasks that needed done made his home life simpler; knowing Lexi was there with Shay and that the mail would be sorted and the toilets scrubbed made it easy for him to focus at work and not worry the way he would if Shay was with a babysitter or in a typical daycare situation. It also made coming home so much nicer. Chores were done, the house was running well, and he didn't have a to-do list to worry about.

And he did the laundry, toilet-scrubbing, grocery thing when he was off and Lexi was at work. It was like having a spouse to share the day-to-day burdens without the fights about money or trying to carve out date nights or arguing about where they were going to spend Christmas.

On the other side was his social life. That was simple and straightforward as well. He could spend a hot, fun, no-strings-attached hour here and there with Ana and not worry about her not giving him a blow job because she was pissed that he didn't get the dishwasher fixed.

Not combining his home life with his social/sex life was really quite perfect.

Nice and easy.

Exactly the way he liked things.

"I didn't know you'd be in tonight," Ana told him, lifting on tiptoe and pressing a kiss against his cheek.

"I didn't, either," he told her. "Just got off an extra-long shift."

"Need a beer to unwind?" she asked. Her hand was still resting on his arm and he felt the little squeeze that he knew meant she'd be up for unwinding him three blocks over in her apartment above the art gallery she managed.

And strangely he didn't feel the need to unwind after his shift. That was interesting. Usually after that many extra hours, he'd want exactly what Ana was offering. But he'd nearly forgotten about the shift. He'd been too focused on

Lexi and all the amazing things that were going on with her. "Actually came down to pick up a friend," he said. He glanced at Lex. The woman who made his home life so easy and steady.

She was watching him and Ana, her arms crossed, a frown pulling her brows together.

That made him straighten. What was that look about? She looked annoyed. Lexi almost never looked annoyed. And never at him.

It had never occurred to him before but it was true. She didn't get annoyed or mad at him.

That was part of what made their setup so great. There really wasn't anything for her to be annoyed or mad at him about. They had a very comfortable, mutually helpful, and supportive situation. Where Lexi thought he was a superhero.

He supposed that made him her...friend. Though that seemed like a strange term. It was more like they were co-parenting without a messy breakup or rough divorce between them.

And without the relationship, and sex, that had created the two little people they were parenting together.

He cleared his throat. "Um, Ana, this is Lexi."

"Oh, Lexi," Ana said with a smile. She held out her hand. "I've heard a lot about you."

Lexi's frown deepened. "You have?"

Caleb frowned, too. She had? He'd talked about Lexi to Ana? He supposed he'd mentioned her. But...why would he have mentioned her? Ana knew he was raising Shay, but that was about it, and he'd only mentioned his niece because she was the reason he rolled out of bed and got dressed shortly after "unwinding" with Ana. So when and why would he have talked about Lexi?

"I know that you're the reason he sometimes gets to stay out later with me," Ana said, dropping the hand Lexi hadn't shaken.

She glanced up at Caleb with a smile. "And I appreciate that you're always willing to babysit for Shay."

Suddenly Caleb felt very uncomfortable. Which was ridiculous because he and Lexi were...friends. Or whatever. There was no reason to feel awkward about her meeting a...whatever Ana was. She wasn't a girlfriend. She was a...fuck buddy.

He winced and looked at Lexi. She was watching Ana. And she looked, well, a little sick.

Caleb's first instinct was to do anything he could to get her smiling again. Oh, and looking at him like he was her favorite person in the world. Of course. Because he fed off of that shit. "I couldn't do *anything* I do without Lexi," he said. Truthfully. "Don't know what I'd do without her."

Lexi gave him a look that said, rather clearly, *really?*

He was fairly certain he'd never seen that look on her face, either. And she suddenly looked older. Was it the black eyeliner or the unfamiliar displeased expression?

"I love Shay," Lexi finally said to Ana. Her voice sounded funny. But she wouldn't look at Caleb.

"Oh, I'll bet she's adorable," Ana said.

Caleb didn't introduce the women he...unwound with...to Shay.

"She really, really is," Lexi said, with a sincere affection in her voice.

Caleb started to reply when she turned to Zach.

"I could *really* use another drink."

Zach nodded. "I've got you."

Caleb frowned as Zach steered Lexi to a barstool. He didn't like that Zach was the one intervening.

"I think it's time to go." Caleb wrapped a hand around Lexi's other arm and stopped her from climbing onto the stool.

"I'm going to have another stupid, sweet, kiddie bubblegum shot," Lexi told him. "You can go with Ana."

He didn't want to go with Ana. That thought snuck up on him

a little, but if Lexi was here, he had no intention of going anywhere with Ana.

A realization that would no doubt bother him tomorrow. But for right now, he wanted to get Lexi home. Where he understood her and how he felt about her and what she was in his life.

Maybe it was seeing her light up about her work—work that he hadn't even been aware she *wanted* to do—dressed in clothes that made him damned grateful she wore baggy stuff at home, and acting annoyed about Ana that made him feel like he needed to remind *himself* about everything. Or maybe it was watching her respond to the praise of other men. He knew he'd complimented her on the clay cats she and Shay had made last week. And the delicious pistachio dessert she'd baked the other night. But that wasn't quite the same as telling her she'd been kick-ass in a medical emergency today.

Caleb was *not* an asshole to her. He was the complete opposite, in fact. He was fucking sweet to her. Something that sometimes amused his friends and often amazed *him*. He helped her and took care of her and very much wanted her and Jack to be safe and happy. He did not take her for granted. He didn't think she was only good at doing Shay's hair or teaching the kids their colors and shapes. She was *really good* at all of those things. But he knew there was more.

Even if his next two thoughts were how good she was at disguising vegetables in casseroles and getting Shay to pick up her toys.

He grimaced. He did *not* take Lexi for granted. But he had a little trouble thinking of her beyond the house and kids. In his defense, that was where he saw her the most, and their happy domestic situation was the majority of their involvement in each other's lives. They were good together. He just didn't think of her as a skewer-pulling-flight-nurse. That didn't make him an asshole. He hoped.

"I don't think these are actually *kiddie* shots," Zach told her.

Josh, Gabe and Logan's other bartender, handed one over even though Caleb was preventing her from taking a seat at the bar. "Oh, they're definitely potent," Josh told her with a smile.

Lexi looked directly at Caleb when she said, "Well, they're not exactly mature or classy, right? They're the kind of thing you'd expect someone who likes PB and J more than any other food, has seen every episode of *Phineas and Ferb* a dozen times, and happens to be fucking amazing with a set of Legos to drink, right?"

Then she tipped the shot back and swallowed.

He hated all of this. For one thing, he'd never heard Lexi say the word "fucking". Then again, that was only one thing on a pretty long list of never-befores tonight. It was clear she was talking about herself—he'd come home to her watching reruns of the old cartoon, *Phineas and Ferb*, several times, and he knew she ate as much PB and J as the kids did. And she was, in fact, amazing with a set of Legos. Yeah, bubblegum shots seemed to fit her. But *he* hadn't ordered them for her. So why did he get the impression she was blaming him for something here?

He frowned. "I think five shots is *more* than enough."

Maybe Lexi was just a surly drunk.

He almost laughed at that thought. Lexi Scott didn't have it in her to be surly. But she was suddenly frowny and sassy—also things he didn't think she'd ever be.

"I can get her home," Zach offered.

"No," Caleb said immediately and firmly.

"I'll get an Uber and ride along," Zach said. "We'll drop her off on the way to my place."

"No," Caleb said again, simply.

"Lex?" Zach asked, ignoring Caleb. "You want to stay for a little longer?"

Lexi swallowed the shot and shook her head. "I'm good. I'm already home."

Oh baby, she was even drunker than he'd realized. "Lexi, I—"

"I'll walk her upstairs personally," Josh said from across the bar. "She'll be okay. Promise."

Josh had been bartending for Gabe and Logan for a while now. Ever since Gabe had gotten together with Addison and needed more family time at home. Josh's hours had increased as Logan also needed to be home before two a.m. every morning. Josh was a good guy. But Caleb wasn't going to let Josh take her upstairs. There was an apartment over the bar where Logan had lived prior to getting together with Dana and where Josh now crashed after he closed down the bar rather than making the twenty-five-minute drive back to Autre, the little bayou town where he and his family ran a swamp boat tour and fishing company.

"You're not taking her upstairs," Caleb said. He was sure his tone conveyed exactly what he thought of that idea. "*I* will take her *home.*" And he meant *his* home. She wasn't going to her mom's house, even if her mom was home. Lexi was now to the so-drunk-she-needed-a-babysitter stage. And if anyone was going to be babysitting a drunk Lexi, it was going to be *Caleb.*

"This *is* my home," Lexi said. Then she laughed. A drunk-giggly sound that made Caleb shake his head. "Josh sleeps on the couch."

"Well, you said that Jack is a wild sleeper," Josh told her with a grin. "I don't need a little foot kicking me in the balls in the middle of the night."

Lexi giggled again.

What the fuck was going on?

"You talked about sleeping in the same bed?" he asked Josh.

Josh might not be part of the support group, but he was a part of the group of guys—including his cousin and brother at times, along with all the guys from the support group and several members of Engine 29—who hung out at Trahan's. And all of those guys knew about Caleb's feelings for Lexi. Mostly because his friends loved to give him shit about it. Still, Caleb knew that

Josh understood exactly how Caleb felt about Lexi being in Josh's bed.

"Not really," Josh said. "That bed isn't very big and if we're not spooning, it just wouldn't work."

The idea of Lexi spooning with Josh sent one word through Caleb's mind.

Mine.

That was a problem.

Lexi laughed. "It's too hot in New Orleans for spooning," she said.

Josh gave her a smile and a wink. "If you're thinkin' about the weather, he's not spooning you correctly."

She laughed, and blushed, and Caleb slapped his hand down on the top of the bar. "What the fuck are you two talking about?"

Josh looked over, amused and not at all intimidated. "Lex and Jack are livin' upstairs. I crash on the couch on the nights I close up. Though," he said, looking back at Lexi, "I'm always happy to help if you do get chilly."

Caleb knew Josh had said that simply to get under Caleb's skin. And it worked. He gritted his teeth and focused on the woman on the stool in front of him. "You're living upstairs? What the hell is that about?"

She shrugged, running her finger around the top of the now-empty shot glass. "My mom and Greg got married and moved to Shreveport."

Caleb frowned. He knew who Greg was. Lexi had talked about her mom's boyfriend at support group before. Amber hadn't dated much at all while Lexi had been growing up, but now that Lexi was older, Amber had started seeing Greg. They were madly in love. And Greg thought Lexi was a burden on her mother. Caleb remembered when Lex had told the group about overhearing Greg trying to convince Amber to make Lexi grow up and get out on her own. She'd been hurt, but she'd admitted that he was right. She was old enough to start taking care of rent and things on her own.

Caleb had wanted to punch Greg in the face.

"When?" he asked shortly.

"Two weeks ago."

"You've been living here and your mom's been in Shreveport for two weeks?" he asked. She hadn't told him. He hadn't noticed anything was going on with her or was wrong.

Lexi nodded. "They didn't renew the lease for the house. I couldn't afford it on my own anyway. I needed a place to go and Ashley told Gabe and Gabe insisted I move in upstairs." She looked up with a smile. "And it's great. It's really close to work."

But it wasn't that close to his place. Where she came every morning, either to stay while he went to work, or to drop Jack off while she worked.

"You should have told me." His voice was gruffer than he'd intended.

"Why?" she asked. "It all worked out."

"You're not going to live above a bar," he told her.

"Why not?"

"Because..." It was a bar. Josh was sleeping on the couch. Jack was two. Her mom had moved away and essentially abandoned her. She'd never lived alone before.

All of those were ridiculous reasons. Josh was a good-looking guy who couldn't breathe without flirting, but he wouldn't make a move on Lexi. Lexi was a grown woman. There was no reason for her to not live alone. Her mom hadn't really *abandoned* her. She'd gotten married and moved to another town with her new husband. It wasn't like they'd never be in touch.

The truth was, he just didn't like it.

Because Lexi had had a problem and he hadn't been the one to solve it. But he'd never say that. So he latched on to the only reason that could even possibly be legitimate. Jack.

"Jack's two," he said. "You really think he should be living above a *bar*? And," he added, as the thought occurred to him. "The bar's open 'til two a.m. In the Quarter. No way are either of you sleeping well with the noise below and around you."

That had to be true. He'd been in the apartment over Trahan's. This was a two-hundred-plus-year-old building. It wasn't like the insulation was amazing. You could hear the laughter and music of the Quarter no matter what. A woman who needed to be up at five a.m. to get her and her son ready so she could be into work by six thirty couldn't be kept awake until two a.m.

"It's okay," she said. "It won't be forever. I'm saving up for another place. But for now, it's great."

Great meant it was free. Caleb knew that Gabe wouldn't be charging her rent and he appreciated that. But he did *not* appreciate that no one had told him about Lexi's situation.

"You're moving in with me," he said, before he'd fully, consciously formed the thought.

She looked at him with eyebrows up. "No."

Caleb stared at her. He couldn't recall Lexi ever saying no to him. "Yes." He said it low and firm. And because he was staring at her, he didn't miss the fact that her eyes widened slightly and her pupils dilated.

"This is fine."

"It's not." He sighed. "Come on. I have that huge house and you and Jack are there eighty percent of the time anyway."

She focused on the shot glass again. "I need to be out on my own. It's time."

Goddammit. Now she sounded almost sad. That was not okay. Lexi Scott wasn't sad. Or worried or anxious or stressed out or upset. In large part because of *him*. And this sure as hell wasn't going to be any different.

"It's okay to need people," he told her. Meaning, of course, that it was okay for her to need *him*.

She swallowed and didn't look at him. "I don't want to be a

burden."

Okay, that was enough of that. Her step-dad had gotten into her head. Caleb had met Lexi's mom a number of times. It had always just been Lexi and Amber. Amber had been a single mom, working hard to support her kid, so Lexi had needed to grow up fast, take care of herself to an extent. But Amber had always kept a roof over their heads and had paid all the bills while Lex went to nursing school. He didn't think Amber felt Lexi was a burden. But Greg, the guy who'd wanted Amber to himself, to have her able to take off on a weekend getaway or, yeah, move to Shreveport with him, would have probably felt that way about his girlfriend's adult child and grandson, who kept Amber tied to New Orleans.

Well, fuck Greg.

"You are the exact opposite of a burden to me," Caleb told her. His voice was low and firm. She looked up at him. "You know that."

She did. He knew she did. She knew *he* needed her. She took a deep breath and then nodded. "At least I do stuff for you."

And for a split second, Caleb's dirty-old-man mind spun off to the whole list of things he'd like her to do for him. He shook his head and said. "Let me take you home. My home."

He held his breath. He would pick her up and carry her out of here if needed, but he'd rather she choose to come home with him. She was drunk. She'd clearly had a big shift in the ER. She was dealing with some not-so-great emotional issues with her mom.

And he wanted to fix it all.

He wanted to see her lit up and happy and excited and giggly...with *him*.

And he could much more easily do that if she was at his house.

She finally sighed. She looked at Zach. "I guess I need to go."

Zach lifted a brow, but Caleb gave him a look that kept the

other man from saying anything but, "Okay, well, it was fun. You did great today."

With that, Lexi's face lit up again. A typical bright, glowy Lexi smile. That gave Caleb a definite sense of it's-gonna-be-okay. Except, of course, for the fact that it was directed at Zach. Until he'd seen it directed at someone else, Caleb hadn't realized how much he loved being on the receiving end of those sparkly smiles. Or how much he'd taken for granted *he* was the only one she smiled at like that.

Damn. Maybe he *was* kind of an asshole where Lexi was concerned.

"Thanks. It was a great shift," Lexi told Zach, sincerity clear in her expression and tone. "I'm so happy to be full-time now."

There was the happy, bubbly Lexi Caleb knew. The one that disappeared when she looked back to him. She wasn't frowning now, but her expression was resigned. Or something. Which bugged him just as much.

She even sighed as she slid off the stool. "Okay, we can go now."

"It's not a root canal," he muttered.

She rolled her eyes.

Yeah, bubblegum shots clearly made her surly. Or at least Lexi-surly.

"It was good to see you, Caleb," Ana said as they moved past her.

"You, too," he told her. It was always nice to see Ana. She was a gorgeous, sexy woman.

Ana gave him a little smile. "Hope to see you again *soon*."

But his attention was immediately jerked away from the sophisticated redhead and to the tiny brunette beside him when Lexi made a funny sound, almost like a growl.

He looked down. "You okay?"

"Great. Peachy. Fine."

Uh, huh. "Okay, let's go."

2

S he should argue.

There was a little place in the back of her mind where Lexi knew she should argue with Caleb about going to his house tonight. She should insist on staying and being on her own and actually run her life like a grown-up for more than two freaking weeks.

But she just...she sighed...she just didn't argue with Caleb.

"Where's the rest of your stuff?" Caleb asked, stopping by the passenger side of his truck. "Jack's bed and everything?"

"Storage," she said.

"Address."

She had to think about it through the cloud of schnapps surrounding her brain, but finally rattled off the address to the storage unit that held her stuff. Her mom's old stuff actually. Lexi didn't have much of anything that was really *hers*.

"Key."

She sighed, but dug in her purse and handed over the key to the unit.

"I'll have the guys pull Jack's bed out and bring it over. What else do you need?"

She could tell he was mad that he hadn't known anything about the situation. Concerned, too—Caleb was always slightly concerned about her and Jack. But she hadn't told him because, dammit, Greg had a point. She'd overheard her step-dad telling her mom to stop worrying about her. Amber had supported Lexi through her pregnancy and nursing school, but now she was finished and had a good job, and was old enough to take care of herself. She shouldn't be a burden on Amber anymore.

And he was right.

But the apartment over the bar had been the best she could come up with only two weeks' notice. Oh, and no money. But it was temporary. She *could* actually be independent. Maybe. Eventually. She blew out a breath.

The thing was, she didn't really want to be totally independent. At least not in the do-absolutely-everything-for-herself-and-never-lean-on-anyone sense. The single parent support group, the team in the ER, and yes, Caleb, all made her happy. She was a people person. She didn't feel bad about leaning on other people once in a while and she was there for them, too. She loved when she was the one that someone in the group called for help or when she got to step up in the ER. Going it all alone didn't work for her. She loved being a part of something bigger and wider than her own situation.

But should she be paying her own rent and stuff? Well, yeah. Probably.

"Lex?"

She realized her thoughts had been spinning. A combination of schnapps and...okay, mostly schnapps. And maybe the crash after an ER shift full of adrenaline. She shook her head. "Nothing. I don't need anything else." Caleb would have everything she and Jack needed. As always.

Caleb gave her a long look, but finally said, "Okay. Get in the truck."

Maybe she should pretend that she was only doing this

because he was insisting. But why? She wanted to go to Caleb's. He wanted her there. She and Jack were there so much of the time anyway and she loved being at his house. Going home with Caleb tonight made sense.

Besides, she didn't want to be alone.

She was good at a lot of things, but being alone was not one of them.

Okay, that wasn't entirely true. She *was* good at it. She had a lot of practice, after all. But she hated it. Now that she knew what it felt like to belong to a group, being alone was depressing.

She'd spent a lot of time alone as a kid. It had always been just Lexi and her mom. Always. Her dad had never been around. He knew about her but he'd been a tourist, in town for—cliché as it was—Mardi Gras. He'd gone home to Wyoming, of all places, long before Amber even knew she was pregnant. She'd let him know, but had told him he didn't have to do anything or give her anything. So he hadn't.

That meant Amber had needed to work two jobs—one with her social work degree and one as a waitress—to support them. Which left Lexi on her own a lot. They'd had neighbors who checked on her and who she could go to for anything she needed, but a lot of the time it was just Lexi hanging out by herself. She'd been fine. But she'd been lonely. And jealous of the people who had families. Who sat around and ate dinner together every night and watched TV together and talked about their days. Who made plans for the weekend and holidays. She'd had friends, for sure, but she couldn't be at their dinner tables every night or crashing their family outings every weekend.

But now she had the support group that shared the highs and lows and celebrated and cried together, and work friends—a team that did difficult, horrible, and amazing things together— and Caleb and Shay. And hell yeah, given the chance to live with Caleb and Shay, she'd take it.

Lexi looked up at Caleb. The guy who saved her time and again. "Thank you," she said softly. Sincerely.

There was a long moment where neither of them did or said anything.

Then, Caleb muttered, "Dammit, Lex." He reached up with both hands and cupped her face. "Why didn't you tell me about everything?"

She stared up at him. He'd never touched her like this. He'd never looked at her so...intently.

"We're okay," she said softly. She was exhausted and feeling sheepish about her aversion to total independence, but she had the instinctive need to reassure Caleb. She reached up and gripped his wrists. "We're good. And even better now."

He stared down at her, his jaw tight. Then he gave her a nod, dropped his hands, and stepped back.

Lexi took a deep breath. Damn. This guy did something to her. His protectiveness had been a turn-on since the first time he'd said, *I'm going to take a look at your car. I don't want you driving it until we know it's not gonna let you down.*

It was that "we" he'd thrown in there. As if suddenly her problems were his. And the bit about wanting to be sure she was safe. And just the confident way he'd approached her and said he was going to take care of things. He didn't ask if he could look at her car. He'd told her was going to. And that had set the stage for their relationship.

It didn't take a shrink to figure out that it was because she'd never had a protective male in her life.

Of course, Caleb's big hands and thick biceps that bunched while he worked on her car were part of the attraction, too.

Caleb pulled the truck door open. Then his hands went to her waist and he lifted her up and into the seat.

Her eyes were still wide as he slammed the door, rounded the front of the truck and got in. He'd never actually *put* her someplace before. Hell, they barely touched. Her hugging him earlier had been a first. Their hands brushed sometimes when they were passing kids or supplies back and forth. Sometimes they passed close by one another in the hallway. But they didn't even sit next to each other at support group. It was like they purposefully kept space between them. Maintained a professional-ish distance.

In spite of the fact they were basically co-parenting their children.

It was a weird relationship, that was for sure.

He slid behind the wheel. "We'll talk about everything tomorrow. But you're not coming back here, you got that?"

And that professional-ish distance was really important. Because him talking to her in that protective, firm, I'm-in-charge voice made her nipples hard.

It was really too bad that she was exhausted and drunk and had only a fuzzy memory of how it felt to be pressed up against all that hot hardness.

Lexi sighed and put her head back and let her eyes slide shut. "Okay," she told him.

It felt good just to keep her eyes closed and let Caleb take care of things. It always felt good. It had become a very easy habit over the past two years. Because she wasn't an idiot. If a big, hot guy wanted to take care of her and actually got pleasure himself from doing it, why would she fight it?

Oh yeah, the being-a-burden thing.

Okay, so there might be one wrinkle in the perfection of living together twenty-four-seven.

———

The next thing she knew, she was being lifted out of the truck.

She recognized the arms holding her immediately. Actually, she recognized the smell of the man attached to the arms holding her.

"Hey," she protested weakly. "I can walk." But she didn't want to. She wanted him to hold her and carry her just like this. Maybe forever.

"Uh-huh, I know."

His low voice rumbled against her ear. And she might have snuggled a little closer to it. "Where're Jack and Shay?"

"In bed. I took them in first."

She'd apparently slept through the stop at Bea's to pick the kids up. "Are they asleep?"

"Yep."

"Oh, good." Now that she'd closed her eyes, she wasn't so sure she ever wanted to open them again.

She felt him push the front door open, and the smell of his house hit her. She loved that smell. It was so familiar, so comforting. She felt so safe here.

Yeah, well, this sugary cloud around her brain was *really* nice.

"You're so *hot*," she told him as he started across the foyer, presumably toward the stairs.

He coughed, the sound loud against her ear. "Thanks?"

She wiggled, kicking her shoes off. They hit the hardwood floor with two *thunks*. Then she took her arm from around his neck and reached for her top. She was suddenly burning up. She stripped it off and let it drop.

"Uh, Lex?" He'd stopped walking.

"Yeah?" She pried her eyes open, focusing on his chin. And his beard. She reached up and ran her hand over it. It was softer than she'd expected and she gave a little sigh as every part of her body said, *We want to rub against that, too!*

"Lex." His voice sounded strangled now.

She looked up at his eyes, her hand still on his jaw. "Yeah?"

"What are you doing?"

"Feeling your beard."

"Why?"

"I've always wanted to. And it's right here."

He stared down at her and Lexi met his gaze. Damn, he was gorgeous. And big.

She felt the shift as he started up the stairs, but didn't look away from him.

"I could get used to this," she said.

She felt his arms stiffen. "What?"

"You carrying me up to bed."

He hit his toe on the next step up and he pitched forward. His arms tightened around and her arm went around his neck. He recovered his balance quickly, though, and finished the steps without another incident, but Lexi could have sworn he was moving faster now.

And the heat soaking into her from his body intensified.

"You're *really* hot." She reached for the bottom of her tank and stripped it up and off.

Just as she was tossing it away, she felt Caleb's hold under her knees drop away and her feet swung to the ground.

She wobbled slightly as he stepped back, just one hand on her upper arm.

"Stop." His voice sounded *really* funny now.

She frowned at him. "I'm *hot*, Caleb." She unbuttoned her shorts and pushed them to the floor. "I have to cool off." She kicked the shorts away.

Caleb sucked in a quick breath, then turned her by the shoulders and nudged her toward the bed in the guest room. "You need to go to bed."

Yeah, that sounded like a good idea. But he'd turned her so fast that she needed a second to stay upright as her head swirled. She gripped the edge of the doorframe.

"Lex—"

"Just give me a second," she said crossly. She took a couple of breaths and forced her eyes to stay open. Finally feeling stable— or at least stable-ish—she started toward the bed. But she drifted a little to the left before she felt Caleb move in behind her, guiding her to the mattress. The damned bed was really tall. She knew that the thick foam mattress was why she felt like she was sleeping on a cloud on top of a bunch of cotton on top of a mound of whipped cream. But it wasn't easy to get into.

She put one knee up and pulled herself onto it from the bottom. She heard Caleb groan behind her, but she didn't look back. So he was a little annoyed by her right now. So she was drunk and stumbling and she probably shouldn't have touched his beard. Or taken her clothes off. But it wasn't like he was going to *do* anything. She'd been wanting him to do something for a long time, but nothing pushed him over that edge. Not her wearing see-through tops or short shorts or licking ice cream sensually from a spoon or sitting on hot Santa's lap at the Christmas party or pulling red furry handcuffs out of the box from said Santa. Nothing shook Caleb. Either he had amazing willpower, or he wasn't attracted to her.

She didn't like that second answer, so she'd convinced herself that he considered her a really good friend and didn't want to mess that up. She could respect that. And it was far better than thinking that he just didn't find her sexy.

Lexi pulled the comforter back and slid in against the cool sheets.

She sighed as her head hit the pillow. She really fucking loved the pillows in here. Clouds on top of...something else amazingly soft.

"There's water and ibuprofen on the bedside table," Caleb said from the foot of the bed. "You should take those before you fall back to sleep."

"Okay," she mumbled, burrowing further into the pillow.

A second passed. "Lex. Take the ibuprofen."

"I will." She let out a long sigh. She loved staying here.

"Lexi."

She didn't answer him that time. It was late. She needed to sleep.

She felt the mattress shift a second later as he sat down next to her. "Lex, sit up. Take this stuff."

"I'm okay."

"I really want you to. It will help tomorrow."

"You're always taking care of me."

"Yep. Always."

"Sorry about that," she mumbled.

He didn't say anything for a second, but then she felt him tuck her hair behind her ear. "Please don't be sorry for that."

"I just—" Her lips were dry and when she tried to wet them, her tongue felt dry, too. Fine, she'd drink some water. She pushed herself up to sitting, the comforter slipping down. She made her eyes open.

And she realized that Caleb was *right there*. Again. Right in front of her. Only inches away. Close enough to smell. Close enough to feel the heat from his body. Which made it ironic that her nipples tightened like they'd been hit by a cold draft. She could have stroked his beard again. She wanted to stroke his beard again. Instead, she just looked at him.

But he didn't notice. Because he was looking at her breasts.

She was only in her bra and panties now, so of course he was looking at her breasts. If he was sitting there without a shirt on she definitely would have been looking at *his* chest. And she didn't have one single urge to cover up. She had pretty great breasts, as a matter of fact, and having Caleb looking her like *that* was...awesome. She was sure he'd noticed them before. They were one of her best assets and they were, okay, more than a handful. Even for Caleb. But he'd never let on that he'd noticed them before. He always looked her directly in the eye. Which was nice, of course. *Of course.* But the thing about knowing, and being mostly in love with, a guy who would look at your eyes versus your pretty-great-size-Ds when you talked, was that you kind of wanted him to look down once in a while, too.

She reached for the water bottle on the side table, her eyes still on him, feeling the comforter slip down even further. But, because of the eyes-still-on-him thing—and maybe the too-much-schnapps thing—she bumped the bottle with her hand and it started to fall.

Caleb leaned forward quickly to grab it.

Which brought his chest within inches of hers. And his mouth within inches of hers. The hand he was leaning on, next to her hip, made the mattress dip even further and she tilted toward him. Her hand went to his shoulder to keep from tipping over. And they both froze.

The bottle hit the table and rolled to the floor, but neither of them moved.

She was suddenly not at all tired. And feeling pretty sober.

Lexi could feel Caleb's breath on her lips, and his bunched muscles under her palm were hot and hard. She stared at his mouth. He stared at hers. And she decided that if he wasn't going to look at her breasts, looking at her mouth like he was starving and she was a grilled BLT—his favorite food in the world—was just fine with her.

Being compared, even in her own head, to a grilled BLT might not seem sexy, but in her mind, it so was. Caleb devoured those sandwiches. He'd do almost anything for one. He made sexy moaning sounds when he first tasted them. And he'd proclaimed that hers were the best he'd ever tasted. Yeah, put that way, along with the schnapps still coating her brain, it was strangely sexy.

"Caleb."

She watched his pupils dilate and his jaw clench.

Her hand went to the front of his shirt and she bunched it in her fists, watching his eyes. He didn't try to stop her. Then she tugged, urging him forward.

And he came, the hand next to her hip pressing into the mattress as she tipped her head to one side.

Their lips touched. Softly. Briefly. But she felt it all the way to her bones. Heat, want, *relief*. She suddenly *had* to have more. She made a little almost-a-sob sound and licked her tongue along his lower lip.

"Lex."

Her name was more of a groan than a word. It was the sexiest thing she'd ever heard.

"Caleb," she breathed.

Then the *next* groan became the sexiest thing she'd ever heard. It was a combination of hunger and resignation, and she felt like he'd just set her nerve endings on fire.

Suddenly, Caleb's hand came up to cup the back of her head, his fingers diving into her hair. And he took over.

His mouth opened over hers and his tongue stroked deep and hot. Every glide of his tongue felt as though he was running a finger over her clit. Some were firmer, some softer, some longer, some shorter, and her need ratcheted up with each one.

She ran her hands over his chest to his shoulders and up the sides of his neck, loving the hard muscles and the heat under her palms. Then she slid her hands down his sides to the bottom of his shirt. She slipped her hands underneath, moaning as she met hot, bare skin. He sucked in a quick breath and she smiled against his lips, loving having an effect on him.

And suddenly she was on her back and Caleb was moving over her. Her hands slid to his back, the muscles there bunching as he braced himself above her, still kissing her like it was his job. Instinctively, she slid her legs apart and he settled between them. The comforter was between them, but she felt him hard and hot and deliciously heavy against her. The feel of his cock pressed against her made her ache. She'd done that to him. She'd made him hard. *Hallelujah.*

Lexi shifted, trying to get the comforter lower, wiggling against him. He groaned and pressed into her, making her clit throb even with her panties, the comforter, and his clothes between them.

Two years of wanting him were coming together and she felt

like if he pressed just a little harder and she moved her hips just a certain way, she could come like this.

"Caleb."

His mouth trailed from hers to her throat and down to her collarbone. He cupped her breast, the silk of her bra the only barrier, and she arched into his hand. His thumb rubbed over her nipple and she felt her desire winding tighter.

"God, you're gorgeous."

She pried her eyes open at his gruff words. The heat in his eyes as he stared down at her, his thumb and finger plucking at her nipple through her bra, made the ache between her legs intensify times ten. "You feel so good," she said, her voice barely a whisper.

He looked down at her breast and watched his fingers play with her. Then, *thank god*, he peeled the cup down, exposing her nipple.

"Holy fuck, Lex," he said reverently. He plucked at the hard tip again, rolling it between his thumb and finger.

She lifted her hips, pressing against him harder, needing relief for the ache that was building.

Then he lowered his mouth and sucked on her and she cried out. Her hand came up to the back of his head and she tipped her pelvis, needing pressure and friction. She ground against him as he sucked. She was so, so close. "Please, Caleb, please."

"What do you need, Lex?" he asked huskily.

"You."

He looked up and gave her a little head shake. "Tell me what you want. *Exactly*."

"You. Touching me. Taking me." The words tumbled out without her really forming them.

His eyes flared at her answer. "How?"

"Anything. Whatever." Relief was *right there*. She swore that if he just sucked a little harder, or circled his hips just right, or even just said something dirty, she'd be there.

"Anything?" he asked. There was something new in his tone. And his eyes. He looked more turned on and more intent than before.

"Anything," she agreed, breathlessly.

"Would you spread your legs and touch yourself?" he asked. "Would you slide your fingers inside your pretty pussy and let me watch you make yourself come?"

The word *pussy* from this man's lips, the idea of him watching her touch herself, made a shudder of pleasure ripple through her. Damn right she would do all of that. And somehow she knew it would take about three seconds if he was watching her. She wet her lips. "Is that what you want? Just tell me."

What she *really* wanted was to have those red fuzzy handcuffs here right now, Caleb clamping them around her wrists, and doing any dirty thing he could think of to her while she was restrained. But she wasn't quite ready to tell him that for some reason.

The heat in his eyes intensified. "What if I told you I wanted you to bend over the end of the bed so I could get on my knees and make you come with my tongue?"

God, yes. Caleb's tongue. His commands. The very idea of all of that made her pelvic muscles clench hard.

She lifted her hips again, pressing against him. "Yes. That. Whatever."

He groaned. "Jesus, you would, wouldn't you?" He lowered his head again and took her nipple in his mouth, sucking hard.

His hand squeezed her hip and at first Lexi thought it was him just touching her, but when she tried to lift up against him again, she realized he was holding her down. Heat flooded her system and she moaned.

He lifted his head, giving her nipple a last lick. "I want to blow your mind, Lex," he told her. "I want to do anything and every-thing you need."

Of course he did. That was Caleb. Always wanting to give her

what she wanted and needed. But in this case, she really just
wanted him to *take* her.

"I want *you* to tell me," she said, nearly panting. "I want you to
just take over."

"Can't." He shook his head. "I need it to be exactly what
you need."

She almost groaned in frustration. He was a good guy. A
protector. The only male in her life that wanted to take care of
her. And she should be wallowing in that. Instead, she wanted
him to tie her up and say something like, *You know, all this time
I've been taking care of you? Time to pay up.* And then fuck two
years of car repairs and childcare and groceries out of her.

Caleb would never think, not to mention say, something like
that. Which was exactly the reason she completely trusted him
and at the same time, wanted him to tie her up and do any dirty
thing he could think of to her.

It was very confusing. She wanted to be dominated by the one
guy who would do anything to protect her and cherish her.

"*You* are what I need. Anything you want. All of it," she told
him, breathlessly, moving restlessly against him. "Just tell me
what to do." Her entire body was vibrating.

But just as she was anticipating him pulling the comforter off
of her, she felt him freeze. She frowned. He knew she trusted
him. Implicitly. "Caleb—"

Before she could finish the sentence, he looked down at her
partially bared breast, swore under his breath, and pulled her bra
back up. Then he shifted back and got off the bed. He pulled the
comforter *up* and then, only when she was completely covered,
looked into her eyes.

"Good night, Lex," he said simply. But he shoved a hand
through his hair and blew out a breath. He took a step back from
the bed. "Take the ibuprofen, okay?"

"Um..." What the hell? It was clear from his fly that he was
still rock-hard. He ran a hand over his face, looking pained.

"Now, Lex."

Suddenly her cheeks were burning.

He was rejecting her.

She'd kissed him, he'd gotten wrapped up and carried away, but as soon as he'd realized just how ridiculously crazy about him she was, willing to do anything, he'd realized he'd better get away.

But he still wanted to boss her around. Not in the "get on your knees" way, but in a "take your medicine" way. She sighed. Of course he did.

Lexi threw the comforter back and turned so she could reach for the water bottle lying on the floor. She leaned over —which was almost a mistake as her brain swished in her head—and then sat up again. This fucking mattress was too tall for her to reach to the floor. She slid off the bed, grabbed the bottle, then climbed back up. She reached for the ibuprofen, took the medication, and then set the bottle down. She pivoted her legs back up onto the mattress, but didn't cover up.

Caleb was still there. He was looking up at the ceiling instead of at her.

Well, excuse the hell out of her double-Ds.

She frowned and grabbed for the blanket and pulled it up, tucking it under her arms.

"You should get some sleep," he said.

"Yeah, I really should." She slid down under the covers.

He pulled the door open and flipped off the light. "'Night, Lex."

All that was missing from him putting her to bed like a little kid now was him saying something about bedbugs. She frowned. "'Night."

"I'll handle the kids in the morning. Sleep as long as you want."

Of course he would. He was taking care of her. At least her

basic everyday ibuprofen-and-roof-over-her-head needs. As usual.

"Okay." She turned to her side and closed her eyes.

He seemed to hesitate, but a few seconds later she heard the door shut.

Well, great. Tomorrow morning—and every morning after that, pretty much forever—wasn't going to be awkward at all.

"Shay! Breakfast!" Caleb called into the TV room that was just off the kitchen.

The house was a big old Victorian in the lower Garden District, and he was forever wishing there was less space. A tiny little girl could find lots of nooks and crannies to get into. She'd found the cupboard under the stairs. She'd found the cupboard under the window seat in the main living room. She'd found the cupboard in the pantry. And she'd found the attic. Thank God she hadn't found the dumbwaiter yet. But Caleb was ready for it.

He'd finally put bells on her. Literally. Thank God Shay was into cats. He'd bought two cat collars, with bells, and threaded them through her shoe laces. Now she could pretend to be a kitty and he could find her wherever she was. That idea had come from Addison, in one of the support group meetings. Because of course *he* hadn't thought of it. But parenthood had a way of making a guy swallow his pride and take whatever tips and tricks other people would hand out.

He wondered if Addison would have any ideas about how to strengthen Shay's left side, or help with her balance, or work on the learning disabilities that the doctor had said were "inevitable."

But no, that was what the therapists, who were scheduled to evaluate Shay a week from now, were for. Physical therapy, occupational therapy, speech therapy had all been ordered by the doctor, and Caleb couldn't wait to talk to them and get some answers.

He also dreaded talking to them.

As long as their evaluations were still in the future, then nothing was for sure. He could still pretend it was all going to be fine. That the doctor had simply given him the worst-case scenario. That Shay could catch up.

Caleb beat the chocolate powder into the glass of milk far harder than it needed to be stirred.

"Hi!"

He looked over his shoulder to see Shay coming into the room. And she was wearing Lexi's tank and top from last night. Along with Lexi's shoes. Without bells.

"Hi," he greeted with a smile, despite the memories of Lexi stripping off those clothes last night thundering through his mind. "What are you doing?"

"I'm Lexi!" Shay told him with a huge grin. She started across the hardwood floor in the too-big shoes, sliding them along so they'd stay on her feet.

He noted that she dragged her left foot even more than the right. Now that he knew it was because her left side was weaker than the right, it seemed completely obvious. But he'd missed that for four years. Caleb felt his neck knotting up and worked to breathe and relax.

Even before she'd been in his care full-time, he'd watched her learn to roll and crawl and walk. Of course, that had been before the accident. He assumed she had been on track then. Just like he'd assumed she was fine afterward.

"Geez, Lexi, you got a lot shorter," Caleb told her, making his tone light, watching her climb up onto her seat at the table, losing the shoes in the process.

She couldn't keep the shoes on, but she could climb onto the chair. It wasn't like her physical weaknesses were *that* obvious.

She's only four. It's hard for a first-time parent to know all the func-

tional milestones, especially when a child is young and still developing so much of her strength and coordination. Don't beat yourself up, Caleb.

He heard Dr. Franklin's voice in his head. He knew she was right. Everything she'd said to him yesterday about it not being his fault that he'd missed the indications that Shay was lagging behind in her physical function and learning was true. He'd never been around kids her age before. She had barely been walking and talking when he'd become her guardian. How was he supposed to know that she should have been doing more at that point? And all the points since?

"No Wexi!" Jack declared, pointing his spoon at Shay.

Caleb gave him a grin even though only half of his mind was on the conversation with the kids. He screwed the lid onto the sippy cup of juice and set it in front of Shay. "She's not? How do you know?"

"That Shay!" Jack pointed his fork at Shay, scrambled egg bits flying across the table.

He was in the high chair at the table, wearing only his diaper. That was how they fed him every single meal, because Jack had the odd habit of putting food in his pockets. When it had been things like pretzels or raisins, it was one thing. The raisins got warm and sticky, but they were easily removed—once they'd finally remembered to start checking the pockets before putting his clothes through the washer and dryer. But Jack didn't just put hard, or even semi-hard, food in his pockets. He stashed whatever he had that he might want to save for later. They'd found Jell-O, grapes, noodles, and even pudding in his pockets. They'd caught that last one pretty early because getting pudding into his pockets had made a huge mess all over *everything* else as well. But it was amazing what the kid could get into his pockets. And how.

Caleb wiped up the egg chunks and nodded. "You're right. That *is* Shay. But why is she wearing Lexi's clothes?"

"Mommy wear Shay cwothes!" Jack decided, then shoveled a handful of eggs into his mouth.

Yeah, Shay's clothes wouldn't cover even one of Lexi's gorgeous breasts. That he'd seen mostly naked last night. Caleb coughed and handed Jack the blunt-tipped fork.

"Fork, buddy."

It was probably completely inappropriate to be thinking about the kid's mom's breasts while feeding him eggs. Then again, dads probably thought about their wives' breasts while feeding their kids once in a while, right?

But he wasn't Lexi's husband. And thinking about her breasts —regardless of if it was appropriate with Jack right next to him— was a bad idea.

Jack took the fork and used it for the next bite. But it scooped up fewer eggs than he could get with his hands, so he dropped it and took another handful. Caleb sighed and went to the stove for Shay's breakfast. As he brought her the eggs and toast, his foot kicked one of the shoes under her chair.

Even seeing those shoes lying on the floor made his gut tighten.

Because they made him think of Lexi's tank and shirt that Shay was wearing. And the fact that Lexi had stripped them off and dropped them as he'd carried her up to bed. And the way she'd been sitting in that bed in nothing but a pale blue bra and panty set. And the way she'd tasted, and sounded. The way her nipple had been perfect against his tongue. The way she'd arched and ground into him like she'd never needed anything more. The way he'd *needed* to satisfy every need she had. And the way she'd agreed that she'd do anything he said.

He'd believed her. Even now, the idea of it knocked the air out of his lungs. She would have stripped naked and let him do anything he wanted to her.

And that was a big part of why he felt a mix of emotions he didn't want this morning. Frustration and worry and knotted-up-desire unlike any he'd ever felt before. And, of course, fatigue. Because he hadn't slept worth a shit last night. And because he was failing Shay.

And maybe Lexi, too.

Lexi had needed to move out of her mom's house and into an apartment that was completely inappropriate for a two-year-old and hadn't said a word to Caleb.

His gut knotted and he had to take a deep breath.

But...*fuck*.

Caleb forced in another breath. He was not *failing* Shay. He'd missed a couple of things. Shay was behind in some areas of development and if he had intervened before this, maybe she'd be a little further ahead. But she had a brain injury from the car accident that had killed her mom and dad and that meant that some of her deficits were just...deficits.

Even thinking the words *brain injury* made Caleb's stomach drop. They wouldn't necessarily get better. She was only four, which meant that her chances of learning to compensate and adapt for her limitations were better than an older kid or an adult. But the changes in her brain were permanent. And because she was so young, things like major physical disabilities and personality changes and memory problems that older kids and adults experienced after a traumatic brain injury were muted in Shay. It was hard to see a personality change in someone who had still been developing their personality when the injury happened. Eighteen-month-olds didn't have amazing long-term memory anyway, nor did they have the language to talk about things they remembered—or didn't—so it would be almost impossible to notice memory issues in her. And she'd just been learning to walk well. She hadn't been running, jumping, kicking or climbing when she'd come to live with Caleb, but neither were other kids her age.

And he was a first-time dad, starting eighteen months in,

while having to change his entire life and mourn his sister's death, all at the same time.

The doctor insisted on cutting him some slack, but Caleb wasn't feeling that generous with himself.

On top of all of that, yesterday he'd found Jack and Lexi living above a bar, essentially abandoned by her mother, and then, in the process of giving Lexi ibuprofen, for fuck's sake, he'd almost stripped her bare and buried himself balls deep inside her. While she was exhausted and drunk and…grateful.

Jesus, Lexi being grateful to him was the thing that made him happiest and the most frustrated. He loved helping her. But he'd also love to have her begging him to fuck her when he *hadn't* just saved her ass.

And he definitely hadn't missed the fact that Lexi and Shay's situations were feeling pretty fucking similar. They were both people he took care of, who depended on him to have the answers, who had shit going on with them that he'd been clueless about.

As Shay picked up her fork and started eating, a thought—specifically the thought of Lexi being naked in his house and all the issues that could raise—occurred to him. "Hey, Shay, don't you think Lexi is going to need her clothes?" He was barely holding it together just thinking about her upstairs in nothing but that bra and panties. If she came down here looking for her clothes with nothing else on, he was going to lose it.

Yeah, okay, he'd gotten over her being too young for him. That had just been an excuse anyway. His attempts to not get involved with her were more about his worry that he'd use his influence to talk her into something she didn't really want. But hey, if she wanted to initiate things, without any pressure from him, he wasn't going to say no.

Shay shook her head. "These are extra."

"They…are?" Caleb looked at his niece. "What do you mean?"

Shay shrugged. "She left them here."

Oh, right. Shay didn't realize that Lexi was actually *here*. Because Lexi was never here when Caleb was here. And if Lexi's *clothes* were here and she wasn't, they must be extra.

"Actually, Lexi didn't leave them here. She slept here last night. In the guest room," he added quickly. Though he wasn't sure a four-year-old would even question where Lexi had spent the night. Or care. It probably wouldn't even occur to Shay that Lexi might sleep in *his* bed. Because why would it? There was no reason for Shay to think that Caleb and Lexi might share a bed. She was four. Just because in *his* mind Lexi could quite possibly end up in his bed...

"Why did she take her clothes off?" Shay asked.

That was a fair question. And the reason was innocent. He didn't think that Lexi had done it to torture him. She'd been drunk and hot, so she'd taken her clothes off. "She said she was hot."

"Oh." Shay chewed a bite of eggs.

Caleb started to reach for his coffee cup. Yeah, *oh*. It made sense. You get hot, you take your clothes off. Simple.

"Were you cuddling?"

Caleb froze with his cup halfway to his mouth. He looked at his niece. She bit into her toast as she looked back at him.

"Lexi and I were not cuddling, no." At least, not the way Shay meant it. And now all he could think about was cuddling with Lexi. Even real, regular cuddling. The type Shay *was* talking about. That would be...awesome. Lexi smelled amazing, she *felt* amazing, and he was sure that he would get very, very hot.

"How did she get hot?"

"I was...carrying her," Caleb said.

"Why?"

"She was really sleepy and didn't feel very good." He often carried Shay up to bed when she was sleepy. She'd understand that.

"Oh, that's good." Shay reached for her juice. "But you should cuddle her. That makes me feel better when I don't feel good."

Caleb cleared his throat. Not only because cuddling Lexi sounded like a fantastic idea—a fantastically horrible idea—but because, honestly, he needed to know that he could make something better for Shay. He very much needed some reassurances today that he could still help his girls.

"Did she sleep here because she's sick?" Shay wanted to know.

"No." He glanced at Jack. "Jack's grandma moved away and they need a place to stay."

"They're going to stay here?" Shay asked, her eyes round as she stared at Jack.

"Yeah."

Shay's grin was huge. "That's good! Our house is so big! We have extra rooms! And they come here a lot! Oh, yay!"

Because it really was that simple.

Or it should be, anyway.

Caleb smiled at Shay. God, she was beautiful. She looked so much like Cassie it made his heart hurt. Cassie, who, at age twenty, had agreed to become *his* guardian when their dad's job moved him and their mom to Singapore. Without Cassie, Caleb would have had to move to another *continent*, away from school and his friends and the only home he'd ever known, and start his life over again at age fourteen. Cassie had believed he was the best person to raise her daughter. Cassie had seen a love and loyalty in him he hadn't even known existed.

Shay hadn't had the brain injury when Cassie had made that decision, though. Would that have changed her mind? Would Shay be better off with her grandma and grandpa? His parents still lived in Singapore. That would take Shay away from her home and friends and what she knew here. But she was four. She would adjust. And his mother was a teacher. She hadn't taught since moving to another country more than a decade ago, but surely her background in education would be better for Shay than Caleb's firefighting experience. His mother probably wouldn't have missed that Shay was behind in learning her letters and numbers or that she was weak on the left side. She was right-handed so it had always made perfect sense to Caleb that she used her right hand and arm far more than the left. And how the hell was he supposed to know how many letters Shay was supposed to know by this point?

"All kids develop at different rates, Caleb, and you haven't done this before. You can't be so hard on yourself," Dr. Franklin had said.

"Can she catch up if we work on it now?" he'd asked.

"I think we can expect to see some changes," the doctor had hedged.

"But she won't catch up with the other kids her age?" he'd pressed.

"Research shows that kids with severe injuries don't catch up and can even fall further behind their peers," the pediatrician had admitted. "But Shay's injury is not classified as severe. She was classified mild. But—"

"*But*?" Caleb had asked.

"She was only eighteen months old, and they estimated that the accident happened more than thirty minutes before emergency personnel got to her. Her age means that it's impossible to accurately measure any post-injury amnesia she might have had, it is very difficult to compare her personality and temperament prior to the accident to after, and there's no way to know for sure if she lost consciousness for any period of time," Dr. Franklin had explained. "A CT was done, and it didn't show a brain bleed or skull fracture. That's about all we know."

Even remembering the conversation had Caleb's gut in a knot. He'd always hated the knowledge that there was at least thirty minutes between the accident and when emergency personnel had shown up. Had Cassie and Stephen died instantly, or had they been alive for a while? Shay had to have been terrified. He hated thinking about all of it.

"So they knew she had a brain injury," Caleb had said.

"Yes. It's in her chart."

Penelope Franklin was a pediatric neurologist. She'd never seen Shay before being referred by Shay's pediatrician almost two weeks ago. That was a good thing. Or so Caleb would have thought. No one wanted their child to need to see a neurologist. But, in this case, he couldn't help but think that if Penny Franklin *had* seen Shay, they could have started intervening and helping her with her issues earlier.

"Why didn't they tell me?" Caleb had asked.

Dr. Franklin had looked at him with sympathy. "I'm sure they did. But you were going through a lot at the time," she'd said. "It's possible they didn't explain the implications fully. Or perhaps it didn't sink in for you. But really, Caleb, it's okay. We can do what needs done now."

That hadn't made Caleb feel much better. They should have been working on things before this. The pediatrician Shay had been seeing with Cassie and Stephen had moved to Houston and with Caleb she'd seen a rotation of doctors at the clinic, just depending on who was there when she had an ear infection or a cough. But she really didn't get sick much and, in spite of her stumbling, she didn't get hurt.

Now that he knew what was going on with her, Caleb realized that Shay was a quieter kid who preferred to sit and color or watch television or play on her tablet possibly because physical activities were challenging for her and she didn't enjoy them.

Or maybe she was just a quieter kid.

Fuck if he really knew.

Despite what Dr. Franklin had said, Caleb couldn't shake the idea he should have been paying more attention. He'd actually started noticing things, and getting concerned, as *Jack* got older. Now that he was two, a little older than Shay had been when she'd come to live with him, Caleb had been noticing the things that Jack could do that Shay hadn't at his age. But for a long time, Caleb had been chalking it up to Jack being exceptional. Maybe he was just naturally more graceful and coordinated than the average child. Maybe he was genetically athletic. Or maybe he wasn't. How *was* Caleb supposed to know what to worry about and what was fine?

Of course, the answer was obvious.

He pulled his phone from his back pocket, pulled up Google, and typed in *how many letters should a four-year-old know?*

Thirty-seven articles popped up in two seconds.

Like many parents, you may be wondering what developmental milestones to be watching for.

Yeah, he clearly should have been wondering. His eyes scanned the list of things a four-year-old should know. He paused over *can walk heel-to-toe and run.* He'd never had her try heel-to-toe, but she could run. She stumbled a lot, but how was he supposed to know that wasn't normal? Dammit. And the standing on one foot for four to five seconds? Yeah, he knew she couldn't do that.

Caleb blew out a breath and made his eyes keep scanning.

May be quick to get angry but tries to control it or express it through words.

Okay, see, this was what was frustrating. Shay had a short temper and was easily frustrated and Dr. Franklin said that could be part of her injury. But it looked like four-year-olds generally had some trouble with that. No, Shay didn't really try to control it, but surely other four-year-olds had that problem, too.

Knows what tasks are expected but may lose focus on following through.

Yeah, she had that. So her difficulty with concentration might be her injury, but it might *not.*

He muttered a word he did not want either kid to learn and shoved his phone back into his pocket.

"So, since Lexi is still here, she might need her clothes back," Caleb said to Shay, finally taking a drink of his coffee.

"She's okay for now."

He whipped around to find that Lexi had come into the kitchen when he hadn't been paying attention. And she was dressed. Kind of. She was covered, anyway. In one of *his* shirts. And that was almost as bad—as in sexy—as her in bra and panties only.

3

C aleb swallowed and came to his feet. "Uh..."

Lexi crossed to Jack and kissed him on the head. "Morning, Boo."

Jack grinned up at her as Lexi reached into the side of his diaper and removed a small corner of toast.

Caleb sighed.

Then Lexi looked over at Shay. "Like your new dress, Shay-shay."

Shay giggled. "I just got it."

Lexi laughed and looked at him. "Hope you don't mind." She plucked his white T-shirt away from her breasts. "I had to borrow something."

His shirt hit her nearly at her knees and hung loose on her small frame. Though her magnificent breasts still pressed against the front. And the bagginess did nothing to dim his memory of those glorious things encased in fitted blue silk. Or the memory of one bare, the hard nipple wet and shiny from his mouth. Or the memory of the sound she made when he sucked on it.

"That was in the guest room?" Did his voice sound hoarse?

She headed for the coffeepot, her bare feet padding against the floor. "No. I got it from your room."

She'd been in his bedroom? In only her bra and panties? Yeah, that was fine. Great. No problem at all.

She filled her cup and then turned to face him. "I went searching for my own stuff but I realized that some of it was down here."

The memory of her stripping off the blue top as he carried her up the stairs hit him again. He cleared his throat. "It's fine."

She lifted a brow, clearly noting that he didn't sound fine. "I didn't rummage around in your room or anything. I knew exactly where to find them," she pointed out. "I've put them away more than once." She lifted the cup to her lips.

That was true. She'd done laundry at his house many times. He'd done her laundry, too, though he just folded it into the basket and left it for her to take home while she actually put the clean clothes away in his and Shay's rooms. But he was fairly certain she'd never put his laundry away wearing only her bra and panties.

"Besides, if I wanted to look for your secrets, I've had plenty of opportunities."

Also true. Good thing he didn't have any secrets. That he could think of.

"Guess you shouldn't have left your top down here," he commented. She *definitely* should not have left her top down here. He never would have seen her bra and breasts if she'd kept the thing on. He wouldn't have *needed* to taste her. He wouldn't have—

"Did you get hot with Uncle Caleb down here?" Shay asked, interrupting his thoughts.

And Caleb realized that he and Lexi didn't have many conversations around the kids. At least not about things that the kids shouldn't hear and understand.

Lexi shot Caleb a look, then looked back at Shay. "Well, yeah, I guess I did."

Caleb coughed in spite of his effort not to react. Or read things into her comment.

Shay nodded. "I get hot when I cuddle Uncle Caleb."

This time Lexi coughed. "Well, Uncle Caleb and I weren't cuddling," she said.

"I told her that," Caleb felt compelled to add for some reason.

Lexi looked confused. "He, um, helped me up to bed."

Shay nodded. "But he should have cuddled you in your bed. He cuddles me when I don't feel good." She looked up at Caleb. "Why didn't you do that?"

Caleb knew that there was no way his little niece had any idea how complicated her question really was. "Well, Lexi just—" He didn't have an answer.

Okay, that wasn't true. He didn't have an answer that was appropriate for a four-year-old. Because the answer was that he'd realized Lexi really would have let him do anything he wanted to do to her. And that if he'd done that last night, it would have been because he'd been left out of a part of her life. He would have wanted to *consume* her. To prove that he could. He would have wanted to fill her up—her mind, her imagination, her body—so that she never thought of leaving him out of anything again.

He dragged in a breath.

"It's been a long time since I needed to be...cuddled," Lexi said after a moment, in answer to Shay's question.

Caleb's eyes flew to her and she winced slightly, as if realizing how that sounded. At least to the other grown-up in the room.

"Cuddled by a guy, I mean." Again she winced.

And this time Caleb smiled a little. Because the kids had no idea that any of this sounded like an innuendo. So really this was just about him and Lexi. And he kind of, probably stupidly, liked the idea that her mind was in the same naughty place his was.

Lexi looked stoically at Shay. "I mean, I love cuddling with you two," she said pointing from Shay to Jack. "But that's all I need."

"I think you'd change your mind if you knew what a good cuddler I am."

Lexi's gaze collided with his and her mouth dropped open.

Okay, why the hell had he said that? But he didn't regret it a bit as a blush stained Lexi's cheeks. They never teased. Or flirted. Or used innuendo. Or stood around in his kitchen talking while she wore one of his shirts and looked fucking adorable in it. Then again, they never did, well, any of the stuff they'd done in the guest bedroom last night.

So he did something else unprecedented. He gave her a wink.

Lexi's eyes grew wide and Caleb realized he was having a really good time. Which, considering everything, including the helplessness and frustration, was really amazing.

Lexi took a deep breath. "Uncle Caleb gave me water and medicine," she told Shay. "So he did take care of me. No cuddling required." She shot him a little frown.

It just made him grin. Because she'd liked the cuddling they had done and she'd been willing to do *a lot* more. And now, in the light of day, when she was sober, and he was proud of himself for holding back last night, the idea of taking her to bed and listening to her tell him everything she wanted and needed was hotter than hell.

And probably inevitable.

"Did he make you feel better?" Shay asked Lexi.

Caleb waited for the "yes." But it didn't come immediately. He arched an eyebrow. Lexi seemed to be thinking about the question.

"Lex?" he asked. Had he made her feel better? He'd kept her from having to climb the stairs. He'd given her ibuprofen. He'd made her moan and writhe and pant. And *hadn't* ravished her in her inebriated state. "Do you feel better?"

She met his eyes as she said, "My *head* feels okay. But some other things hurt."

Some other things hurt? He immediately frowned. "Are you okay?"

She shrugged, looking away from him. "I will be."

There was something in her tone and the way she emphasized *head* that made him frown. What the hell was she getting at?

"What hurts?" Shay asked, before he could. Bless her.

"My pride," Lexi told her.

Caleb frowned.

"What's that?" Shay asked, wrinkling her nose.

"It's what feels bad when you do something you wish you hadn't done," Lexi said.

Wait a damned minute. She'd done things last night that she now wished she hadn't?

"Like when I took the marker away from Jack and he cried?" Shay asked.

Lexi tipped her head. "Kind of. But that's called guilt. You feel bad for something you did to someone. Pride is...like embarrassed. Do you know what embarrassed is?"

Shay shook her head.

"Caleb?" Lexi asked, looking from Shay to him. "How would you explain embarrassed?"

He lifted a brow. She was *embarrassed*? Oh, hell no. Everything she'd done and said last night had been hotter than anything he'd had in...he couldn't even remember. But he couldn't say that. They were with the kids now. But this was equally interesting. They also didn't talk *to* the kids much together. "Embarrassed is when you did something wrong or silly and then people find out about it and they might make fun of you or be mad at you for it."

Shay scrunched up her face.

"Would it make you feel even worse if you knew that your friends knew you'd taken that marker away from Jack?" Lexi asked.

Shay thought about that. "Maybe."

"Because then your friends would know that you were mean to Jack," Caleb said. "And that might make them think you're not nice."

Shay nodded. "Yeah. I guess."

"And that would make you feel embarrassed. It's a yucky feeling when everyone knows something about us we wish they didn't," Lexi added.

Caleb felt a strange emotion ripple through his chest. He and Lexi were teaching Shay something. Together. They didn't do that. This was…nice. And they fell into the conversation together easily.

That shouldn't surprise him, he knew.

Shay nodded again. "Okay." She looked over at Lexi. "Did your friends find out you did something bad or silly?"

"Kind of. One of my friends found out that I wanted to do something with him. But he doesn't want to do it with me. So I feel embarrassed that he knows I want to do it," Lexi said. "And that he wants to do it with other people, but not me."

Caleb felt surprise rock through him. He knew that she was talking about him, but there was *nothing* she wanted to do with him that he wouldn't want to do with her. In fact, his list of things he *did* want to do with her would very likely shock her.

"Like you want to play with him, but he wants to play with other people instead?" Shay asked.

"Yes, that's exactly what it is."

Caleb swallowed wrong and coughed while Lexi nodded solemnly.

"But," Shay said, going up onto her knees on the chair, her expression suddenly earnest. "Why doesn't he want to play with *you*?"

It was clear that Shay couldn't imagine a world in which someone would not want to play with Lexi.

He concurred.

"Are you bad at the game?" Shay asked.

Caleb choked again and set his coffee cup away. He was going to kill himself if he kept trying to drink during this conversation.

Lexi lifted a shoulder. "I don't think so. But I've only played it with one other person. He thought I was good at it. But I'm not sure if he really knew."

Holy shit. On second thought, he did need something to drink. Like whiskey. Or maybe some of the schnapps from last night.

Which made him think of bubblegum. Which made him think of how Lexi had tasted last night. And how he didn't think he'd ever get his fill.

Caleb reached for Shay's sippy cup, unscrewed the top, and downed the orange juice.

"You should play it again with your friend. You're probably good at it," Shay told her.

In spite of the fact that Shay was hardly an unbiased opinion —his niece thought Lexi walked on water—Caleb was quite certain Lexi was *damned* good at it.

"But I think he's worried that if we play that game together, it might make the other things we do, not as good anymore."

Shay seemed confused about that and Caleb almost laughed. She *should* be confused about that. People who liked each other were supposed to play games together, and playing together made people like each other more, not less.

"My friend Kayla is a brat when we play hide-and-seek," Shay said. "I don't like to play that with her. But I like to play in the sandbox with her."

Or maybe his four-year-old niece completely understood the world and relationships in a way Caleb simply didn't.

What was that famous poem? About learning everything you needed to know in kindergarten? Looked like Shay had figured life out even before kindergarten. And this was why he wasn't worried about her. Or hadn't been. Until Jack had carried a huge armful of books across the room without help or tipping over. Shay couldn't do that. She also couldn't sort all of her shape blocks by color. But Jack could. Still, Shay was a bright, sweet, happy little girl. Until she was trying to do something that was hard. Or when she had an emotion that she didn't know how to handle. But wasn't that essentially true of everyone? Caleb had told himself that she was completely fine.

It was definitely a bit of denial...mixed with him not knowing what the fuck he was doing.

He blew out a breath. Damn, this was going to be hard.

He really liked when things were easy. When he thought he had it all handled. When he felt on top of things and like the fixer and protector he wanted to be.

Fuck.

"It's just like you and Kayla," Lexi told Shay. "Some friends you play hide-and-seek with. Other friends you play in the sandbox with."

Caleb frowned. He fucking wanted to play *all* the games with Lexi. And he sure as fuck didn't want Lexi playing any games with anyone else. He wanted hide-and-seek and the sandbox and TAG and any other damned thing that girl would ever want to play. And he'd be the best playmate she'd ever had.

"Is your friend a brat sometimes?" Shay asked Lexi.

Lexi smirked as she lifted her coffee cup. But he saw it.

"Yes, he is definitely a brat sometimes."

Well, that was nicer than *over-protective asshole*, he supposed.

"He should play a different game with you then," Shay said. "You should still be friends."

Lexi nodded. "You're a sweetie, Shay."

Yeah, he had a whole list of games he and Lex could try. Caleb couldn't help the thought. He shifted on his chair. This was a dangerous conversation to be having with a two- and four-year-old around.

ERIN NICHOLAS

"Do you want some strawberries?" Lexi asked Shay and Jack, avoiding Caleb's gaze, changing the subject just like that.

"Yes!" Jack shouted.

"Yes," Shay said.

And they were off the playing-games-with-people-who-didn't-want-to-play-with-you conversation. Except that Caleb was not as easily distracted.

Lexi went to the fridge and retrieved the strawberries from the drawer. She went to the sink, washed them, then transferred them to the cutting board. She started taking the stems off and slicing the berries as Caleb watched her, absently handing Jack pieces of banana and pushing Shay's toast closer so she'd finish it.

"Did you put your hands on Uncle Caleb when he carried you upstairs?" Shay suddenly asked.

He saw Lexi freeze just before he looked at his niece.

Lexi looked over her shoulder. "What, honey?"

"Is that why you got hot?" Shay put a bite of eggs in her mouth, looking at Lexi innocently. "When my hands get cold, I put them on his neck and they get warm fast."

Lexi coughed and turned back to the strawberries. He heard her swear softly and move toward the sink. He covered the curse with, "Your cold hands on my neck make *me* cold, you know," he told Shay, leaning toward her.

She dodged his tickle-fingers with a giggle. "Did Lexi make you cold?"

Well, that was a definite no. He glanced over at Lexi. She reached for a paper towel.

"No," he said honestly. "Lexi didn't make me cold at all."

He saw Lexi's shoulders rise and fall as she took a deep breath. She moved back to the cutting board full of strawberries. He watched her for a second, realizing that something looked awkward about what she was doing. "Lex?" he asked.

"Yeah?"

"You okay?"

She sighed. "Yeah. I just need to run upstairs. Can you finish these?"

He got up and crossed to her. "What's going on?"

She held up her hand. "I just cut my finger."

He saw the red stain coming through the white towel and his heart lurched. It was a finger. A paring knife cut. Nothing horrible. But he reached for her immediately. And she pulled back.

He lifted a brow. No. Lexi wasn't going to pull back. Not figuratively or literally. "Don't," he admonished softly.

"I'm fine," she said.

"I don't think so."

"There's nothing you need to do."

And suddenly they were not talking about the cut.

"There is if you're hurt."

"I'm fine. I've got this." She started to turn away.

He caught her wrist. "Lex."

She stopped and sucked in a breath. But he knew he hadn't hurt her finger. He had, however, hurt her feelings.

"Let me take care of you."

She pressed her lips together and looked up at him. "I need to stop needing you to do that all the time."

His gut twisted.

"I can handle it," she said. "I know what I'm doing here."

He tugged her over to the cupboard where he kept first aid supplies anyway. He had stuff upstairs, too, but it didn't hurt to have things readily available all over the house. "I'm a first responder," he reminded her. Maybe he couldn't fix what she saw as a rejection last night—at least not at this very moment—but he could fucking fix her finger.

"And I'm a nurse." She let him move her toward the cupboard, though. "You guys just keep people going until they can get to us, right?"

That was true. And he was a firefighter first. The majority of the calls they went on were medical emergencies as opposed to fires, and he was trained as a first responder, as were all the firefighters, but he wasn't the main medic on the team, and the ambulance always rolled out with them to medical calls. He could keep someone alive until the ambulance arrived—usually... probably—if needed, but he was a lot better with the hoses. And for a second, he thought about saying that. Trying to recapture the teasing and innuendo from earlier.

But Lexi was bleeding and he needed to be the one to fix it.

"I think I've seen more blood than you have, Lex. I've been doing this for ten years. You just started." He peeled the paper towel away from her finger. The cut was small but deep. He frowned. "I should glue this."

"You're not gluing it," she said, tugging on her wrist. "I'm fine."

"Like I said," he told her, looking up. "I've done this more than you have."

"It's a *cut*. On my *finger*," she said.

"That might need glue."

"Caleb," she told him, her voice firm. "If you come at me with glue, I will—" She glanced in the direction of the kids. "Put my knee somewhere you don't want it to be."

He felt his eyes widen. Wow. Lexi had never thought she knew better than him about something. Damn, she was feisty this morning. And Lexi was never feisty.

At least that he knew of.

"What's your problem?" he asked. "I'm trying to help."

"I'm a *nurse*," she said. "I think I know when a cut, especially on *my own finger* needs glue. And I can put a bandage on myself."

That irritated him. And he couldn't even say why. Because of course she could. Even without her medical training.

"What would be *helpful* would be if you'd go cut up the strawberries," she said.

He let go of her and stepped back, hands up. "Fine. Do it yourself." He stomped over to the cutting board. He tossed the knife she'd been using into the sink and grabbed another one, slamming the drawer harder than necessary.

"Use the kitty Band-Aids," Shay said from the table. "They're the best ones."

"Thanks, honey, I will," Lexi said.

Caleb chopped up the strawberries and dumped them into a bowl. There, at least he was useful for *that*. And why he was acting, and feeling, like this, he couldn't have explained for a million dollars. Unless he was being honest with himself and admitted that he was mad because Lexi hadn't let him help her. And he *really* needed to feel helpful this morning.

But that didn't make him feel better, so he decided not to be honest with himself.

Lexi bandaged her finger as he carried the bowl over to the table, then Lexi took the chair next to Jack.

"Uncle Caleb has to kiss it better," Shay said, reaching for the strawberries. "That's what he does after Band-Aids."

Lexi looked up at him, her cheeks suddenly pink. "Oh, but *I* kiss both you and Jack after Band-Aids," she said. She lifted her finger to her lips and kissed it. "See? All better."

Spurred on by all the emotion of the last two days, Caleb caught her hand and bent as he lifted it. He met her eyes and said, "I don't think kissing yourself counts." Then he pressed her finger against his lips. He lingered there, watching her as her eyes locked on his mouth. He saw her swallow and her hand seemed to instinctively curl around his.

When he finally let her go, Shay announced, "There. All better."

Lexi slowly nodded as he straightened. "Sure. All better."

He gave her a half grin. "Glad I could help."

C aleb did always make things better. Sure, the kiss on her finger had made all kinds of sparks and tingles go racing through her body. And now she was thinking about all of the other places she'd like to have his mouth. But she definitely wasn't thinking about the stinging from her cut anymore. Or even, much, about her annoyance over the cut and Band-Aid and everything.

That was still there, though, at the back of her mind. She'd cut her damned finger because of Shay's comments about Lexi putting her hands on Caleb. Then he'd completely overreacted about her possibly needing glue. For God's sake. She would have known if she needed *glue*. And she would have taken care of it.

But she'd almost let him do it.

That was the most irritating part of all. She'd almost let him glue the little cut on her finger because she knew how much he loved taking care of her. It also felt really freaking good to have Caleb Moreau fussing over her. She figured the tough, life-saving hero wouldn't love the term "fussing," but it was exactly what he did sometimes. And dammit, it was *nice*.

It was also a little pathetic. Except that it really worked for both of them.

Right now, he was upstairs showering and Lexi was sitting on the floor by the coffee table in the living room where she could see the kids playing in the next room, but could spread the newspaper out to look for apartments at the same time.

She wasn't sure she'd ever been more distracted in her life.

She'd drawn twenty-seven circles around the same apartment listing in the paper. And it certainly wasn't an apartment worthy of twenty-seven circles.

Of course, it wasn't entirely her fault. It was biology that she was attracted to Caleb. He had all the characteristics of the alpha that appealed to women on a primal level. He was a protector, a provider. He commanded attention. He'd stepped in to raise his niece. He walked into fires to save lives. And he had really great hands. Big, and a little rough, strong, confident, and yet very gentle when he was playing with or taking care of Jack and Shay. And yeah, hot. His hands were hot. Literally and figuratively. So was his mouth. She'd replayed last night and the feel of his hands and mouth on her, the dirty words, the way he'd looked at her like he'd never seen anything he wanted more, a million times since waking up.

If she *wasn't* attracted to him, she'd wonder what was wrong with her. It was like her ovaries...and her nipples...strained toward him whenever he was around. And now he was naked and wet just upstairs. She groaned and leaned to put her forehead on the table, thunking it a couple of times against the hard surface on the off chance that it might help. Though with what she wasn't sure. She didn't really want to *not* be attracted to him.

She just wanted him to be attracted back.

She just wanted to make their pseudo-family into a real one.

She just wanted him to be madly in love with her.

She gave her head one more thunk against the table.

She just wasn't used to being here *with* him. She'd always loved being surrounded by his things and his scent and the pieces of his life that were obvious here—his hunting gear in the garage, his favorite foods in the kitchen, his running shoes by the front door—but *he* was never here when she was but for the few minutes by the front door. So now she felt jumpy and distracted. Especially after the kiss last night, and the stupid kiss on her finger this morning. How could those two things be equally affecting?

Lexi sighed and watched the kids for a minute. They'd set up the miniature soccer goal and the six little balls that went with it.

She heard the water shut off upstairs and pictured Caleb reaching for a towel and wrapping it around his waist. She thought about him leaning over the sink to look into the mirror while he trimmed his beard, and she realized that she wanted to watch that. That beard did things to her and she was fascinated by it.

One of the little soccer balls bounced off the wall and came rolling into the living room, and Lexi saw that she'd started drawing circles around another apartment listing while daydreaming about Caleb and his beard. She'd tuned right back in to Caleb the second she heard a sound from the upper floor.

Damn, that right there was a good reason she couldn't stay here. If he was in the house, the kids could be setting things on fire five feet away and she wouldn't notice.

She glanced over at Jack and Shay. They were fine. They were right there and nothing was burning. But then she heard Caleb's footsteps overhead and sighed. Caleb was right there, too, and if the past was any indication of how things would go, she'd never *not* be able to tune in to him if he was near.

There was something about him that just made people listen. He said things in this firm, confident way, but with a true concern tingeing the edges that made her melt. When Caleb said he was going to do something, he did it, and when he wanted to take care of you, there wasn't a lot you could do about it.

But he really wasn't a very good listener, come to think of it.

She frowned and circled the apartment listing again. When he made his mind up about something, it was really hard to change it.

Not that she ever argued very hard with him. It was like she had this instinct to please him. To make sure that he was happy. And the best way to make him happy was for him to think *she* was happy.

It sounded nice—them wanting to make each other happy.

And also sounded kind of messed up.

And embarrassing when she thought about the things he'd asked her last night and how willing she'd been to do any and all of it. It was no wonder he thought she was a crazy wannabe girlfriend.

Because she was.

Yes, there was a part of her that wanted Caleb to just take over and take care of her in the bedroom the way he did everywhere else.

Lexi realized she was almost breaking through the thin newsprint with her repeated circles. She laid the pen down and sighed, massaging her temples. She turned her head and watched Shay and Jack kicking the balls into the net, trying to focus on the two little people who had brought her and Caleb together instead of the man upstairs who caused so many complicated emotions for her.

The playroom was supposed to have been a formal dining room, but Caleb—or maybe his sister—had decided the wide-open room just off the living room on one side and the kitchen on the other was the perfect place to put Shay's toys. Either way, it made the big, old house a lot less assuming. With the right table, that room could easily seat twenty people for a holiday feast. But the toy box, the sunshine yellow, kid-sized picnic table, and the brightly colored plastic tubs of art supplies and puzzles and books made it seem like a home.

The room was big enough that the kids could play with balls if they didn't get too crazy, and Caleb had set the soccer goal on the end away from the other rooms so the wall would stop any errant kicks. Once the kids were older and kicking and throwing harder, they'd have to move the sporting activities outside, but for now there wasn't much they could hurt.

Lexi frowned as Jack kicked the ball into the net. She was impressed with his seemingly natural abilities to catch, throw, and kick. According to the child development stuff she'd read—for class and for mom-hood—Jack was ahead of the average for his age. But he wasn't the one she was really watching now. Shay was having a hard time with the kicking. It was as if when she tried to swing her leg, it threw her balance off. She managed to stay upright, but the ball barely rolled.

Lexi resisted the urge to go over and help her. This wasn't the first time she'd noticed Shay having trouble with something, but she knew that kids needed to figure things out on their own sometimes. Shay was perfectly safe, but Lexi's protective instincts with that little girl were incredibly strong, and Lexi knew she was just overreacting to watching Shay struggle.

Jack lined three of the six balls up again. At two, he still carried the balls with two hands and had to half-bend/half-squat to set them down, but he had no trouble balancing to wind up or staying on his feet as he contacted the ball with his toe.

Shay, on the other hand, always tried kicking with her right foot first, but had trouble balancing on her left. But she also couldn't swing her left foot, even though her balance on the right was much better.

"Hey, you guys," Lexi said, setting the pen down and crawling across the floor. "Let's play bridges and highways!"

She'd made up the game several months back. Jack and Shay both loved playing with little cars and trucks, and Lexi had thought up a way to get Shay using her seemingly weaker left side while playing.

"Yes!" Jack ran to the bin with the miniature vehicles and grabbed his favorites—a fire truck and a black pickup that looked a lot like Caleb's.

Lexi smiled even as she rolled her eyes. Jack's idol worship of Caleb was so obvious and so sweet. She felt a pang in her chest. She was so grateful to have Caleb in Jack's life. Jack's dad, Seth, had chosen medical school over marriage and a baby. He'd written her a ten-thousand-dollar check—well, his dad had—and had told her that he'd come find her after he was finished with his residency. She wasn't holding her breath.

Shay brought a dump truck and a blue sedan over, but Lexi said, "How about you be the bridge first?"

Shay grinned and got on her back, lifting her butt up off the floor. Lexi and Jack drove the cars and trucks under her and then up her legs, over her stomach, and down her arms.

"This highway is getting bigger!" Lexi exclaimed tapping Shay's left leg.

Shay lifted her leg off the floor. Jack made siren noises for the fire truck, driving it faster than the pickup from Shay's foot to her hip. Shay giggled as the little wheels tickled her and Lexi smiled, but she noted that Shay's leg didn't stay up for very long.

"Other highway!" she said, tapping Shay's right leg.

That leg went higher, but she couldn't keep her butt up as high pushing with just her left leg.

"Earthquake!" Lexi announced. They'd played the game several times before so Shay knew that meant she was going to march her legs up and down, and Jack and Lexi had to drive their cars up her leg before it lifted off the ground and threw them off.

Shay marched her legs three times but then her butt collapsed to the ground.

"Okay, country roads," Lexi said.

Shay lifted her arms and they drove on the smaller roads for a few minutes before Lexi parked on Shay's forehead and grinned down at her. "Jack's turn?"

"Your turn!" Jack told Lexi.

She grabbed him and kissed his cheek. "I'm the bridge now?"

"Big bwidge!"

She laughed. "I might be offended by that." She got on her back and lifted her butt in the air. "You better drive fast," she told them. "This is a *monster* bridge that is going to try to crush your trucks!"

She lifted and lowered her butt as the kids laughed and tried to get their vehicles through the space underneath her before she smashed them.

"*Damn*, I've really been missing out on playtime around here."

4

The deep, low voice from the doorway made Lexi freeze with her butt in the air. She craned her head. Caleb stood with a shoulder propped against the doorframe, watching. Shirtless. Lexi quickly dropped her butt, felt the sharp edge of the fire truck poke into her back, winced, and worked to pull Caleb's shirt down over her butt. She was wearing her shorts under the big shirt but with her hips in the air, the shirt had ridden up on her stomach, and she felt strangely exposed by the way Caleb was watching her lift and lower her hips.

She cleared her throat. "Bridges and highways," she said, gesturing to the kids holding the cars.

"Come play!" Shay told Caleb, going to him and grabbing his hand.

"Yes!" Jack agreed, running at Caleb. "Big bwidge."

Lexi laughed. "Yeah, this way *I'm* not the biggest bridge."

Caleb scooped Jack up, tossed him over his shoulder. "A bridge? Maybe I'm the troll under the bridge that eats the little kids who try to cross the bridge." Caleb found a ticklish rib and Jack shrieked and laughed. Lexi felt herself grinning.

"No, on the floor," Shay insisted, pulling on his hand. "You be the troll under Lexi!"

Caleb looked at Lexi and she felt her stupid cheeks heat. It was a *game*. With the *kids*.

"I'd love to be under Lexi," Caleb said.

His voice was huskier, though Lexi doubted the kids noticed at all.

Yeah, well, you are definitely more of an on-top kind of guy, Lexi thought before she could stop it. "He's too big to be under me," she told Shay. And yeah, she met his eyes when she said it, meaning the innuendo as well. Two could play *this* game. He'd seemed annoyed or confused by the conversation that morning about her being embarrassed over him not wanting to *play* with her last night. But if he was going to keep making comments like that one, she wasn't going to just let them go.

"Oh, I promise that we can make it work," he said, holding Lexi's gaze. "Might take some stretching. And spreading. But we can do it."

Geez. She felt the heat in her face. How could he be so dirty with the kids right there, talking innocently about a *game*? An actual game.

It might have something to do with the fact that he wore a loose pair of black athletic shorts...and nothing else.

"Lexi could be the troll!" Shay decided. "She's little and can fit under you."

"She sure can," Caleb agreed.

Lexi could only think, *Yes, please.*

"But she's way too pretty to be a troll," Caleb added.

Caught off guard by the compliment, Lexi said nothing. Even when Caleb gave her a wink before he bent to sweep Shay up with his other arm.

Shay giggled as he tossed her over his shoulder.

"But I think both of *you* could be little trolls," he told them.

The kids giggled and wiggled. "We're not trolls!" Shay said. "We're pretty, too!"

"No twolls!" Jack agreed.

"I don't know," Caleb said. "If we're playing bridges, don't we have to have trolls?" He turned to face Lexi squarely and suddenly she couldn't swallow.

He had a child that she loved with all her heart over each shoulder, he wore a huge, happy grin, and her damned heart flipped over in her chest.

Holding the wiggling kids, she could see all of his muscles bunching and rippling. From his shoulders and arms, down to his abs, and her mouth went dry. And she was vaguely aware she was staring. She was also vaguely aware that she wasn't doing anything to stop it.

"So what do you think?" he asked.

He had both arms up, keeping the kids from sliding off his shoulders. His feet were spread, his legs braced. He was big and wide and hard and...she had no idea what he'd just asked her.

"Lex?"

She managed to drag her gaze from the trail of hair that ran from his belly button into his shorts. But she dragged it slowly. Up his abs, over his chest, and finally to meet his eyes.

She'd never seen Caleb naked. She'd never seen him even *this* naked. There weren't a lot of reasons for him to go shirtless when she was around. Unfortunately. She wasn't going to waste the chance to check it all out.

"Yeah?" she finally asked.

He didn't say anything for a long moment. Then he shook his head. "I don't remember what I was going to say."

The fact that her looking at him had distracted him made a ribbon of heat curl through her belly. "Sorry," she said, not sorry at all.

"Uh-huh."

He wore a half grin that made her swallow hard as he seemed

to snap out of—whatever—and bent to set the kids back on the floor.

"Bridges and highways!" Shay said, reminding them both of what they'd been talking about.

"Okay, so someone show me how to be a bridge," he said, crossing to where Lexi sat cross-legged on the floor. He dropped down next to her.

"Lay on your back," Shay told him.

He did and all Lexi could think about was running her tongue up the middle of his abs from the waistband of his shorts to the base of his throat.

"Tell him the rules," Shay said to Lexi as she reclaimed her vehicles.

Lexi cleared her throat. "Um, okay. For a bridge, you just lift in the air."

He did and her eyes were immediately drawn to the front of his shorts where the material molded around his cock.

Caleb coughed. "You keep looking at me like that and we're gonna have a big roadblock in the middle of this bridge," he said.

Shay was already driving her car up his right leg, and Lexi knew exactly what he was referring to as the blue four-door approached his hip. She cleared her throat again.

"Well, there can be road construction," she said, not meeting his eyes.

"Put your hand here," Shay told him, pulling his right hand to his thigh. "Now I have to go around." She drove her car down the side of his leg.

"Swing!" Jack said.

Lexi glanced at Caleb. His eyes were on her. "You can be a suspension bridge, too," she said. "Sway your hips back and forth."

"Yes, ma'am." He moved his hips side to side.

And yeah, Lexi had a hard time taking a deep breath.

The kids moved their cars and trucks over him, even with the movement, making engine noises.

"How about a racetrack?" Lexi asked.

"Yay!" Shay told her.

Lexi looked at Caleb. "Now you get on your side and curl up."

He did, turning toward her, propping his head on his hand, and pulling his knees up to curve into most of a circle. He just watched her as the kids raced their cars around and around him, pretending there was a ramp that launched their cars into the air to get over the gap between his shoulders and knees.

"Oh, no, another earthquake!" Lexi announced. She met his gaze, which hadn't left her face. "Roll back and forth."

The kids giggled and played through it all.

"Okay, Golden Gate Bridge," Lexi said. "Shay, you want to do that one, too?"

"Okay." Shay got on her hands and knees, then boosted her butt in the air.

Jack drove his cars over her and Lexi followed with the dump truck.

"Now do the drawbridge with me," Shay told Jack.

The two-year-old got on his hands and knees, facing Shay. Then they both raised their hands up, going up into a kneeling position. Lexi drove three of the cars between them.

"Draw bridges you can drive under?" Caleb asked.

She looked at him over her shoulder and shrugged. "Sometimes we use boats."

"Or my hippo!" Shay said. "Then he's the lock-mess monster!"

Lexi laughed. "Loch *Ness*." She looked at Caleb. "Yeah, sometimes there's water and we have monsters and even sword fights on the bridge with our soldiers." The stuffed animals and plastic army men became all sorts of great things when they pretended.

Caleb pulled himself up to sitting. "This is all quite a game. I've never played bridges before."

"It's Lexi's game," Shay told him.

"It is, huh?" Caleb looked at Lexi. "Very creative."

"Balls!" Jack announced, heading back into the playroom and straight for the soccer balls.

"Can I color now?" Shay asked.

She often asked for a quiet activity after they'd done something more physical. "Of course," Lexi told her. Shay went to the cupboard for her coloring books and crayons and settled at the picnic table in the playroom. Lexi got up and crossed the room. She grabbed a pad of blank paper out of the same cupboard and took it to where Shay was sitting. She watched Shay open her coloring book. "Hey, after you color that picture, would you draw me something?" Lexi asked.

"Okay."

"And I want you to draw something using only blue, red, and orange, okay?"

"Okay," the little girl said agreeably.

Lexi made a mental note to ask Shay which colors she'd requested in a few minutes.

She went back to the coffee table in the next room. Caleb was stretched out, propped up on one elbow again, watching her. She sat down behind the table, putting the solid object between them. For some reason.

Him watching her so intently made her jumpy and she couldn't really say why. Except that this was all new. Different for them. They never all hung out, just playing and lounging together. One of them was always at work when the other was here with the kids.

This was all very...domestic. And comfortable. And sexy.

Sexy? But yes, hanging out in the living room together casually, while the kids played and they watched, was sexy. Strangely. Though the shirtless Caleb didn't hurt.

And she was in big trouble.

"What's that all about?" he asked when she was settled.

"What?"

"The drawing with just three colors?"

She glanced at Shay. "Oh. Well, sometimes she has trouble remembering things so I give her little tasks like that so she can practice. I'll ask her which colors I wanted in a few minutes and see if she remembers."

Caleb frowned slightly. "You play memory games with her?"

Lexi nodded. "And other games."

"Like?"

"Naming things that are green. Counting the lamps in the house. Naming things that are bigger than her shoes, or what things would fit inside her cereal bowl. Just little learning things like that."

He looked puzzled. "Why?"

She shrugged. She'd noticed that Shay had some trouble with her colors and numbers and categorizing things. "They're just some things I've noticed she needs a little practice doing."

Caleb just watched her for several long moments. Then he said, "Is that what the bridge game is about?"

"That's more about her strength and coordination."

Caleb pushed himself up to sitting. "That's to help her get stronger?"

Suddenly she felt very self-conscious. She could admit that she'd been a very intense student during nursing school. She'd gone over and over her assignments. She'd asked a million questions. She'd been hyper focused. Nursing wasn't something, in her opinion, that people should fuck around with. People were depending on them to make the right decisions to help them. People trusted them to take care of them.

And she loved that. She loved having people put their faith in her, listen to her, and respect her opinion. She'd never really had that before. She'd always been the one who felt she needed help and had so much to learn from other people. But in the ER, she had to know what she was doing and she took that seriously. Patients listened to her. Her coworkers listened to her. She'd even convinced a cardiologist to take a closer look at a patient the other day. He'd listened...and realized that they'd missed a heart murmur.

She got a little high off of all of that, but she knew she needed to dial it back outside of the ER. She didn't know everything. She definitely didn't know everything about pediatrics. That had been only one unit in school and she hadn't worked with kids much, and definitely not outside of the ER. In an emergency, there wasn't much time for involved assessments and she left all of that to other professionals.

"It's just some stuff I've noticed," she said. "I don't really know what I'm doing, but it just seemed that she's *so* right-handed, well, right-*side* dominant, that I thought it might be a good idea to encourage her to use her left side more. And I've noticed that she doesn't like to do a lot of intense physical play. I know Jack is on the other end of the spectrum and can barely sit still, so I try to balance it all out for both of them. I make up these games to get her playing more and then we do quieter activities with animal sounds or playing I-Spy around the house and stuff so that Jack does some quieter stuff..." She trailed off. She was going on and on. She pressed her lips together.

"Lexi," Caleb said quietly.

She looked up, realizing she'd been drawing even more circles in the newspaper rather than looking at him. This time circling an ad for motor oil. But she didn't need to buy motor oil. Caleb took care of that for her.

"You've been working on this stuff with Shay for how long?"

"Always. I mean, a long time. Whenever I noticed something, I'd try to figure out a way to practice it with her."

Caleb had a *really* strange look on his face now. He looked amazed and confused and...turned on. But that couldn't be right, could it?

———

H e was so damned turned on he almost couldn't stand it.
Sure, he'd seen, touched, and tasted her nipple last night. He wasn't able to completely forget about that. But it was so much more than that right now.

Lexi had been working with Shay on the things that were hard for her.

Not because she knew there was a problem. Not because the doctor or therapist had told her to. Just because she'd noticed it and decided to help the little girl she loved get better at things.

That also meant that Shay's issues hadn't been completely neglected. She wasn't as behind as she would have been otherwise.

Of course, as the intense sense of relief crashed over him, he also felt a huge wave of guilt. Lexi had noticed something that he hadn't.

"Does this all help?" he asked, his voice a little hoarse.

"The play and exercise?" Lexi asked. She lifted a shoulder. "Yeah, of course." She gave him a little smile. "If you practice something, you get better at it, right?"

Of course.

Shay was better because of all of this. *Of course* she was. He loved that. The bubble of hope that expanded in his chest made it hard to take a breath for a moment.

And then reality surfaced.

Shay might be getting a little stronger or a little better at remembering, but none of it was going to improve drastically. Some of the things going on with her were permanent. The weakness in her left side was because of damage to her brain. Damage that couldn't be reversed.

And there was nothing in that moment that could have made him tell Lexi that. He was the guy who fixed things for Lexi. And Shay. It was who he was. It was why he was important to them both. Until he had some idea about how to fix this and could reassure Lexi that he had a plan, he didn't want to say anything.

"Are you concerned about her?" he asked.

Lexi glanced at Shay, her face relaxing into a soft smile, her eyes full of love. Caleb sucked in a quick breath before she looked back at him and noticed all of the emotions that had to be obvious on *his* face. "No, I'm not concerned about her," Lexi said. "She's amazing."

"But that left side..." He trailed off, wanting to see what Lexi's reaction would be.

She laughed softly. "She's a little klutzy. So what?"

"What about her memory?"

Lexi glanced at Shay again and then lowered her voice. "Listen, maybe she's not going to be an Olympic athlete or Valedictorian, but that doesn't matter. She's sweet and she loves cats and she loves to color and she does the things she *can* do with excitement and curiosity. Who knows? Maybe she'll own a cat rescue, or a cat café." Lexi grinned. "That would be amazing. I'd go every day."

Caleb couldn't help his smile even as his heart clenched.

He was still dealing—okay, honestly, he hadn't even started dealing—with the idea that Shay wasn't going to do a lot of things he'd assumed she'd do. He'd thought she might do dance like Logan's little girl, Chloe. Or that she might play soccer or be a swimmer. He realized that somewhere in the back of his mind, he'd assumed that he'd be watching her play sports and win ribbons for science projects and participate in music programs.

He had no way of knowing if any of those things were possible or would still happen. He knew next to nothing about her brain injury, including the specific area of the brain affected, or even all of her symptoms. Shay had just always been Shay.

Over the next few weeks, though, with the therapist assessments and sessions he was going to learn all about it. He was bracing himself for all of that, even knowing that some of it might not be obvious until she was older. But he was mourning the loss of the things he'd assumed and taken for granted. And that made him feel like an asshole.

He also couldn't share *that* with Lexi. He couldn't be the asshole who didn't know what to do with a little girl who had challenges. Until he *did* know what he could do for Shay, he was keeping this to himself.

"You've never said anything about her being klutzy or her memory," he commented.

Lexi shrugged. "I don't say things about her getting a scrape on her knee or throwing a fit about her mac and cheese touching her hamburger or her asking if ladybugs go to heaven, either. It's just a part of her life that happens when I'm here and I...take care of it."

And here was Lexi, accepting Shay for who she was right now in this moment and taking care of things that came up, taking it all in stride, maintaining that as long as Shay was happy, it was all good.

He drew a deep breath. That made him feel better.

"But you think she's a little...slow?" Caleb asked.

Lexi smiled over at Shay, then back at him. "I don't know. Maybe. I mean, we're not all going to be Nobel Prize winners or NASA scientists. But I also think maybe we haven't read to her enough or gone over her colors with her enough or encouraged her to play and exercise enough."

Caleb felt his chest tighten at that. "You think I'm not doing enough?" He *knew* he wasn't. Now. But he hadn't realized Lexi thought so. And Lex was supposed to think he was amazing.

"I said *we*," Lexi said with a little frown. "We have crazy schedules and we're in and out and so we don't have, or take, the time to really sit and concentrate on things sometimes. But that's all stuff we can change."

Okay, that was fair. "We can do better." *He* could do better. Lexi was doing more already.

She nodded. "Always." She gave him a smile. "And hey, maybe we're doing fine, too. Maybe it's just Shay. I mean, I'm horrible at spelling. I don't know why. No matter how much I worked on it, I just was never good. So I compensate. My phone has autocorrect and my computer has spell check and I look stuff up."

He didn't want Shay to have to compensate. He wanted everything to be perfect and wonderful and easy for her. He took a deep breath. His whole mission in life for the past two years had been to make Shay, and Lexi, and Jack safe and happy and healthy. To make their lives as good as they could possibly be. To make things easier for them. But no matter what he did or tried, no matter how much he cared, no matter how much he wanted it, he couldn't fix this for Shay.

And he couldn't tell Lexi that.

At least, not yet.

Lexi loved Shay. She loved that she was helping. And she was probably in denial that it could all be something more.

She saw Shay's limits just as a part of who Shay was and nothing more. Nothing to worry about. Lexi didn't have anything to mourn because she just loved Shay as she was, without building up crazy dreams and plans.

Of course, Cassie hadn't given Shay to *Lexi* with the idea that she would do everything in her power to make Shay's life good. Not that Cassie would blame Caleb for any of this, but he'd let the whole hero-thing go to his head. He'd built up this idea that whatever successes Shay had would reflect on *him*, and people would be even more impressed with the way he'd stepped into Shay's life.

Maybe all parents felt that way. That they wanted their kids to be huge successes because it would make their *kid* happy, but also, at least a little, because it would mean *they* had done a good job.

Or maybe he was just an asshole.

Shay's injury was not a failure. Not for her. Not for him. And it could have been so much worse. He should be thankful for where she was at. And he would be. Eventually. He'd get there. He loved her and she *was* happy and she would find her talents and the things she loved. He'd do everything he could to help her do that.

But, right now, only a day after finding out that things weren't going to go exactly according to plan, he was still dealing.

That was okay.

Probably.

But no, he was not going to be able to tell Lexi about this right now. It would bother her, too. She'd worry. She'd have questions that he couldn't answer. Yet. He'd figure all of this out and then fill Lexi in. When he could honestly reassure her that everything would be okay. Because that's what he did.

"What are you doing with that?" Caleb asked, gesturing to the newspaper in front of her. And changing the subject.

"Uh...apartment hunting."

He looked up with a frown. "Why?"

She lifted a brow. "Because I need a place to live."

"You have a place to live."

"We can't stay with you permanently."

Yes, they could. That was his first reaction. And his second. And even after he thought about it for nearly a minute, it was still his reaction. "I think you should," he finally said.

"Um, no."

"You just said that our schedules are crazy and we're in and out and that might be negatively affecting the kids." Okay, that wasn't *entirely* fair. She hadn't said things were *bad* for the kids and she'd said they could make the necessary changes. Which they definitely could. Obviously, all of Shay's issues were not because of their schedules. But then again, it wasn't like their strange routine was a *good* thing, right? And what about Jack? The kid needed a place he could be stable and secure. Permanent.

"The kids are fine," Lexi told him. "Don't overreact."

Yeah, well, that was kind of his MO with these three people. Especially in the past twenty-four hours. "I'm not," he said. "I just can't come up with any reason that we *shouldn't* live together."

Both of her eyebrows flew up. "Really? None? Because I can think of a couple."

"Yes, you're messy. But I can live with that." The girl left glasses and cups and pens and notes and hoodies all over the house. But honestly, it made him smile to clean up after her. He liked how comfortable she was in his house.

"Yeah, okay, that's a good point and not even one of the reasons I was thinking of," Lexi said.

"Okay, what're your reasons?"

She pressed her lips together, regarding him thoughtfully. "The naked thing," she finally said after several seconds passed.

"The naked thing?"

"The reality that we will both be naked in this house at times and if we're both always here together, the chances of seeing the other without clothes goes up exponentially."

He wondered if she'd been talking to Logan. "I'm not really seeing that as a reason to *not* live together." He gave her a slow grin.

She just tipped her head to the side and gave him a *Really?* look. "That could make things awkward, don't you think?"

It could make the fit of his pants a little tighter. But it could also make his day start off on a fucking amazing foot. "How so?"

"Naked time doesn't really go with this big-brother-little-sister thing we have going on, does it?"

Big-brother-little-sister thing? He leaned in. "Lexi, I can honestly tell you that I've *never* thought of you as a sister."

She sighed. "Then what? A stray cat? A charity case?"

"No," he said firmly. "A...friend."

"Okay. So our *friendship* doesn't really go with naked time."

Yeah, he knew where this was coming from. And there were a few things they needed to get straight. Mainly, that he'd never given in to all his feelings for her because it wasn't right for him to initiate it. But not because he didn't have them. *She* had started things last night. She'd wanted him. But she'd also been drunk and grateful.

However, if she wanted to do that again, when she was sober and things were good and safe and stable in her life, then she needed to be aware that he was definitely *not* going to be so noble he'd resist for the sake of their friendship.

In fact, she needed to be *very* clear on that.

5

―――――

"I pulled back last night because you were drunk. And exhausted. And you were feeling especially indebted to me. And I was keyed up about finding you living over the bar—with Josh on the sofa—and realizing you hadn't told me what was going on. There were too many things going on for us to go there last night."

Lexi blinked at Caleb. So they *were* going to straight-up talk about the make-out session? Good. Yes, she'd pushed him here, but he'd started it with the whole thing about living together. She was just going to move in as if he was just some friend who had an extra bedroom? He was just going to make that offer as if he didn't know she had feelings for him? Like he hadn't seen her nipple last night? *Really?*

"And now? Now that I'm sober and you've calmed down?" she asked. She wanted to have this conversation. Mostly. After last night and then the innuendos flying around this morning, not to mention this very domestic scene they were experiencing, they needed to get on the same page with everything.

Because she wanted this. Badly.

She wanted to live with him. She wanted relaxed mornings

playing with the kids together. She'd seen the spark of admiration in his gaze when she'd told him about making up games that would help Shay. She'd seen the soft look of affection when he'd been watching her and Jack. She'd also seen the heat in his eyes when she'd first come into the kitchen in his shirt. She wanted all of that, too. Those emotions from him. The sense of really doing this together. Not just handing the kids back and forth and leaving sticky notes that they were out of cereal, or that her car was making that weird clunking noise again. She wanted to actually do it all *together*. And she wanted him to *see* her. To let her be his partner in this. To not just be the guy who took care of her.

She did not want this if he thought he was just doing her a favor. Or if he thought this was just a more convenient setup for them both with the work and home balance bit they juggled.

She wanted a home. She wanted Jack to have a home. And she wanted it to be with Shay and Caleb. They were her family, no matter how puzzle-pieced together their situation was.

And she wanted Caleb to feel the same way.

She held her breath as Caleb glanced at the kids. They'd already moved on from soccer and coloring to some game of their own that involved the soccer balls, three teddy bears, and turning the picnic table on its side.

Caleb looked back at her. "I want you here. I want you and Jack here where I know you're safe and comfortable."

She nodded. Okay, so this *was* a favor. "I appreciate that."

"And last night I realized how much I hate not knowing what's going on with you."

Lexi sighed. "I promise to give you my new address. You can even help me look for apartments."

"That's not enough. I want you *here*. This feels...good, right? Being here together. All four of us."

She swallowed and nodded. He knew what the sense of family meant to her. She'd shared that much in their support group meetings. She'd referred to the group as her pseudo-family and told them how much that meant to her and why.

"I like taking care of you," he said, his voice low and gruff. "And I can do that best if you're here *with* me. All the time."

Her mind wandered just a little in the direction of ways he could take care of her—that had nothing to do with her car or where she lived—before she reined it back in. She couldn't fight her body's response to his natural dominance, but she could keep her head on straight.

Honestly, until Caleb had come along, she'd had no idea that she was turned on by that alpha-I'm-in-charge-power thing that Caleb exuded. But she was also mostly convinced that it was only true with *Caleb*. She'd never been attracted to other men who had power—bosses or teachers or cops or anyone else who could somehow tell her what to do. Seth, the only guy she'd ever had sex with, had been a guy's guy. He liked sports and drank beer and talked dirty sometimes. But even when they'd had sex, he'd never made her feel the things Caleb could make her feel with a slow, sexy grin. It was just Caleb who made her think things like, *Yes, please, sir*. And again, it went back to the fact that she trusted him more than any other man who had ever been in her life. Actually, she trusted him more than any other *person* in her life.

So letting him have some hot-bossy-protective power was just fine. In fact, her body thought it was more than fine.

Still, she lifted both brows. "You do know how that sounds, right?"

"Sweet and protective?" he asked dryly.

"Controlling and crazy."

"I'm not going to tie you up or anything," he said. Then after a beat added, "at least not for that reason."

Lexi felt a strange, hot clench in her gut—okay, lower than her gut. Had she imagined that response? Because that was *exactly* the kind of thing she wanted him to say. And do. And she shifted slightly as tingles went through her.

A heavy silence stretched with the words hanging in the air. Caleb's gaze dropped to her mouth again. Not lower. Not to her breasts. But her nipples hardened anyway.

She cleared her throat when it was obvious that he wasn't going to elaborate. Or try to clarify his statement. Or reassure her. He just let the words linger in her mind.

"So I wouldn't be a prisoner," she finally said. "Good to know."

"Right," he agreed. His eyes were back on hers. "Unless you try to go back to that apartment. Or something as bad or worse."

She wet her lips and decided to look at the newspaper in front of her instead of at the hot, alpha man who was threatening to tie her up. Her nipples sent out yes-please-we-want-that signals to the rest of her body, but she tried to ignore them.

"Fine," she finally said, noting the pleased, almost smug, glint in his eyes with her answer.

Well, she wasn't stupid. Living here really was a good solution to her current situation. But it could also be temporary. Until she really got on her feet and had some money saved up. And until she saw how things went with her and Caleb. If there was even a chance that this could all be real, that they could be actual partners, that they could be compatible beyond liking the same pasta sauce and laundry detergent, then she needed to try it. It was a risk, for sure. But it was one she was willing to take.

"But I'm paying you rent," she said.

"No."

"Caleb."

He lifted a brow. "Fuck no, even."

"Caleb—"

"*I* don't even pay to live here," he said. "Cassie's life insurance money paid for the house so I don't owe anything. It would be ridiculous for you to pay me to stay here."

"But electricity—"

He gave a short bark of laughter. "I think I can handle the price of you blow drying your hair, Lex."

She sighed. "Then I'm going to do more around here. I'll do all the laundry and—"

"No."

"Stop it," she said firmly. "I'm going to contribute. I want to feel like this is even." She *needed* this to be even. Not just for her own pride's sake, but so that Caleb could see that he could depend on her, too. "I want to give you something in return."

He looked at her, his gaze tracking over her face, and lingering on her lips.

Lexi had the strangest sensation that he was thinking of some inappropriate ways she could "pay rent." *She* definitely was. And a not-so-little part of her *really* wished he'd just say it. The dirty talk from him last night had been a fantasy come true.

Well, part of a fantasy. She had a whole library of full-blown fantasies that included a lot more than just talking.

"What?" she finally asked.

"Just working to get my image of you in a French maid's costume out of my head."

Lexi felt her mouth drop open. So he *had* been thinking inappropriate thoughts. *Yes.* "Do you realize you just said that out loud?"

Then he grinned. And she wanted to go straight to the costume shop.

Role-playing with Caleb? Having him give her dirty commands as her boss while she played his maid? Or the employee he was punishing for embezzling money from the company? Or the college professor who was going to make her "earn" her A? Or the sexy firefighter who wanted repayment for saving her kitten from a tree? Or the hot single dad who had a special benefits package for his babysitter? Okay, that one was even closer to reality. And all she could think was, *Yes, please.*

"I—"

Suddenly Jack came running and jumped on Caleb. Shay tumbled into Lexi and she had to drop her pen to catch the girl. They were both making monkey noises and Jack climbed up to sit on Caleb's shoulder.

"Monkey attack?" Lexi asked, laughing as Shay "ooh-ooh-ahh-ahh-ed" in her ear.

"From Boston!" Shay announced.

Caleb chuckled as Jack climbed all over him like he was a tree. "Brazil, baby girl."

Shay nodded, scratching under her arm like she'd seen the apes at the zoo. "Brazil."

Caleb grabbed Jack and swung him down to the floor and started tickling him.

Jack shrieked and wiggled. "Help! Shay!"

Shay jumped off of Lexi and hopped over the table and onto her uncle's back.

"Ack! Double monkey attack!" Caleb said. "Help me, Lex!"

Laughing, Lexi crawled around the edge of the coffee table and reached for Jack. She pulled him away from Caleb, who promptly flipped Shay off his back and reached for one of the throw pillows on the couch. Lexi pulled Jack's shirt up and blew a raspberry on his belly while Caleb bopped Shay on the butt with the pillow.

Both kids were laughing so hard they couldn't talk. Lexi reached for a pillow as well. They were the perfect size for a kid-level pillow fight. But as she stretched, she felt someone whop *her* butt with a pillow. She looked over her shoulder. Caleb still held the pillow. And he didn't look apologetic. Or like it had been an accident.

She lifted an eyebrow. "Really?"

"I just want to be sure that you know I am a friend who *definitely* wants to play with you."

Lexi turned on her knees to face him. "You also said *that* out loud."

The kids had grabbed pillows and were now bopping each other and still making loud monkey noises.

Caleb nodded. "Yep," he said, under their noise. "You need to know that me pulling back last night had nothing to do with not *wanting* to play with you. Or you being good at...the game."

Lexi felt that down-deep clench again at the huskiness in his voice.

"What did it have to do with?"

"The drunk and exhausted thing," he reminded her.

She nodded. "Right."

"And that I've got some power over you."

She froze at that. She stared at him. "Excuse me?"

He did. Kind of. But she didn't realize that he really acknowledged that.

"I'm older than you. I give you a lot of things. I help you out a lot."

She tried to say something, but she had no idea what *to* say.

"You feel indebted to me."

Again, she tried to make a sound. And couldn't.

"And, you respond to me bossing you around."

Her eyes couldn't go any wider.

"So I have to be careful with you."

"You better be careful," she finally muttered.

He gave her a cocky grin. "I'm right."

He was. About the bossing thing. And the influence thing. But he did *not* have to be *careful* with her. And if he couldn't tie her up and make her scream, well, this wouldn't work out.

Probably.

She *really* wanted him to tie her up and make her scream—in the good way, of course—but he was still Caleb. And he still had Shay. And she still wanted this family for real. For good.

Dammit.

"You're careful with me because I always seem in over my head and because I need your help all the time." What would he think if she told him that she often *let* him help her because she knew how much he loved doing it?

"I'm careful with you because it doesn't take much for me to influence you."

She wasn't sure she'd put it quite that way. *I want you to tell me not to wear panties while I dust the house. And to be sure to bend over a lot. And to use the arm of this couch for something other than propping up to watch TV.* Okay, so the French maid costume thing maybe needed to get bumped up her Want-To-Do list. But she wasn't sure he was *influencing* her. She just wanted him to boss her around. "You think...you *influence* me?"

"I do."

There was a screech from one of the kids, who were only a few feet away, but Lexi couldn't pull her eyes from Caleb's face. If the screeching got louder or kept going, she'd look over there. She waited for a heartbeat. The next second there were two loud giggles and Lexi's full attention was back on Caleb in an instant.

"Give me an example." Maybe they were actually talking about the same thing.

He gave a soft chuckle. "I talked you into a new car seat for Jack. I talked you into using a new salad dressing."

Yeah, that wasn't the direction her thoughts had gone. Or the direction she'd hoped *his* thoughts had gone. "Car seats and salad dressing?" She rolled her eyes. "Really?"

"I told you that I thought you looked beautiful in red and you wore red the next time I saw you."

She felt a flush of embarrassment. She hadn't thought he'd noticed. Well, she'd thought he might notice she looked nice, but not that she'd done it on purpose. "So?"

"I told you that I loved pistachio pudding. You made me a dessert with pistachio pudding two nights later."

"Because I'm *nice*."

"Because you love to please me."

Okay *that* sounded more like what she'd been thinking. And

hoping he was thinking. That sounded a lot more—she swallowed hard—submissive.

And damn if there wasn't a streak of that in her. As surprised as she had been to realize it.

Lexi felt her cheeks get warm. He said it with such confidence, watching her face, *knowing* that he was right no matter what she said. And he clearly liked it. Which made her pulse race.

"You're a good guy. We make each other's lives better. Easier. And you're older and have more experience than I do, so of course I listen to you."

"You love to please me," he repeated. He leaned closer. "You light up when I thank you or when I say you did something well."

She took a deep, shaky breath. None of this should be sexy. But...it so was. It had been when it had just been in her own thoughts, but now hearing that he realized it, hearing him talk about it, was making her feel very hot and squirmy. "I like you, Caleb. I respect you. You're nice to me, so I'm nice to you."

There was a loud, "No!" from Jack just then and Lexi glanced over. But Shay was already handing him back the stuffed dog. Lexi watched as he tucked it into the driver's seat of the huge fire truck, then brought her attention back to the hot, intense man in front of her.

"Austin and Gabe and Logan and Bea and Addison and Dana and Corey...they're all nice to you," Caleb said, continuing their conversation as if nothing was happening in the playroom.

And nothing really was. Nothing that needed their full attention or presence, anyway.

Lexi wet her lips. "And I'm nice to them, too."

"You don't light up for them, Lex." He paused. "You don't wear red for them."

And in the midst of the heat—and yes, hope—that this all inspired, she also felt a little mortified. He knew all of this. He knew how she felt about him. That she wanted him. And he'd still pulled back last night. "You're kind of an ass sometimes, you know that?" she asked.

"Yeah," he agreed. "But not last night. I was a good guy last night. I couldn't... influence you last night."

"Because I was drunk."

"Yes. And because I had you in that bed for a lot of reasons besides sex."

Hearing Caleb saying the word *sex* did funny things—*nice* funny things—to her stomach. "Wha—" She swallowed hard. "What do you mean?"

"You were in that bed because you needed a place to *sleep*. You were tired and drunk. *I* needed you in that bed because I needed you to be safe. And close to me."

"And sex couldn't be a part of that?" she asked softly. Partly because the kids were there, but also because she had lost her breath.

"I was worked up last night, Lex. Really worked up. Because of how much I needed you to be safe, because of how much I had to assure myself that you were okay with your mom gone, and that I could still take care of you. Because of how mad I was that you didn't tell me about everything." He gave her a pointed look. "And I knew that I could *influence* you into just about anything. And I wanted to. I wanted you to need me in a way you never had. So I had to pull back. I didn't want my frustration and fear to be the reason for getting you to say and do all the things I want you to say and do. That's not how it's going to be when that happens."

Holy. Crap.

Lexi felt hot. And wet. "*When* that happens?" she asked, keying in on that one word.

"Yeah. When."

"You're pretty sure of yourself." But if she *lit up* when she saw him and he'd noticed just how influential he was with her, then yeah, he should be sure.

Everything he said was true. She did listen to his opinions

more than the others. She did love it when he was pleased with her. It was pathetic. But true. And it was something she'd never experienced before.

"I am sure," he agreed.

She took a deep breath and then asked, "So, how's it going to be?"

"All about pleasure. All about giving you exactly what you need. All about taking care of you," he said, his voice gruff.

Well, holy damn, that sounded all right to her. "All about me? What about you?"

"Oh, darlin'." He gave her a slow smile that went straight to her core. "When it's about taking care of you, it *is* about me. Haven't you realized that?"

She did know that taking care of her made *him* happy. It gave him something. She hadn't really thought about how that might translate to sex, though.

Now she wasn't sure she'd be able to *stop* thinking about it.

"It won't be about fear or frustration or exhaustion or intoxication," he said.

That was fair. Neither of them had really been at their best last night. "Okay," she said. "You're forgiven."

That seemed to take him by surprise. But he gave a low chuckle that made heat scoot through her belly.

"Thanks."

She took a deep breath, feeling completely overwhelmed. Which made sense considering she and Caleb were talking about having sex. With each other.

God, she couldn't wait.

If it actually happened.

Because what she wanted from him was going to push him out of his comfort zone.

Caleb's worldview really was all about taking care of her. Protecting her. Tying her up, making her do dirty things, maybe even spanking her—a little shiver of desire went through her—

was going to be at odds with all of that. With how he usually treated her. With how he thought of her.

But he wanted to make her happy. He wanted to give her what she needed. And *this* was what she needed. Caleb being completely dominant, telling her what to do, taking charge, and *taking* his pleasure from her.

She took another shaky breath. She wanted to be everything he wanted. To show him that he was everything she needed.

She cleared her throat. "This might really...rock our boats," she told him. This was going to change everything.

"It might," Caleb agreed. "Then again, some things are worth getting a little...wet for."

Wow. She felt her cheeks heat. She was no shy innocent but Caleb had simply never talked to her like this. It was taking a little getting used to. And some things, like slow sexy drawls, were impossible *not* to get wet for. She blew out a breath.

"But," he added, "all of this means you're in charge."

That jerked her thoughts away from the fuzzy handcuffs Santa had given her at the support group's after-hours Christmas party. She frowned. "What do you mean?"

"Because of my influence over you, you're going to have to be the instigator of whatever happens."

She had not been expecting that. "But...really?"

"Believe me, it's going to be hard on me," he said. "I'm pretty used to calling the shots. If I think something needs to happen, I just bust in and make it happen."

She couldn't argue with that. Caleb had a natural dominant streak.

"And," he said, his drawl lengthening slightly. "I really like the effect I have on you."

Dammit, she blushed deeper. She'd known that he was aware of her crush, but she hadn't realized just how many details he'd picked up.

"But because of that," he said, "*you* have to be the one to make whatever happens...happen."

Wait, what? That was not at all what she wanted. He had to do this. He had to take charge. He had to be in control. She wanted him telling her to strip, to bend over, to get on her knees...

She got where he was coming from. Appreciated it on some level. He didn't want to use his *influence* over her to maybe make her do something she didn't want to do.

But she *wanted* him to take charge here.

Her stomach clenched. Would he even be *able* to take charge with her? Could he say things like *suck my cock* to her? Could he restrain her? Could he pinch her nipples hard enough or spank her ass or deny her an orgasm because prolonging the pleasure would make it even better?

She knew the answer.

No. Caleb wouldn't deny her anything. If he tied her up and she begged him to make her come, he would. And yeah, it sounded ridiculous for her to *worry* about that. But there it was.

"Okay, so, we're on the same page there." She pushed up from the floor, unable to help the swirl of satisfaction when she saw his eyes track down her bare legs. "And now, I need to head to the s-t-o-r-e for a couple of things."

"You're going like that?" he asked, blatantly checking her out as she crossed the room, still in his shirt.

She shook her head. "Heading up to take a shower."

"Am I going to get my shirt back?" Caleb asked.

She let her gaze wander over his shoulders, chest, and abs. Damn, she *really* wanted a chance to get her mouth and hands on all of that.

"Sure." She stripped the shirt off and tossed it to him. Then she turned on her heel, in only her shorts and bra, and headed for the stairs.

———

C aleb was certain that Lexi could hear Jack's tantrum even in the upstairs bathroom.

But she was sure taking her sweet time getting back down here.

She, obviously, knew that Jack wasn't *actually* being tortured —despite the sounds he was making—but she could come check.

Caleb propped a shoulder against the arched opening between the living room and the foyer where Jack was currently pounding out his frustrations over the injustices in the world on the wood floor. Caleb took a bite of the banana he held as he watched the little boy. Jack was a pretty easygoing kid most of the time but...he was two. There were just moments where he was an unreasonable monster.

Caleb's post in the doorway let him keep Shay in sight where she was coloring at the coffee table—with the three colors Lexi had requested but that Caleb had needed to remind her of— while also keeping his eye on Jack. He always watched the tantrums, making sure the kids didn't hurt themselves. Or any of his belongings. But he didn't try to talk them out of whatever was pissing them off. Anymore. In his experience, once a toddler had decided that everything sucked, you just had to wait them out.

Five minutes—that felt like five weeks—later Caleb heard footsteps on the stairs. He supposed maybe Lexi's hair dryer had given her some reprieve from the noise. But now she was on her way down. Caleb suddenly frowned at Jack as it occurred to him that this might be bad. What if Lexi didn't appreciate Caleb's approach to dealing with her son's tantrums?

He swallowed and straightened away from the doorway as her legs came into view. It also occurred to him that this was maybe the first time he'd been concerned that Lexi might be displeased with him. *That* was interesting. But honest. In the time they'd known each other, they didn't spend a lot of time one-on-one and when they did, it was almost always situations where Caleb looked pretty good. He was fixing something or hauling something or delivering something or telling a story or offering advice at the support group. He wasn't bragging when he said that he gave pretty good advice. It was always easier to be objective about someone else's parenting than your own. At the same time, he knew that Lexi liked hearing about Jack and Shay from his perspective, and yeah, maybe he chose the stories he shared and the questions he asked in order to show her that he was doing a good job and really cared.

Huh. It hadn't occurred to him that he'd been trying to impress her until that moment. When she was about to come upon her child prostrate on the floor, sobbing as if his last friend had just left him, while Caleb watched on. Eating a banana.

She came down the stairs, stopping on the last step, and looked down at her son. Then she sighed, crossed the foyer, and stepped over Jack without a comment.

She stopped in front of Caleb. "Wow. What's that about?"

She didn't look concerned. Or angry. Caleb gave her a grimace. "I wouldn't unwrap the string cheese he brought me from your purse."

One of her eyebrows lifted. "Oh?"

"It was a tampon."

Now both brows went up. "Oh."

"Yeah."

Then she grinned. "He freaked out on me the other day because he broke his cracker and I wouldn't put it back together."

Caleb laughed, relieved and amused and...something else he couldn't quite name. "You're so mean."

"I know, right?" She smiled up at him.

"So—" Caleb glanced at Jack. "How do you usually handle this?"

"His my-life-is-over fits?" Lexi glanced back at her son. "I ignore them." She looked back to Caleb. "I used to try to redirect him and sometimes that would work, but now—" She shrugged.

"I tell myself that it's time he learns that tantrums aren't going to help him get his way. But sometimes I think it's just that I'm really...tired."

Caleb felt that something-else-he-couldn't-quite-name again. His hand itched to lift and tuck her hair behind her ear. But he couldn't. Then he realized that yeah, he could. She was living here and he'd laid everything out—that he wanted her and that she was in charge. He could touch her now and not worry about sending mixed messages or confusing her. His messages would be very clear. *I love touching you and I want to do a lot more of it.*

Was the sex thing in her court? Yes. But did that mean he wasn't going to encourage her to take charge sooner rather than later? No. Hell, no.

He brushed the back of his knuckles over her cheek and tucked her hair back. He was gratified to see her wet her lips. "So we handle these the same way."

She looked pleased by that. "Well, that's good."

His hand fell away because he couldn't think of a good reason to keep it there, but neither of them made a move to leave the spot.

Lexi tipped her head. "It's interesting. We've never really talked about that, have we?"

"The tantrums?"

"Well, that," she said. "But also the discipline thing or how to handle this stuff."

He thought about that. "I guess you're right."

"But what we're doing is working."

She *almost* put a question mark on the end of her statement. He could practically hear it. But no matter what was going on with Shay and her brain injury, she was well-behaved—for a four-year-old—and generally happy. She got frustrated sometimes and ended up in time-out, and Caleb didn't know how much of that had to do with her condition and what was just being four. He supposed that was another question for the experts—should he be disciplining her for things like frustrated breakdowns that were caused by things she simply *couldn't* do? Probably not. But how did he tell the difference?

Forcing the tension out of his shoulders, Caleb nodded, "It is," he told her. "The kids are both happy." That much he could say for sure.

"Yeah." She pulled her bottom lip between her teeth.

Her lips distracted him. Even more so now that he'd tasted them. And told her that he was all in on tasting them again.

"Oh my God, I can hardly think straight," she finally said, glancing at Jack again.

The kid could go for a solid twenty minutes so Caleb just shrugged. "I'm hoping he can find a well-paying job that requires him to yell. I haven't come up with anything yet, but we've got a few years."

Lexi gave him a smile, though she shook her head, as if confused.

"What?" he asked.

"It's nothing."

"Come on."

She took a breath. "I just...when you talk about 'we' and things that are years down the road as if we'll still be doing all of this...I just..."

They *would* still be doing all of this. The idea of *not* being there to see Jack graduate high school or get his first job—a yelling job or not—stabbed Caleb in the chest. As did the thought that Lexi might not believe he'd be there. "Lex—"

"I just really like it," she said, finishing her thought. "A lot of the time I feel like I'm functioning day to day, maybe week to week. While I was in school it was semester to semester. But I don't really think long-term." She swallowed. "I guess that's why my mom moving to Shreveport with Greg kind of surprised me. But it shouldn't have." She shook her head. "I think that's why I'm so...unprepared all the time. I don't think ahead. I just take things moment by moment or day by day."

Maybe that was good. Just take it as it came. Not think about what things Shay wouldn't be able to do when she was eight or what things might frustrate her in high school. Just take today for what it was and do his damnedest to make it as good as he could. If he couldn't fix today, he sure wouldn't know what to do with a teenage girl who couldn't keep up with her peers.

Lexi was staring at his chest now instead of looking him in the eye. As always, Caleb had the instinctual urge to reassure her and tell her that he'd take care of whatever she needed so she didn't *have* to think ahead.

But before he could speak, she looked up at him again. "I have to quit assuming that everything will always stay the same," she said. "Right? Things will *always* change."

They did. Always. And often times it didn't matter how prepared you were. Caleb saw it every day. Knew it firsthand. You could go to bed with the next day's lunch packed and Thursday's report done and weekend plans confirmed in your day planner, and you could wake up in the middle of the night to the smell of smoke and your whole world turned upside down and shaken. You could go out to mow the lawn in preparation for the barbecue you were hosting the next night and fifteen minutes later, you could be lying in your too-long grass, praying that the ambulance would get there before your heart completely stopped.

You could go to the pediatrician for a checkup and walk out with your entire reality altered.

"That's why you have to wallow in the moments when everything is good and just how you want them to be," he said.

Without thinking about it any further, he cupped the back of Lexi's head and pulled her in as he bent. She was a lot shorter than him, but he didn't mind leaning over to cover her mouth with his. He kissed her, lips only, for several long moments, just relishing the feel of her, the taste of her, the scent of her. But she didn't pull back. In fact, she leaned into him, and soon it wasn't enough. He parted his lips. She followed his lead, and a moment later he was stroking his tongue along hers, slowly and deeply.

He felt her go on tiptoe and fist the front of his shirt and he slid his other hand from her shoulder to her ass, bringing her up even more fully against him. Damn, that was something he'd wanted to do for so long.

She smelled sweet—that ever-present bubblegum scent— and tasted even sweeter. Then there was the feel of her ass in his hand, her silky, warm hair between his fingers, and her hands holding the front of his shirt as if he was all that was keeping her upright. But it was the *sound* of her that really fired his blood. The soft whimpering sound against his mouth was needy, a wordless plea, the sound of a woman who, yeah, *needed* him, and what he was doing—and could do—to her.

He started to turn her so her back would be against the wall and he could press closer. Harder.

But suddenly he heard a sniff and, "What doing?"

6

J ack's tantrum was over.

Of course it was.

Damn, Caleb hadn't even noticed the little boy had stopped crying.

But nothing could distract a guy from a good pissed-off conniption like some dude kissing his mom like he wanted to... Caleb cleared his throat. Truly, just kissing her was probably enough to get Jack's attention. That was definitely something they'd never done in front of the kids.

Then again, they hadn't even sat around the coffee table and talked about new apartments, or had breakfast together, or played with the kids while the other showered. Today was full of firsts.

Lexi stepped back from him and combed her fingers through her hair. It took her a second to look away from Caleb, but when she did, she turned to her son and said, "So you're finished with your fit?"

Jack was sitting in the middle of the foyer, his face red and wet. He rubbed a fist in one eye and sniffed again. "Uh-huh."

"Good," Lexi told him. "That one was pretty loud."

Jack just nodded.

She crossed to where he was sitting and squatted down in front of him. "It's okay to get mad about stuff. Sometimes things don't go the way we want them to and that's not very fun." She reached her hand out and set it on top of his head, looking into his eyes.

Caleb found himself shifting so he could see both of their faces more easily, mesmerized. He'd seen Lexi with Jack, of course. Mostly when he greeted her at the door when she came to pick him up, or at the family events for the support group. But there, Jack was playing and distracted by the games and other kids. Caleb was sure that in two years he'd seen her discipline Jack or talk to him seriously, but for the life of him, Caleb couldn't remember a time. Of course, Jack had just turned two a few months ago. Maybe her tactics had changed. It made him feel strangely...strange to not have witnessed this before. Or to even know how she generally approached disciplining the little boy they both loved so much.

They really were parenting more like exes who had joint custody. They both had a hand in the parenting, but they didn't do it together and rarely saw the other one doing it.

He wanted that to change. The thought hit him suddenly, and hard. But it felt right to think about doing this, all of this, together.

"But screaming doesn't mean you're going to get your way," she said. Jack sniffed and then suddenly launched himself into her arms. She gathered him close and said, "Sometimes I just want to scream and cry, too, honey. I understand."

And Caleb had to force oxygen into his lungs.

Damn. That was the most beautiful thing he'd ever seen. It was crazy, really. He'd seen Lexi looking beautiful many times. Most times. Every time he saw her. Hell, he'd seen her breasts— finally—last night. And yet *this* was what drew him like a bee to honey. Of course Lexi hugged Jack. He'd seen Jack go running to her and fly into her arms before. But there was so much love pouring off of them in this moment, Caleb swore he could feel it across the five feet that separated them.

Jack's breathing had calmed and he was no longer sniffing by the time Lexi stood with him and turned to face Caleb fully.

She gave him a funny look. He could only imagine what expression was on his face at the moment. A mix of wonder and affection and lust, he was sure.

"Looks like everything's okay," he said, his voice gruff.

"Yeah." She swallowed. "Being held is sometimes all a person needs."

Caleb felt a jolt and his knee-jerk reaction was to open his mouth to say he'd hold her anytime. But she quickly looked down at her son, almost as if wanting to interrupt before Caleb said anything at all.

"Everything's okay, right?" she asked Jack.

"Yep," the little boy told her.

"Okay, then." She crossed to Caleb and handed Jack over. "I'm heading to the s-t-o-r-e, then."

She was leaving? They didn't need any groceries. He usually stopped by the store on Wednesday and Lexi went on Saturdays. She got the bulk of what they needed and all of the staples. Caleb's trip was usually to pick up the stray extras they either forgot to put on the list or ran out of.

They were almost never both off on Fridays and if they were, Lexi wasn't *here*. She was at home with Jack. Except now *this* was her home. And they were all going to spend the day together.

"Oh, no, it's zoo day," Caleb said. A family outing. That wasn't something they'd done together before.

Lexi looked up at him quickly. "Zoo day?"

"Zoo!" Jack crowed.

Lexi winced and Caleb grinned. Once the kids knew about it, she wasn't getting out of going.

"Yep, it's Friday. Zoo day. Right, Jack?"

"Zoo day!" Jack agreed.

Fridays really were zoo day for him, Jack and Shay. It wasn't *completely* manipulative to put it into the two-year-old's head that they'd all go out together.

Lexi sighed. "Really?" she asked Caleb.

"Sure. We've never done that together before. It'll be fun." He started into the living room with Jack to grab the kid's shoes. "Shay, zoo day."

Shay looked up from her coloring page. "Now?"

"Yep."

Shay immediately grinned. "Yay! We can see that girl I like!"

Caleb grinned. There were actually three girls that the kids liked. He was ninety percent sure that Shay was talking about Lauren, but, for some reason, Shay had a hard time remembering all their names even though they saw them every Friday. Kara was Jack's favorite, though Naomi was a very close second.

Shay got up and ran to get her shoes and Caleb dropped onto the couch with Jack in his lap to pull the boy's shoes on. Thankfully, he remembered to do a swipe and fished a dried orange slice out of Jack's shoe before he stuck the boy's foot in. He did, however, note that something crunched in Jack's left pants pocket. It wasn't anything from breakfast. He'd made sure Jack left the table with nothing in his hands. But sometimes Shay got snacks from the cupboards for him. Caleb was getting pretty good at figuring out what Jack had squirreled away just by touch through a pants pocket, though. This had to be cereal or the tiny cheese crackers shaped like dinosaurs. Caleb didn't have time to clean Jack up right now. Lexi might use that as an excuse to leave for the store without them. And hey, smashed cheese crackers wouldn't be any messier in an hour or so than they were right now.

Caleb didn't look up until he set Jack on his feet and sent him to grab Caleb's cap from the pile of shoes, caps and jackets by the front door.

Then he noticed Lexi watching him with a hand on her hip.

"What?" he asked getting to his feet.

"Who's the girl Shay likes?" she asked.

He smiled. "Lauren. I think. It could be Naomi. But Lauren is the one who feeds the monkeys."

Lexi's eyebrow went up. "There are two girls that the kids are excited to see?"

"Three, actually." God, he wanted to kiss her again. The kids were preoccupied. He could just get a quick taste.

"Three?"

His eyes were on her mouth as he nodded. "Your son has lots of girlfriends he needs to say hi to."

He took a step closer to her, his attention on her lips. Hell, they didn't do things just the two of them, either. And he'd really like to change that soon.

"My *son* has lots of girlfriends he needs to say hi to," Lexi repeated.

She sounded dubious, and Caleb's gaze bounced back up to her eyes. Ah, she thought maybe *he* was the one who wanted to go flirt with the girls who worked at the zoo. Well, they were all very cute and yeah, Naomi had given him some signals. But he hadn't taken her up on it. Mostly because you didn't pick up one-night stands at the zoo. You might pick up a woman you actually wanted to date, if you were into that kind of thing. Because she'd then know, up front, that there were kids involved, and he'd know up front that she was good with it. And yeah, he knew that guys with kids, guys with the dad-vibe, were attractive to some women. He'd have to be dead or stupid to not know that. If not from personal experience, then from trips to the park with his friends who were dads. Or trips to the water park. Or trips to the grocery store. Or...just about anywhere else he and his single-dad friends had ever been with their kids.

Women loved a guy who was good with kids.

But he had never, not once, used that to pick up a woman. Because what he wanted from the women he spent time with had nothing to do with Shay and Jack.

And because he already had the perfect woman involved with Shay and Jack.

And she was standing in front of him right now.

"I'm very sorry to break it to you, but your son's a ladies' man," Caleb told her.

"My son is, huh?" she asked. "Why do I think maybe these ladies didn't notice *Jack* first?"

He laughed as Shay and Jack came running back in just then, ready to go.

He'd just take her to the zoo and show her that there was nothing with these girls and him. The girls and *Jack* on the other hand...this little mama was about to see her son flirting for the first time. Caleb grinned as he swung Jack up into his arms and took Shay's hand, heading for the door.

"You're sure we *all* have to go?" Lexi asked as she watched him load the kids into the car.

He pointed to the buckle on Shay's booster seat. "Buckle up, Shay-doodle."

She giggled at the nickname and strapped herself in. She managed to get the thing buckled after three tries of inserting the metal tab into the right slot. Caleb put Jack into his seat and got him secured.

He'd bought an extra car seat for each kid within a month of him and Lexi figuring out how to swap childcare and work schedules. It was simply easier than loading and unloading the seats each time they exchanged the kids. She'd protested, of course, and he'd insisted, of course. And he'd gotten his way. Of course.

"We don't *have* to go," he agreed, turning back to Lexi. "The kids and I can go. You can stay here and relax."

But he knew she didn't want time alone at home. She just wanted donuts. And now she was curious about the zoo.

"No, I'm fine, I guess," she said, moving toward the front seat.

He moved to block her. "I'll stop by the store on the way home and buy you the coconut crunch donuts you're jonesing for."

The grocery store where they shopped made their own mini-donuts every morning. He knew Lexi didn't splurge on junk food much at all. Not for the kids or herself. He was the one who bought the pudding cups and the occasional package of cookies. But he'd been, well, charmed when he'd found that she'd stashed donuts. Charmed wasn't a particularly manly word, he knew, but it was how Lexi made him feel. Often, in fact, if he really thought about it.

Her eyes got wide. "I don't know what you're talking about."

He grinned. "You really thought you could stash them in the Crock-Pot and I'd *never* find them?"

She frowned. "You found them in the Crock-Pot?"

"Hey, I use the Crock-Pot sometimes."

"I'm just...surprised there were any left. I never forget about donuts."

He laughed at that. "They were pretty stale."

She nodded, a slight curve to her lips. The lips he still *really* wanted to kiss.

"I forgot about those. But I promise you won't find any in the crystal serving bowl in the high cupboard over the fridge or in the box of kale chips in the back of the cereal cupboard."

He narrowed his eyes, enjoying this more than made sense. "You ate the kale chips and then kept the box so you could stash *donuts*?"

She wrinkled her nose and shook her head. "I got that box from the break room at work. Kale is disgusting. In every form."

She gave him a grin and Caleb felt a kick in his gut. She was teasing, almost flirting, with him. It wasn't sexual but, apparently, it didn't have to be. Just that little smile, that little spark in her eyes, just the idea that she was stashing food in his house in places she knew he'd never find them—kale chips, really? He was so glad that even she didn't actually eat those.

She was...charming. That was the only word that really applied.

"The donuts don't stay in that box very long, though," she said.

"But you definitely don't share them, right?"

"These kids don't need that much sugar." She cast an affectionate glance at the little ones in the backseat.

"But you do?"

She looked back at him, her expression serious now. "Yes, Caleb. Yes, I do."

He laughed. "I won't tell anyone."

"And you better not eat any of my donuts." She pointed a finger at his nose.

Impulsively, he grabbed the finger and tugged her close. She stepped on his foot, but he didn't mind. Because now he could smell the bubblegum. "Or else?" he asked.

"Yeah." Her voice was breathless.

He fucking loved that.

"Or else what?"

"Um." She swallowed. "I don't...know."

He loved affecting her. And he was questioning this let-her-take-the-lead thing. Already. But that didn't mean he couldn't *encourage* her to take the lead. "Well, lucky for you, donuts aren't my favorite thing to eat."

Her pupils dilated, responding to the way he was looking at her, and the innuendo. "Oh. Good."

"Ask me my favorite thing to *eat*, Lex," he said, dropping his voice to the low drawl that he knew she loved. Or that she responded to, anyway. Which *he* loved.

"Um…"

"Bubblegum," he said, leaning in and taking a long draw of air near her ear. He leaned back. "And all things that smell or taste like bubblegum."

She blew out a breath. "Holy crap."

It was practically a whisper, but he heard it. And grinned.

"Should we go?" he asked, stepping back.

"Yeah. I…guess."

"What are you unsure about?"

"How to prepare myself for you to be…so *you*, no matter what we're doing."

He lifted a brow. "So *me*?"

She nodded and licked her lips. His cock twitched.

"What's that mean, Lex?"

"You're just…" She took a deep breath. "We don't spend a lot of time together. Doing normal stuff. I guess, I didn't think that…I didn't realize that you'd just take up so much *space* even doing everyday stuff."

He pretended to be offended, but he knew what she meant. He still wanted to hear her say it. "So you're saying I need to lay off on the junk food?"

She shook her head, almost looking frustrated. "Not physical space. Well…"

She trailed off, looking him up and down and his cock liked that, too. He coughed slightly and shifted. "Well?" he prompted.

"I'm not used to having you *around*. And you're definitely hard to ignore," she told him. "But you're so…"

"I'm taking up a lot of your attention," he finally supplied. Because he knew exactly what she was talking about. They'd spent half a day in the house together and he was acutely aware of where she was and what she was doing every minute. He felt like he was on alert. Ready for…something. Seeing her. Hearing her. Smelling her.

"You do," she agreed.

"We're just getting used to sharing a space." But he didn't think it would actually change. He couldn't imagine his mind not being on her if she was in the house with him. Hell, he thought about her when she *wasn't* there. Hearing the water running upstairs and knowing she was in there, wet and soapy and slick, was pretty damned hard to ignore.

"Do you think if we—" She glanced at the kids. Shay was kicking her feet and looking out the window, humming to herself. Jack was running a toy airplane back and forth over the padding on the front of his car seat. Lexi looked back to Caleb. "Sleep together," she said softly. "That it will be less intense? Is this just anticipation or something?"

Fuck no. That was his initial reaction and he knew it was right after he thought about it seriously. Once he had her, all of her— every sigh, every cry, every orgasm—he wouldn't be able to walk into a room without him wanting it all again.

He slowly shook his head. "I really don't. It might be even worse."

"Worse?"

"Once I know what it's like to be inside you, I'm not sure I'll ever recover."

He wanted to put his hands in her hair, push her to her knees, and slide his cock past the "O" that her gorgeous lips made in response to his answer.

Damn. This was intense. More than he'd expected, too.

But something he did very well, believed in very strongly, was wallowing in the good stuff. And the idea of fucking Lexi Scott every way he knew how was *very* good stuff.

She finally blew out a breath. "I thought I was in charge."

"You are." Stupidest idea he'd ever had.

"Then what's this?"

"Honesty."

"That's what you call it? You want to be *honest* so you're going to go around talking about"—she lowered her voice—"being inside me?"

His entire body went hot and hard in an instant. He was going to die if she ever said *fuck me*.

"Total. Honesty." He said it firmly. In the voice that made her nipples hard. Yeah, he'd seen it. More than once. He'd ignored it —and then used the image later when he was jerking off—but now, he didn't have to ignore it. And he wasn't going to let her ignore it, either. "You're in charge. I won't throw you over my shoulder and take you up to my bed." He leaned in. "I won't tie you to my bed and worship you from head to toe, making sure you come twice before I fuck you." His voice dropped even lower. "I won't lift you up on the kitchen counter after the kids are in bed and eat your pussy until you cry." He paused, taking in her bright, wide eyes and the way she was barely breathing. "Until you say the word." Then he straightened. "But that doesn't mean I won't talk about it."

Then he took her by the waist and lifted her up, the way he'd love to do onto his countertop, and tossed her onto the passenger seat of his truck. He slammed the door and rounded the front bumper, feeling a swirling mix of lust, impatience, and arrogance. Because her nipples were hard. And now she was going to the zoo with him and their kids with all of that going on, along with the images he'd just put in her head, and very wet panties.

Of course, he was going to have to walk around with one of the hardest erections he'd had in a long time, too.

He shifted, trying to ease the pressure against his fly, and started the truck.

———

Jack was wiggling in his seat by the time Caleb had the truck parked at Audubon Park.

The park was made up of acres of land in the Uptown

neighborhood of New Orleans and had everything from a jogging trail to a golf course, soccer and baseball fields, riding stables, a historic café, and the zoo, aquarium, and insectarium. They also held many special events from private parties to Boo at the Zoo in October, light displays in December, and several educational activities throughout the year.

Lexi knew that Caleb had a family pass to the zoo and the kids often talked about the animals, fish, and bugs they'd seen. She didn't, however, realize this was an every-week thing. Or that there were other women involved.

Truth be told, Lexi was wiggling in her seat, too. Sitting next to Caleb, seeing his big hands on the wheel, and his thigh muscles bunching as he stepped on the brakes and gas, after what he'd said to her was driving her crazy.

Caleb Moreau, the guy she'd been fantasizing about for two years now, her hero, had said the word *fuck* to her. About her. Not to mention the word *pussy*. For the second time in twenty-four hours.

She swallowed hard. If she'd thought he was taking up a lot of her head space before, now she was pretty much doomed. The man was hot when he was drinking punch at a single parent support group, for God's sake. Now? She was pretty much melting in her seat.

"Kawa!" Jack squealed as Caleb got out of the truck and came around to the passenger side.

He pulled her door open and Lexi worked on breathing. Just in and out. Simple.

But she was a mess. And a pervert. Because the only thing "in and out" made her think of was sex. She gripped her hands in her lap and told herself that she couldn't touch him.

"Lex?"

His deep voice rolled over her and her nipples perked up. Again. This wasn't the I-know-what-I'm-doing-to-you deep voice, though. This was just his regular voice. It seemed that her nipples had gone from we-like-when-he-gets-bossy to we-like-him-all-the-time.

She swallowed. "Yeah?"

"Need you to get out so I can grab Jack."

"Kawa!" Jack hollered louder.

In her peripheral vision, she saw Caleb grin.

"Yeah, bud, we're going to see Kara."

"I want to see the kitties," Shay said.

She was struggling to unhook her seat belt, and Lexi took advantage of having something to focus on other than Caleb. She pivoted on her seat to reach back for Shay's buckle.

She heard a little groan behind her.

"A thong? For the zoo?"

Lexi's hand flew to her butt and she realized that her sundress had pulled up as she'd twisted and reached for Shay. Yes, she was wearing a sundress. It was Louisiana. It was hot.

But the truth was, she'd loved the way Caleb had checked out her legs when she'd been wearing his shirt and she'd put the dress on with that in mind.

She kept one hand on her half-exposed butt cheek and unhooked Shay's belt with her other hand. Then she turned back and met Caleb's gaze. "It's July in New Orleans," she said. "I try to wear as little as possible as often as possible."

His eyes flared and bolts of electricity shot straight to her pelvic muscles. "Remind me to turn the AC off when we get home."

God. Had she known how he'd be with her if she moved in, she would have begged him to let them live with him long before this. But honestly, if he *didn't* make good on the threat to tie her up, she was going to lose her mind.

"*Kawa!*" Jack yelled.

Caleb leaned in, close, reaching for her. Lexi sucked in a breath. Then he reached past her. He unfastened her seat belt, pulling it off of her. The belt brushed over her breast and she was proud of the fact she held the little whimper in. But it was right there.

Caleb held out a hand. "Let me help you down before Jack loses his shit."

She shook her head and grabbed her purse. "I'm good."

He, thankfully, stepped back and let her slide to the ground by herself. She quickly turned to help Shay, who had climbed into the front seat, out of the truck. With the little girl's hand in hers, Lexi started for the zoo entrance.

"Ow, too tight," Shay protested, tugging on Lexi's hand.

"Geez, sorry, baby," Lexi apologized, loosening her grip on Shay.

Shay started to run, pulling Lexi with her. Fortunately, with Lexi holding on to her, Shay didn't do a face-plant when she caught her left toe on the curb. "Whoa."

Shay smiled up at her. "Oops."

Lexi smiled in return, but something nagged at her. Now that she and Caleb had talked about the fact that Shay was behind on things, that little "oops" bugged her more than usual. Shay said "oops" a lot. Because she tripped and stumbled a lot. Lexi had only recently really started noticing as Jack became more mobile and independent. She hadn't been around kids a lot and hadn't had a clear idea what things were easy or hard for them at different ages until she'd done her pediatric section in nursing school. With Jack two years behind Shay, and Lexi not knowing Shay until she was past the early stages of learning to crawl and walk, she hadn't been fully aware that anything was off. But it was becoming more obvious as Jack started to do more, that Shay wasn't quite where a four-year-old should be.

Caleb and Jack caught up with them as the girls stopped at the ticket counter. Caleb produced their family pass and they went through the gate.

"Kawa!" Jack reminded them.

As if they could forget, Lexi thought, rolling her eyes. She'd never heard of Kara before. Interestingly. This seemed to be a with-Caleb-only kind of thing.

"We're going to see Lauren first," Caleb told the boy as he handed over ten dollars and set Jack in the rented wagon. "She's the first one. Then Kara."

"'Kay," Jack agreed. "Lauwen first."

Lexi tried to ignore the prick of jealousy she felt. So her son had another girl that he couldn't wait to see. Two or three even. That didn't mean anything.

"Lauren!" Shay said bouncing up and down.

And Lexi could also be jealous of *Shay* being this excited to see someone else. Great.

"Where do your hands go, Shay-doodle?" Caleb asked.

Shay moved in and grabbed a hold of his belt loop.

"And how about your hands, Lex?"

Her head came up quickly at the drawled question. So they were even going to do this in public? Sure, her becoming completely turned on and super horny while looking at tigers with their kids wouldn't be awkward at all.

"My hands are good right here," she said, holding them up. *Not* touching him.

"You sure?" he asked. "Wouldn't want to lose you."

There were *so* many things she wanted to say to that. Most especially, *are you so sure you have me to start with?* But she'd never say that. And he did have her. Completely.

"I'm good," she said again.

"Okay, well, you know you can hold my hand while we look at the spiders."

He gave her a little wink and Lexi sighed. She fucking hated spiders. Dammit, he knew her better than she'd thought. Which made her feel warm even while she wondered if he'd be surprised to find out she had a little kink in her. Knowing about her passion for donuts was one thing. Nipple clamps were something else.

She took a deep breath and banished thoughts of sex toys from her mind. "Fine."

They rounded the pond with several pink flamingos and suddenly Shay took off running. "Lauren!"

Lexi's deep, resigned breath turned into a gasp as Shay tripped and went sprawling across the stone path. Lexi quickly knelt next to her, running her hands over her knees. "Oh, baby, here we go," she said soothingly. Shay stumbled and tripped, but she didn't often fall. However, when she did, she ended up with bruised kneecaps along with a bumped chin, a split lip, or once, a huge goose egg on her forehead. Lexi hated that she got hurt and worried that, if her coordination didn't improve, she could seriously injure herself sometime.

"Kiss them?" Shay asked, sitting on her butt and bending her knees up.

"Of course." Lexi kissed each knee. Shay wasn't crying and was, thankfully, too young to be self-conscious about taking a fall in public. It was on the tip of her tongue to tell the little girl that she needed to slow down and be more careful, but she bit it back. Shay was four. She should run and be excited and be fearless. Especially when Lexi and Caleb were right there with her. They'd take care of her. They'd pick her up when she fell. They'd kiss the hurts away. And that was all Shay needed to know right now.

"Shay! Jack!"

A woman's voice from behind her made Lexi pivot. The woman was in her mid-twenties, only a little older than Lexi. Her hair hung in gorgeous long black braids and she wore a tan zoo polo tucked into dark gray shorts that showed off long, bare legs. She was beautiful.

"Lauwen!"

So this was Lauren.

Shay got up quickly and met Lauren halfway between her spot on the ground and the entrance to the Wildlife Stage exhibition.

"How are you, sweet girl?" Lauren asked.

"Good!" Shay said, her tumble clearly completely forgotten.

Lauren took Shay's hand and gave Lexi a quick smile. Lexi got to her feet, returning the smile. Shay seemed fine, or at least distracted as Lauren led her to a little table outside of the exhibition where another woman had a face painting station. But instead of having Shay wait in line behind the two kids already there, Lauren began painting Shay's face, talking and smiling with the little girl as if they'd been friends forever.

Jack kicked his short, denim-clad legs, and Caleb took him out of the wagon and set him on the ground to go running over to where Lauren was just finishing Shay's face.

"I'm a sea otter!" Shay told Jack.

"Me, too!" Jack insisted, grabbing Lauren's hand.

"Well, of course," she said with a laugh. "You have to be ready to meet Ollie today, right?"

Jack nodded enthusiastically. Shay asked, "What does Ollie eat?"

"Oh, that's a good question," Lauren told her. She painted Jack's nose brown with a black tip and added whiskers as she went over Ollie the otter's diet.

Lexi felt Caleb move in next to her, but she had to admit she was fascinated watching Lauren with the kids. She was friendly and clearly adored both Shay and Jack, giving them special smiles as they hung on her every word. Clearly the adoration went both ways.

"No apples?" Shay asked.

Shay hadn't liked apples until about four months ago. Lexi had thought it was strange that Shay would eat applesauce but not raw apples. Then suddenly, Shay had announced one day she *did* like apples and that was that.

"Sometimes they eat fruit," Lauren said. "But that's not usually part of their diet. Fish and frogs and snails and things are."

Shay looked disappointed. "Can we feed Mike instead?" she asked.

Lauren laughed as she led them to another table. "Maybe in a couple of weeks," she told Shay. "But you should try what Ollie eats. Remember you didn't like apples, either, until you met Mike?" She handed them each a little plastic cup. "This is crayfish. Ollie loves it."

Shay wrinkled her nose, but she picked up the tiny piece of crayfish. Jack happily stuffed his right into his mouth, but Shay took her time looking at it and smelling it. Finally, she tasted it.

She didn't look entirely impressed but she swallowed and nodded. "It's okay. I like apples better."

Lauren laughed. "Me, too."

Ah, so that explained the new appreciation for apples.

"So that's Lauren," Lexi said to Caleb.

"Yep. That's Lauren," Caleb agreed.

Lexi looked up at him. He was looking at her. Not watching Lauren with their kids.

"And that's why Shay likes apples now?"

"Well, more Mike, probably, but yeah, Lauren, too," he said. "We met her a few months ago when we stopped by here. She was talking to the kids about Mike, the spider monkey, and feeding him apples. Shay told her she didn't like apples and Lauren said that they were Mike's favorite. So Shay tried a piece with her and that was that."

"Did she paint their faces like monkeys?" Lexi asked. Clearly they bathed before she got home on Fridays. She'd never seen them painted as animals.

"She did. It's a whole thing. They get their faces painted, eat what the animal of the day eats, then listen to Lauren tell about the animal while she handles it. Then, sometimes, they get to touch it and ask questions. It's the main reason we come every Friday."

Lexi sighed. "She's great. She's one of the vets?"

"Zookeeper," Caleb said.

That was cool. Damn. "Does she handle snakes and spiders, too?"

Caleb nodded.

Lexi blew out a breath. She was beautiful, smart, and had a very cool job. "That's pretty awesome."

"It is." He still wasn't looking at Lauren.

"She's also beautiful."

He nodded. "She is."

That made Lexi's stomach clench. Not in a good way. But if he'd denied it, she wouldn't have believed him anyway. Lauren *was* beautiful. It was just a fact.

"And she got Shay to eat apples."

"Yep," Caleb agreed. "She has great melons, too." He was watching Lexi carefully, the corner of his mouth curling slightly.

Lexi lifted a brow. They were just playing, but there was something about his tone that made her wonder if he was gauging her reaction. Did he want her to be jealous? Did he want her to *not* be jealous? Did it really matter how she felt? Caleb dated. She knew that. She ignored it—or tried to anyway—but she knew it. And it definitely made her jealous. She hated that feeling. That feeling of wanting what another woman was getting. The sex, of course. *Of course*. But also just time with him. One-on-one time with him. Talking to him about things other than tantrums and runny noses and counting games and work schedules. Seeing him laugh about something other than a goofy kid joke or something one of his buddies said at support group. *Making* him laugh.

But she could have that now. Living with him would certainly give them more chances for all of the above.

"She knows a lot about bananas, too, I'd guess?" Lexi asked, deciding that she could tease and make light of this.

Maybe that would drive *him* a little crazy. He seemed to think he knew her well. Maybe leaving him guessing, surprising him even—because no one who knew her would be surprised if she *was* jealous—would be good for him.

"I'm sure she does," he said smoothly.

"Cucumbers, too?" she asked. "Or only fruit?"

"I've never seen her handle a cucumber," he told her.

"Hmm," Lexi said, "how about eggplants?"

Everyone knew that the eggplant emoji in texting meant penis. At least, she assumed everyone did. She and Caleb didn't text with emojis. They texted with boring stuff like *stuck in traffic, be there in 10.*

"Never seen her with eggplants, either."

The way he said it, Lexi knew that he knew that emoji. She looked over to where their kids were babbling to Lauren about who-knew-what. Lauren was smiling and listening to every word. She pulled a wet wipe from behind her stand and wiped Shay's hands, nodding at whatever Jack was telling her as she rescued a cup of crayfish from being stuffed in his pocket.

"This is all pretty cool," Lexi said honestly.

"It is. The first time we met her she had a baby tiger in here."

Lexi smiled in spite of the jealousy. "And Shay as a fan for life." She didn't add the *dammit* on the end of that sentiment. "Have you gone out with her?" She didn't really want to know. But she kind of wanted to know.

"I haven't," he said. He met her eyes directly.

"She turned you down?" Lexi asked dryly. Maybe Lauren was married. Which would be great in some ways. But Lexi kind of wanted Caleb to not *want* to go out with her rather than just not dating her because he couldn't.

"I haven't asked."

Lexi glanced over at the other woman. "Well, why the hell not?" She looked up at him. "She's great with kids, loves animals, and is beautiful."

"I don't need a woman who's great with kids, loves animals, and is beautiful," he said.

"Doesn't every guy need a woman like that?" Lexi asked. Okay, maybe some guys didn't care about kids and animals specifically, but it meant Lauren was sweet and patient and loving. Surely all guys wanted that. Even if they also wanted to get laid.

"The smart ones do anyway," he agreed. He reached up, tucked a strand of hair behind Lexi's ear. Then he leaned in and said, "But I've already got one." He kissed the top of Lexi's head and then stepped around her to go to the kids.

Lexi stood stock still and stunned for a moment.

That was...sweet. And uncharacteristic. And hot.

Wow.

Maybe she didn't need nipple clamps. Maybe she just needed *that*.

She turned more slowly, but went over to meet Lauren. The other woman seemed sincere when she said she was thrilled to meet Jack's mom, and she didn't give Caleb any more attention than she gave Lexi, honestly. The only person who she really flirted with at all was Jack.

Lexi watched, surprised and amused, as her son put his hand in Lauren's and gave her a smile along with a "you wook pretty" that made Lauren laugh and hand him another bite of crayfish. Jack took it happily. But kept his hand in Lauren's as he ate it.

Lexi realized she might be in trouble. Jack's charm might be genetic. Seth had certainly been charming and flirtatious and knew how to make a girl feel special. But her son also spent a lot of time with Caleb, who was the most impossible man to resist who Lexi had ever met. Caleb was less playful and more intense than Seth, but there was no denying that it worked on women. If Jack took after either man, or, God forbid, a combination of the two, the women in New Orleans better look out in a few years.

They settled onto the wooden benches that faced a little stage where Lauren brought Ollie out to meet the kids. For the next fifteen minutes she talked about Ollie and how he lived, as he played and showed off for the kids. But Lexi's mind wasn't on the animal or the zookeeper. It was on the big guy next to her.

Caleb had said he already had a woman who was good with kids and animals and was beautiful. That was a little cheesy and probably a lot I-want-to-have-sex-with-you-now-that-you're-living-with-me-and-if-you-initiate-things, but she had to admit it was making her feel good. Even better than when he'd said he thought she looked good in red or when he told her the pistachio dessert she'd made was one of his new favorites.

She blew out a breath as the kids went up to pet Ollie and ask questions. Yeah, Caleb *influenced* her all right. There was very little Caleb could ask of her that she wouldn't want to do. Moving in, pillow fights, a trip to the zoo—maybe even the insectarium. And initiating sex with him.

The show ended and they headed out of the exhibit, turning toward the elephants. "Shay," Lexi said, forcing her thoughts away from all the things she would love for Caleb to just *do* to her without her asking. "Ollie eats crayfish."

"Ollie eats crayfish," Shay repeated. They played this game a lot and the little girl knew what was coming.

Lexi smiled. "Right. But he also eats snails."

"Ollie eats crayfish and snails."

"Awesome job," Lexi told her. "But he also eats one more thing. Ollie eats crayfish, and snails, and frogs."

"Ollie eats crayfish and snails and frogs," Shay said. Then she wrinkled her nose. "I don't like that he eats those things."

Lexi put a hand on her head and smiled down at her. "It's okay. It's what he's supposed to do."

Shay sighed. "Okay."

"Now tell me one more time what Ollie eats," Lexi said.

"Crayfish, snails, and frogs."

"Good job. I'll ask you again in a little bit."

"Okay." Shay went over to the fence around the elephant enclosure and peered in at the big animals basking in the sun.

"Another memory game?" Caleb asked, pulling the wagon. It was empty because Jack was up at the fence next to Shay.

Lexi nodded. "And those three things have meaning for her since we just met Ollie, so they might be easier for her." She grabbed a pamphlet about the fundraising project to expand the elephant enclosure, pretending to study it as she pondered her next question for Caleb. "I hate when she falls like that." She flipped to the back of the pamphlet. "Do you notice that happening a lot?"

Caleb didn't respond right away and she glanced up at him. "She'll be okay, Lex."

Lexi found herself searching his eyes. He met her gaze, and she felt the very familiar sense of comfort that he inspired so easily. She nodded. Yeah, of course Shay would be okay.

"Kawa!" Jack said, pointing down the path to the left and climbing back into the wagon.

Caleb's attention shifted to the two-year-old. "Well, when it comes to beautiful women, this guy has no trouble remembering where to find them."

He took Lexi's hand and they started down the sidewalk. Lexi braced herself to meet yet another sweet, beautiful girl who had a cool zoo job and had captured her son's affection.

Caleb pulled Jack out of the wagon and set him on the ground as soon as they got to the place where the path forked.

"Kawa!" Jack called as he hurried into the gift shop to their right.

Lexi followed, keeping him in site between the racks of T-shirts and bins of stuffed animals.

He came to a skidding halt in front of the cash registers. "Jack! Yay!"

Lexi watched the girl come around the counter and squat down to fold Jack into her arms. She'd been right. Kara was beautiful. She had curly blonde hair, bright blue eyes, a sweet smile, and clearly had Down syndrome.

Lexi looked up at Caleb, but he was watching Jack and Kara.

"Hi, Kara!" Shay headed in their direction, too, and Kara opened one arm to pull Shay in for a hug, too.

"The gift shop is his favorite, huh?" Lexi asked, her voice soft.

Caleb looked down at her with a smile. "He doesn't care about the stuff. He just loves Kara. The first time we met her she was the one renting out the wagons. She's been promoted."

He looked over at Jack, Kara, and Shay and the expression on his face sucked the air right out of Lexi's lungs. He was proud of Kara. Lexi felt her throat tighten. He was just such a good guy. Hot. And a dirty-talker, apparently. But just *good*.

Yeah, she didn't really *need* to be blindfolded in bed.

"I think there's something about a person who's just so damned happy to see you that's impossible to resist, you know?" he asked, his attention back on Lexi now. "But I can never tell who's happier to see the other, Jack or Kara."

He would know exactly how that felt. Lexi was always damned happy to see him.

Blindfolds or not.

"You okay?"

She swallowed and nodded. "Yeah. I, um...need to use the bathroom. I'll, um, be right back." She turned quickly and beelined it out of the gift shop. She didn't need the bathroom. But she did need some space. She kept walking until the path veered off to the left. She stopped and just took some deep breaths.

She thought about Caleb a lot already. Now she was living with him and they were spending the day together. There was just no escaping him. And even hanging out at the zoo showed her how awesome he was and made her want to be *with* him. All. The. Time.

She groaned and looked around. The petting zoo. Great.

"Baaa!"

She looked at the sheep that had come over to the fence. "That's how I feel about it," she told him.

Another sheep joined the one at the fence. "Baa!" she added. "You, too?"

A baby sheep came over next. He just looked up at her.

"I don't have an answer," she said. "I mean, hot sex is important, right?"

"Baa!" This from the bigger sheep. Perhaps the mother telling Lexi not to talk about hot sex with her offspring.

"Yeah, sorry." She looked at the baby. "Sex isn't the only thing that's important." *But it's very important*, she added silently. "I could use some advice, if you've got any," she told the mama sheep.

The older sheep didn't even have a baa for that. Lexi did need advice, though. She pulled her phone out and tapped Ashley's name. Her friend answered a moment later. "Hey, girl."

"Hey, need to talk." Lexi looked around. No one else was in the petting zoo at the moment, thankfully.

"Sure, what's up?"

"So, um, how important is the handcuff sex? Say, on a scale from zero to ten."

7

There was a long pause on Ashley's end. She heard her friend say, "I'll be right back," to someone on her end, then to Lexi, she said, "Hang on. Let me go to the back room."

Ashley was getting her business degree but she was working part-time at a cell phone store. She pretty much ran the place and Lexi was almost always able to get a hold of her.

She heard a door shut and then Ashley said, "*What?*"

Lexi sighed. "I kissed Caleb last night." She rubbed a hand over her forehead. "Wait, let me back up. He helped me up to bed and then he was trying to get me to take ibuprofen before I fell asleep and when he leaned in, I kissed him."

"Whoa," Ashley said.

"Yeah," Lexi agreed. "And it...turned into more. It was a pretty heavy make-out session there for a while." Her body heated as she remembered it. It seemed like a lot longer ago than last night.

"Just a make-out session?" Ashley almost sounded disappointed.

"He pulled back because I was drunk." Lexi had to admit that had been the noble thing for him to do. "And because he knows that he can easily *influence* me."

Ashley laughed at the tone in Lexi's voice. "Well, he can."

"Yeah." There was no point in denying it. "But that kept him from acting on anything else. He says that he was wound up about everything last night and he really wanted to—"

An older woman and two little boys joined her at the fence just then. The boys leaned over, holding their hands out. The sheep ate the food pellets from their palms. Lexi gave them a smile and moved several feet down the fence line where she could talk about having Caleb tie her up for sex without old women and little kids overhearing.

She should probably feel bad about this.

She didn't.

Her sheep and goat friends came with her.

"Baaa!"

"Where the hell are you?" Ashley asked.

"The zoo."

"Why?"

"Caleb wanted to come."

"Baaa!"

"I don't have anything," she told the animals. "You should stay down there with them." She nodded at the little boys. The sheep didn't care.

"You're at the zoo with Caleb?" Ashley asked.

"And the kids," Lexi said.

"And you're thinking about handcuffs and sex?"

Lexi blew out a breath. "Yeah. It's a problem." She dropped her volume. "He said that he was wound up and wanted to make me *need* him."

"So, *that's* good."

Yeah, it should have been. "But then he said that was why he pulled back. He didn't want the sex to just be about proving he had influence over me or that he could boss me around. He said *when* it happens, it will be all about pleasure and taking care of me."

There was a long silence on the other end of the phone, and then Ashley breathed out and said, "Damn, that's hot."

It really was. "And then he said I'm in charge of if and when it happens. I have to initiate it all."

Again, Ashley didn't respond right away.

"Ash? A little advice here, please?"

"What advice do you need?" Ashley said. "Put the kids to bed tonight, take off your clothes, and tell him you want him to hand-cuff you to the bed and have his wicked way with you."

God, even hearing her friend say that made Lexi's breathing speed up. "Yeah, but...I... don't know if he'll do it."

"Really?"

"I..." She glanced around to be sure no one was nearby to overhear and lowered her voice even though she was now alone. "I want him to blindfold me and restrain me and stuff. I don't know if he'll do it. He's pretty protective. He's all about taking care of me. Do you really think he has it in him to...spank me?"

Ashley hesitated then, making Lexi's chest tighten. "I think he'll *want to*," Ashley said.

Yeah, that wasn't the same thing as doing it. "And what if he can't?" Lexi asked, voicing her true fear. "He's...amazing. He's everything I want. I can just let that stuff go, right?" A couple came to the fence with their toddler and, frustrated, Lexi headed in the opposite direction. She ducked around the end of the pen and found herself looking into a pen of goats. She didn't expect them to be any more help than the sheep had been. She took a deep breath. "Right?" she pressed Ashley.

"Well..."

Lexi blew out a breath. "Come on, Ash."

"I'm just saying, I don't think that you should compromise what you want."

"But, it's *Caleb*."

"Yes, but..."

Lexi waited for Ashley to go on. When she didn't, Lexi hissed, "Ashley!"

"Okay, listen. I will go over this with you. Again. Quickly."

Lexi blew out a breath. She was staring at the food pellet dispenser, but instead of the very happy goat on the front of the box, all she saw was Caleb's face.

"What's the most important thing about tying someone up in bed?" Ashley asked.

"Orgasms." She looked to her right, realized a mom and two little kids had come up next to her without her even noticing, and she sighed. "Sorry," she mumbled to the mom, then she skirted around them and went to stand by the water fountains.

"Um, no," Ashley said with a little laugh. "That's definitely one of the important things, but the *most* important thing is trust."

"I completely trust him and he knows that."

"Yep. But he has to trust you, too."

"He trusts me." But she knew what Ashley was going to say.

"He has to trust that you know what you want and how to get it and what your limits are. And that you'll tell him those limits. That you'll say no to him if it's something you don't want or if he's going too far."

And that was the thing. She sighed. "And he doesn't think I really know what I want and I don't ever tell him no and I rarely think he's going too far."

"And he's a really good guy. He's overprotective and he overreacts to things that happen to you and Jack and Shay. He wants to give you things that you don't even know you want. He wants to be the guy meeting every need," Ashley said. "But he's aware of all of that. And he's trying to pull back on the sex stuff. That's pretty gallant, right?"

"But I want him to tie me up!" Lexi hissed.

"So tell him that. And then tell him your safe word and make him trust you."

Make him trust you.

That was exactly what she wanted. Not just for sex but in general. She wanted Caleb to see her as a partner, as someone he could be himself with, that she could be herself with. Not someone that he had to always worry about and take care of.

She blew out a breath. "Okay, I'll tell him."

"Good luck. Let me know how it goes." Ashley laughed. "In sexy, graphic detail if it goes the way I think it will."

Lexi felt herself smile in spite of the butterflies swooping and diving in her stomach.

"'Kay, babe, I'd better get back to work," Ashley said.

"Yeah. Sorry. Thanks for listening." Lexi needed to get back to Caleb and the kids before they started wondering if she'd been kidnapped.

In fact, she headed for the concession stand on the other side of the main sidewalk. This would be a good excuse for her time away.

She chose popcorn and a lemonade for each kid, but just as she took the first step back toward Caleb and the kids, her phone vibrated in her pocket. Wondering if Ashley had thought of some awesome advice since hanging up, she pulled it out immediately.

It was a hospital number.

"Hey, Lex, it's Zach Christy."

"Hey, Zach," Lexi greeted the new ER resident she'd worked with the other night.

"Wondering if you'd be able to come in tonight for about six hours? We've got a couple nurses out sick."

Yes. She needed to get out of Caleb's house. This was the first of his two days off so he'd be home. All. Night. Which meant he could definitely watch the kids and she could go help out in the ER where she felt confident and put-together and knew what she was doing and where she was, for sure, trusted.

"Yes. Definitely. No problem. When do you need me?" she

asked quickly, starting back for Caleb and the kids. With any luck, they'd need her in ten minutes.

"Four to ten?" Zach asked. "We're covered 'til then."

She had to work again tomorrow morning at seven a.m. "Sounds great," she said, hoping the ER would be busy tonight. Then she could get home and go straight to bed. She needed to be distracted and to reduce the amount of time she spent with Caleb until she could figure out how to bring up the nipple clamps.

"Awesome. Thanks. Glad we'll have you on the team tonight," Zach said.

On the team. The other night had been the first time she'd worked with Zach and it really had been awesome. She loved the adrenaline of the ER and how she had to tap into her gut instincts and make quick decisions. She'd felt confident and, yeah, pretty kick-ass down there.

"See you soon," she told Zach.

They disconnected as her phone vibrated with a text.

It was from Caleb and said simply, *monkeys.*

Lexi headed for the primate area. She rounded the corner and spotted Caleb and the kids immediately. With yet another woman.

But this one didn't have a zoo polo on. Nor was she wearing a name tag. She was pushing a stroller that held an adorable little girl who couldn't have been much over a year and who was holding Caleb's finger in one tiny hand.

Lexi stopped and just watched for a minute. Caleb was laughing about something and didn't seem to mind that the baby had a hold of him. Of course not. He was great with kids. But he also didn't seem to mind when the woman leaned in and squeezed his forearm.

She was pretty. Long, blonde hair gathered back in a loose ponytail, fitted pink cotton tee, and short denim shorts. She was toned and trim. And wasn't wearing a wedding ring.

Lexi definitely felt a hot flash of jealousy now. Because, unlike Lauren, this woman's body language was all about Caleb and he sure didn't seem to mind.

But Lexi didn't start forward until the woman turned to *Jack* and gave him a big smile and said something that made him grin in return.

Yeah, Lexi might not have a claim on Caleb, but Jack was *hers*. She'd share him with women who wanted to teach him about otters and give him hugs, but not with women who wanted Caleb. Caleb would just have to pick up women with his own charm.

"I got treats," she said, coming up to the cart and handing the kids the popcorn and lemonade.

"Yay!" Shay said.

Jack already had his hand in the box of popcorn.

The woman straightened and let go of Caleb. Her baby did not. The little girl gazed up at Lexi and stuck the hand not holding on to Caleb in her mouth.

Lexi smiled at her. It wasn't her fault her mom was hitting on Caleb. "Hey, sweetie, who are you?" she asked the little girl.

Of course one of the other adults was going to have to answer.

"Lexi, this is Hannah," Caleb said. "And this is her mom, Jenna."

"Hi, Jenna," Lexi said with a big fake smile. "I'm Jack's mom. And Caleb's roommate."

Jenna's smile wobbled, but didn't drop. "Oh, hi." She glanced at Caleb. "We all run into each other here every Friday. Hannah is always excited to see Caleb. And the kids," she added, as a clear afterthought.

On impulse, Lexi stepped close to Caleb and hooked her finger through his back belt loop. Right where he had Shay hold on to him. She felt his surprise, but a second later he turned slightly toward her and rested his hand on the back of her neck. It wasn't exactly sexual, but it wasn't really *not* sexual, either. Or it was, at least, more than two casual friends going to the zoo together. Wasn't it? She had no idea suddenly.

"That's so nice," Lexi said to Jenna. "I usually work on Fridays, so I'm very glad to be here as a family today." Yes, she'd emphasized the word *family*. She looked up at Caleb and gave him a little smile.

He moved her so she was more up against his side. He looked entertained and did nothing to interrupt her.

"I figured I should get the snacks. Caleb would go for the ice cream or cotton candy," Lex said with a little laugh as if she was *so* amused by the fact. "I guess it's a good thing we have each other, right? I'd have no fun without him, and he'd have too much fun without me."

Okay, that hadn't sounded quite the way she'd meant it to, but she held her smile. She and Caleb were a *team*. That was the point.

"Yes, it's so great that he has you to babysit for him," Jenna said.

Lexi felt her eyebrows rise. This was the second woman to refer to her as the babysitter. Is that how Caleb had described her role in his life to these other women? Maybe when he was explaining who Jack was? *Oh, this is my babysitter's little boy.* And, by the way, did Jenna *not* see Caleb's hand on Lexi's neck?

Of course, maybe that didn't mean anything.

"A single dad with a job like his?" Jenna went on. She was looking up at Caleb and she actually gave an audible little sigh. "I'm just so in awe of everything you do."

And yes, she'd emphasized the word *single*.

Lexi narrowed her eyes. "Yeah, I'd definitely be lost without him during my twelve-hour shifts at the hospital," Lexi said. "We're a great team."

Jenna just gave her a smile. A fake smile. That wasn't even slightly believable.

"Hey, I wanted to be sure to thank you for the chicken recipe,"

Caleb said, probably sensing that the women were squaring off. Or maybe he'd noted Lexi's narrowed eyes. Or felt the tension in her body. After all, his *hand* was on her *neck*. Okay, it wasn't like he was grabbing her ass, but still, didn't it mean *something* to Jenna?

"Oh, you bet. Sorry I got that cheese measurement wrong," Jenna said. "I'm glad you texted me about it."

First of all, no one thought Caleb Moreau was more amazing than Lexi did, and she was a little offended that this woman thought she could get points with Caleb simply by admiring him. If being "in awe" of him got anyone points, Lexi was so far ahead that Jenna had no hope of catching up. Second of all, she was a *nurse* and a single mom, thank you very much. She freaking saved and improved lives, too. This woman could fuck off.

For a moment, Lexi hoped that Jenna wasn't a neurosurgeon or a cancer researcher or something, then decided she didn't care. What *she* did was important, and Caleb *babysat* for her as much as she did for him.

Caleb chuckled and Lexi felt the vibration against her shoulder. It didn't unknot her a bit.

"No problem," he told Jenna. "Never too much cheese, right?"

Lexi fought the urge to roll her eyes. Had Jenna accidentally given him the wrong measurement, or had she purposefully given him a reason to contact her again? Lexi had to admit that was pretty good.

But Lexi knew who he was going home with today. At least from the zoo.

She rolled her eyes at *herself* with that thought. Yeah, that was really sexy.

But last night at the bar, Ana had referred to Lexi as Caleb's babysitter, too, and Lexi hadn't said a word. She hadn't felt she had the right.

That wasn't true now. Not after Caleb had moved them in with him, after the things he'd said to her that morning, after

Lexi had decided she wanted to tell him she had a few little kinks. And that she wanted him to be a part of them.

A lot had changed over the last several hours.

"You know," she said, interrupting something about how the fucking chicken would have been better with Monterrey Jack cheese instead of Swiss. "I just have to say something." She looked from Jenna, up to Caleb. He simply lifted a brow. She focused on the other woman again. "What Caleb and I do for each other isn't *babysitting*. We are raising our kids. Loving them. Teaching them. Taking care of them. *Together*. We aren't just keeping them out of trouble and feeding them for a few bucks an hour while the other person is at work."

Jenna stared at her. "I, um—"

"And yeah, Caleb's job is amazing and him being a dad is amazing, but while he is single, he's not doing the parenting thing alone. So..." She trailed off, realizing she'd said everything she'd meant to say. "Anyway. I just wanted to...point that out."

Jenna swallowed and then gave a nod. "I know he depends on you a lot. And"—she glanced down at Jack—"your son is adorable. And Shay is wonderful. Obviously, you're doing a great job. I'm sorry. You're right."

Lexi felt equal parts *yeah* and *way to overreact, Lex* at that. She blushed. "Okay. Thanks."

She felt Caleb squeeze her neck. She didn't know if that meant *okay, shut up now*, or that he was proud of her sticking up for their situation. She didn't look up at him.

"Let me know if you need any other...recipes," Jenna said to Caleb.

"Sure."

Lexi felt his thumb stroking up and down the side of her neck. She didn't know what that signal was, either, but it kept her quiet about Jenna giving Caleb an opening for more texting.

Jenna said goodbye to the kids, then said, "Nice to meet you, Lexi."

Lexi nodded. "You, too." She didn't mean it, but she was pretty sure Jenna didn't, either.

The woman moved off and Lexi took a deep breath and let go of Caleb's belt loop. He did not, however, let go of her. In fact, he pulled her closer and whispered, "We're going to talk about that later."

Lexi's breathing sped up. She didn't know if he was unhappy with her or what. And she told herself it didn't matter. She was going to stick up for their situation. This was one of those times she definitely knew herself and how she felt about something, and Caleb would just have to be okay with it.

"I have to work tonight," she said, mustering some bravado. He wasn't her dad or her husband. It didn't matter if he was displeased with how she'd talked to Jenna.

"You do?" Finally, he dropped his hand and she looked up at him.

"The ER needs me for a few hours."

"Oh."

"What? You're off tonight and tomorrow."

"Yeah." He shrugged. "Thought maybe we were going to do... something...together tonight."

All kinds of thoughts flooded Lexi's mind. But she nodded. "You and the kids can watch movies."

He looked at her for a second and Lexi wished she could read his mind. His expression was completely indecipherable. "Yeah, I guess we can."

"Okay." Lexi turned toward the kids. She smiled at Shay. "So, Shay-Shay, what are the three things that Ollie eats?"

"Popcorn!" Shay said, then giggled.

Lexi smiled, too, but shook her head. "No. Ollie doesn't eat popcorn. There were three things."

"Crayfish," Shay said.

"Very good. Ollie eats crayfish. What else?"

Shay just shrugged and started fiddling with Jack's shoelace.

ERIN NICHOLAS

Lexi took a deep breath. This was often how it went with Shay and the memory games and it was starting to concern her. But maybe it had been too long since she'd started the game. Or too much had happened. She needed to look up how long a four-year-old could retain new information again.

Lexi started to pull the wagon up the next path. She needed to see the giraffes.

"I'll give you a hint," Lexi said, as Shay walked beside her. Caleb was slightly behind them, but Lexi felt his presence like she felt the humidity when she stepped out the front door. Hot and clingy and inescapable. "They were things that live where it's wet," she said, focusing on Shay.

Shay didn't respond.

"Come on, Shay," Lexi encouraged. "You can do it."

"Crayfish," Shay said quietly.

"Right. What else?"

"Choc-wate milk!" Jack said helpfully.

She grinned down at him. "Chocolate milk is for little girls and boys, not otters."

"Popcorn," Shay said again. Almost hopefully.

Lexi felt her heart squeeze. The games were hard for Shay and dammit, more and more she was feeling like that meant something. "Popcorn is for kids, too." Lexi stopped the wagon and squatted in front of the little girl. "Close your eyes," she said. "And think about when we first saw Lauren."

Shay closed her eyes and Lexi took her hands.

"Remember the pictures Lauren showed you about Ollie's food?"

Shay nodded again.

"Crayfish was at the top. What picture was next?"

"She's getting frustrated."

Lexi looked over her shoulder at Caleb. She had to crane her neck to look up at him.

He was looking at Shay worriedly.

144

Lexi nodded. "I know. Sometimes it's hard."

"Maybe it's *too* hard." He was frowning at Lexi now.

She frowned back. "It's not. I looked it up." She was confident about the things she was doing to help Shay. No, she didn't know a lot about pediatrics, but she looked stuff up when she thought it was pertinent, dammit. Like memory games for four-year-olds. She wasn't bumbling her way around here. She straightened and faced Caleb squarely, a hand on her hip. "I meant what I said to Jenna," she told him.

"I know."

"I'm not just *babysitting* when I'm with Shay."

"I know."

She couldn't read his expression.

"I want the things she and I do together to matter. Some of the stuff we do is to have fun and make memories. Some of the stuff we do is for learning."

"I know."

"So back off."

One of his eyebrows went up again and for a second Lexi was distracted by the fact that that was really sexy. But dammit, this was all important. She had to be sure he *really* got it.

"Okay," he finally said. "I'm sorry."

She was tempted to make him apologize for flirting with another woman in front of her, too, but she had a feeling he knew that wasn't cool.

She nodded. "Okay."

"And now," he announced, looking at the kids, "We need snow cones!"

"Yes!" Jack agreed.

Shay took a hold of Caleb's belt loop and they started toward the next concession stand.

Lexi followed. Damn, he looked good in those jeans, with those two kids hanging on to him.

She really didn't need to be handcuffed to his bed.

Probably.

———

They had lunch and played with the kids for a little while before Lexi had to get ready to go into work. But they didn't talk about what had happened at the zoo—either Jenna or Shay's trouble with the memory game—because the kids were around.

That was frustrating. Caleb had never really realized how little he and Lexi did actually talk. They shared reports on what had happened during the hours with the kids, and he felt like he got general insight into her issues and questions and concerns about parenthood from the support group. But that was about it.

And suddenly it wasn't enough.

She hadn't even been living in his house for twenty-four hours and he wanted more.

To say that he was stunned by her defense of their situation and the way she'd called Jenna out on her use of the term babysitting was an understatement. Lexi had been feisty. Like she'd been that morning when he'd tried to help with her finger. Yet, even while confronting Jenna, she'd been calm and confident about it. As she'd been when handling Jack's tantrum.

And then she'd told *him* to back off.

That was definitely new.

And strangely hot.

Why was that sexy?

But it wasn't really hard to figure out. He loved taking care of her. But it was kind of a relief to think that he didn't have to be so careful with her. If he wandered into asshole territory, she'd tell him. Apparently. That was a really good thing.

And it made him want her even more.

His affection for her wasn't new, of course, but combined with the physical want, he felt things for this woman he'd never felt before. Liking her, being grateful to her, acknowledging how great she was with the kids, loving her smile, feeling protective of her were all very familiar. But the mix of that along with the desire, and now realizing that there might be a side of her he didn't know was combining into a hot, nagging, itching, driving-him-crazy knot of emotions that he wasn't sure how to handle.

Except to take Lexi straight up to bed and pour it all into a few orgasms.

But he'd put her in charge of when and if that happened. And she wasn't fucking here.

Caleb played with the kids some more, they napped, he made dinner, they played some more. Then he did something that had been nagging in the back of his mind, but that he hadn't quite had the courage for until now. He sat down at the computer and pulled up a list of physical activities that a four-year-old should be able to do.

He didn't look at it as he hit the print button. He didn't want to read it because he was fearful of what it would tell him. Just how behind it would reveal Shay was. But Lexi had said something at the zoo that had caught his attention. She'd looked stuff up so she knew what memory games to play with Shay.

He was sure it went into the Worst Dad of the Year column that he hadn't done that. But Shay was happy. She didn't have nightmares. She didn't get sick that much. She felt safe and secure and knew she was loved. He gave her a home and clothes and food and toys and...he'd found Lexi for her.

Caleb blew out a breath. He'd felt secure in the idea that he was doing a good job for Shay because she was happy, and he'd found the single best person to be there for her when he wasn't. And he'd felt that way even before he knew about the exercises and memory games. He'd been so intent on just meeting Shay's basic needs and adjusting to what having a little girl did to his life that he hadn't been reading parenting magazines or blogs or whatever the fuck people read to learn stuff about their kids. He hadn't been worrying or looking for problems because what could be worse than being orphaned before you were even two? Shay had come out of that okay and he'd felt like he was doing pretty well.

The printer stopped and Caleb took a deep breath. He reached for the pages that had printed out.

The article was broken into sections—movement milestones, cognitive milestones, emotional milestones.

He felt overwhelmed just reading those three headings.

He made himself focus on the physical list first. Monday was physical therapy. That one made the most sense to him. They were also going to see an occupational therapist and a speech therapist. He was less clear on what those therapists would be assessing and helping with, but he figured they'd explain tomorrow.

Hops and stands on one foot up to five seconds.

Shay didn't hop.

Right there, the very first thing on the list, and he was already at something she couldn't do.

He made himself suck in a breath and keep reading.

Goes upstairs and downstairs without support.

Support like what? An adult's hand? Or did the banister count? Because she could do it without holding on to him but she used the railing. He was pretty sure. But now that he was thinking about it, he wasn't sure. When had he last watched her go up and down the stairs? He often carried her up to bed. Because she was sleepy...okay, because it was faster. She couldn't dawdle if he was carrying her. But maybe she wasn't dawdling. Maybe going up the stairs was hard. Had he been making it worse by carrying her?

Thoughts and questions swirled, and Caleb ran a hand over his face. *Fuck.* This sucked.

He made a note to have her go upstairs later and to fucking pay attention when she did it.

With a deep breath, he kept reading.

Kicks ball forward.

She had a hard time with kicking, too.

Throws ball overhand.

Huh. They hadn't done that in a while, either. Why hadn't he taken the kids to the park to throw the ball around? When had they last been to the park? What the hell was wrong with him?

Jesus. This wasn't helping at all.

But they could work on this stuff. And maybe it would get better. Maybe some of this was just him being a bad uncle and not because her brain had been tossed around inside her little head as her mom and dad's car had tumbled over the side of the road.

Caleb set the page down and braced his hands on his thighs, closing his eyes and just breathing. In and out. In and out.

Not reading this list or freaking out when you're reading it isn't helping anyone. You're the grown-up. You're the guy with the answers. The one everyone looks to for ideas and solutions. Get your shit together.

After a moment, he opened his eyes and looked at the list again. Okay, solution number one—take each thing, one at a time and...do his best.

"Who wants to play statues?" Caleb called to the kids as he got to his feet.

"Me!" Shay told him.

"Me, too!" Jack said. Jack always wanted to do whatever Shay was doing, and if it was also something Caleb suggested, Jack was all in.

"Okay," Caleb said, moving into the playroom. He was going to take that standing on one leg thing and do something with it. Get an idea of what Shay could and couldn't do. And he was going to channel a little Lexi when he did it. He could be creative. He could make this stuff into a game like she did.

Probably.

It only took about ten minutes for Shay to say, "I don't want to play statues anymore." She was frustrated with the inability to hold some of the positions he'd come up with.

So did he push? Was he even having her try the right things? Maybe he should just wait and let the therapists do it. He was paying them after all. He'd just have to resist the urge to yank her out of there when that happened.

"Okay, honey. We don't have to play anymore."

Even as he said it, he had no idea if that was the right call.

He watched her reach for her stuffed hippo. His heart swelled with love. He hadn't signed up to be the stand-in father to a baby girl, but he couldn't believe the love and awe he felt for her on a daily basis.

And no, no one had said this would be easy. But he'd been so fucking sure that he could *make* their situation whatever Shay needed it to be.

He remembered the night she'd been born. Cassie had called him, excited and scared, to tell him she was in labor. He'd been in the waiting room for ten hours before the nurse came to tell him Shay had arrived. He'd held her before she was even an hour old. He'd seen her at least once a week after that. He'd been there for her first birthday, her first tooth, she'd even taken her first steps to him. And the night that he'd arrived at the hospital after being called about the accident, he'd held on to her like *she* was *his* life preserver.

Shay, and Cassie's trust in him, had changed his life overnight. He'd been a party guy who'd flaunted the firefighter thing and his N'Awlins drawl to any pretty tourist who let him buy her a drink. And more than a few local girls, too. He'd hunted and fished and drank and laughed with his friends like he didn't have a care in the world. Because he hadn't.

Until his phone had rung that misty November night two years and ten months ago.

He'd suddenly had to be a grown-up. And according to the people around him, from his mother to Stephen's sister to the social worker, he'd done a hell of a job. Everyone was proud of him, everyone thought it was amazing how he'd stepped up and how seriously he was taking everything. Even his friends had clapped him on the back and told him he was a hell of a guy. Gabe Trahan, a guy Caleb had always liked and admired, had invited him to the single parent support group where an entire circle of people who were doing just what he was doing—raising kids on their own—had told him he was doing a fantastic job.

He'd believed them. Every single one.

And then he'd met Lexi. And his ego had gotten even bigger.

She was one more person who he could step up for. One more person who needed him. One more person to help and support—and who thought he was amazing.

Lexi and Jack had given him even more reasons to smile and laugh and feel like a big fucking deal. He'd been there for Jack's first word and his first Christmas and his first trip to the petting zoo. And his first earache. Of course, Lexi had been there the first time Shay had gotten strep throat and the first time she'd asked about her mom. Lexi had made his life so much easier.

And he *really* needed to talk to her.

Right now.

He needed to kiss her and touch her and tell her how fucking hot it had been to see her getting a little jealous and possessive. But he also needed to *talk* to her.

Okay, what he really needed was to hear her tell him he was amazing. Right now. Tonight.

He wasn't ready to tell her about Shay. Lexi already knew everything he knew, really—Shay was a little behind in some things and needed some help. He needed a *plan*, he needed to know how to make Shay's life easier and better, before he told Lexi everything. He wanted to be able to say, "Here's what's going on, but here's what I'm going to do about it." The same way he said, "The squealing sound your car is making is the drive belt. I'll get a new one and get it put in tomorrow."

But he'd really love to have Lexi look up at him with that so-familiar, so-addicting I've-never-met-anyone-like-you in her eyes, right about now.

Yeah, he needed to feel like he was amazing at something tonight. Something amazing for one of the girls that he most wanted to be amazing for.

Just after seven, Caleb made his way back downstairs, like he did every night after he put Shay to bed. He usually got Jack ready for bed as well so that he'd have his bath done and pajamas on and could go right down to sleep when Lexi got him home. Then they'd sit together on the couch and watch reruns of *SpongeBob* together. It was their guy time. During which Jack almost always fell asleep.

But tonight, Caleb had tucked Jack into bed across the room from Shay's bunkbeds and it had felt so fucking *right*. And so much easier. Once Lexi got here, she could just...stay. No bundling Jack into the car. No sending them back into the night. No worrying about whether she got home okay.

She could settle down on the couch next to him to watch *SpongeBob*.

And they could talk.

Or something.

Yeah, he liked this a lot. This was how it should be.

With that thought ricocheting around in his head, Caleb started picking up the toys in the living room. He knew he should make the kids do it before they went upstairs, but there was something soothing about the routine. Especially when he was antsy, waiting for Lexi.

An hour later, the living room and kitchen were both clean and he was sitting on his couch, watching his TV, the way he did every single night he wasn't at the station and yet, he felt like pacing.

She hadn't told him what time she'd be home, he realized. He was resisting calling or texting. They only did that if there was something going on with one of the kids. It wasn't his place to check up on her. But he wanted it to be.

Hell, he'd picked his phone up, typed a message, and deleted it twice already.

So as soon as he heard her key in the lock, he was up and off the couch.

8

      Caleb didn't even wait until Lexi had stepped all the way into the house before he asked, "Is everything okay?"

      She was clearly surprised to find him in the foyer. "Hi. Yeah." She closed the door and turned. "I realized I hadn't told you what time I'd be off and I thought about calling but then I got sidetracked and then figured you'd probably put Jack to bed and that it didn't really matter if I was late." She gave him a smile. "That's really nice, I'll admit. Not having to think about getting him back out to the car and then into the apartment and settled down."

      Caleb nodded. "That is nice. You can even lock the door behind you when you get home now." He felt his heart kick at that idea and the use of the word *home* with her. "You're not going out of it again tonight."

      "Huh." She turned back to the door and slowly lifted her hand, twisting the lock closest to the knob, then sliding the chain into place higher up. She faced him again. "That is nice."

      God, he wanted to throw her over his shoulder and take her straight upstairs. She looked tired. Or she looked like she should be tired. Her hair was coming out of her ponytail, and he noted that she was wearing a different scrub top than the one she'd left in.

"You changed clothes?" he asked.

She looked down. "Oh, yeah. Blood." She looked up again. "Lots of blood."

He frowned. "You okay?"

She smiled. "None of it was mine."

"Bad day?" A lot of blood wasn't a *good* night.

"Busy," she said. "Big car accident. Multiple injuries."

He nodded, watching her closely. He'd missed her, which he recognized as a little stupid, but there was something more about her that was pulling at him. Maybe the recognition from earlier today that he was feeling a lot more for her than he'd previously realized.

"What?" she asked, her brow wrinkling as she watched him watching her.

"You're...glowing."

"Glowing? What do you mean?"

He wasn't even sure. "You don't look *happy* exactly, but you don't look tired or worried or anything, either."

She took a deep breath, blew it out, and gave him a soft smile. "I'm feeling proud. Satisfied."

Satisfied. Yeah, okay, that seemed to fit. "Tell me about it."

"About what?" She dropped her bag by the door and toed off her tennis shoes.

"Your shift. What happened. What you're proud of." He meant it. That look on her face was beautiful. Soft but still a little...feisty. And he wanted to know more about what had caused it.

"Oh." She glanced at the stairs. "I was just going to head up to take a bath. Then bed. I have to work in the morning. I didn't think you'd still be up."

That wasn't an invitation to join her in the bath or the bed. Still, he wanted to hear about her shift. "I know." He reached out and caught her hand. "Just for a little bit. Tell me about what happened."

She let him tug her to the couch. Of course she did. She didn't argue with him. She didn't resist him. And her willingness to go along with him now had a whole new meaning.

He coughed and nudged her down onto the sofa. "So tell me about all the blood." He settled next to her, but she turned so she could sit with her back against the arm of the couch, putting her further away from him.

Caleb shifted and put his arm along the back of the couch.

"It was three cars and a truck," she said. "Five injuries. One was a fifteen-year-old boy. Came in unconscious. His heart stopped twice." She took a deep breath. "We finally got him stabilized but he was there alone. He'd been in the car alone and they couldn't get a hold of his parents. So after things calmed down, I went in to check on him. And I hated that he was alone. So...I just stayed. I just held his hand and started talking."

She gave Caleb a sheepish smile that made a hot ball gather in his gut, then slide lower to his cock.

"What did you talk to him about?" he asked, realizing he was curious even as he was fighting the urge to pull her into his lap.

She laughed softly. "I didn't know what to talk to him about. He's fifteen. I don't know any fifteen-year-old boys. So, I started... telling him stories."

"What stories?"

"I started reciting the kids' books," she said, dipping her head as if embarrassed. "I know all of their favorite books by heart, and I just thought he needed to hear a voice and hear something light and maybe something that would be familiar? I mean, all kids know *Goodnight Moon* and *Love You Forever* and *Green Eggs and Ham*, right? So I thought maybe that would be comforting but wouldn't make his brain work too hard."

Caleb smiled at the top of her head. She was fiddling with the bottom of her scrub top and he wasn't sure he'd ever wanted her more.

"That's amazing, Lex."

She looked up with a smile. "He squeezed my hand during *Love You Forever*." Her eyes were bright. "And he woke up before I left."

Caleb felt what seemed strangely like pride. "Wow."

She nodded. "I know. And then his mom showed up so I felt okay leaving. I have no idea if the stories helped, but I just couldn't stand the idea of him being there all alone in the quiet."

"You're—" Caleb stopped and thought about his words. He felt in some ways like he was meeting her for the first time, just getting to know her. And yet, this seemed very in character for her. She was sweet and thoughtful and she took things in stride and seemed to just naturally know how to make the people around her feel better. Except maybe Jenna. Though she'd had the right instincts there, too. And God knew she made *him* feel better when she was around. "I'm really glad for you."

She shrugged, but the glow around her was obvious. "It feels weird to be happy. I mean, this kid has a lot of pain and rehab and hard work ahead of him. At the same time, it did feel good to be there for him."

Caleb nodded and reached out, wrapping his hand around her ankle, unable to keep from touching her. "I know that feeling." He ran his thumb over her ankle bone and watched her lips part. "I've pulled people out of fires and I feel damned good about it, Lex. Yeah, they have a long road ahead but...at least they have the road, you know?" And that was exactly how he should be feeling about Shay, he realized. She had some stuff to work on, some things that would be tough for her as she grew up, but she was going to get to grow up. That was huge.

Lexi's eyes lit up at his words and he had to swallow a groan. God, that was beautiful.

"Yeah. I know," she said. "It's okay to be happy even though he's barely out of a coma, right?"

He realized she was still learning her way around health care. School and training and internships were one thing, but being there, in the trenches, with real patients and being *the* person taking care of things was different. He nodded. "Yeah. It's definitely okay. It's worth celebrating."

She bit her bottom lip but nodded. "Okay, good."

They had this in common. Pulling people through hard, scary, life-threatening situations. He wasn't sure why that hadn't really occurred to him before. He knew she was a nurse, of course, but he hadn't really thought about how this was another way they could relate beyond their kids and single parenthood.

"I like that we share that," he said.

She looked at him for a long moment. "You know that you are the reason I went into nursing, right?"

Surprise rippled through him. "What?"

"Yeah. I have always really admired you and loved your stories about the medical calls and I wanted to be a part of that. You're why I chose the ER, too."

She ducked her head again and Caleb felt his chest tighten. She ducked her head around him. She hadn't ducked her head when she'd been talking to Jenna. Somehow he knew that she didn't duck her head in the ER. He knew that she faced the patients and situations that came in like she did Jack's tantrums. In stride. Straight on. Calm and cool. Confident.

But she fucking ducked her head when she was with *him*.

"Hey." He leaned in and put his thumb under her chin, tipping her head up to look at him. "That means a lot to me." It really did. This was the stuff Lexi did to him. He didn't know if walking around with a huge ego because of her was *all* good, but if her admiration had led her into a career that she was great at and loved, then it was at least a little good.

Her cheeks were pink. "It sounds creepy."

"It does not. It's awesome. What you do is really important and if I had something to do with it, then I'm pretty proud of that."

She smiled and he felt his breath lodge in his chest.

"In fact," he went on. "It's especially amazing because I went into firefighting because of my sister. So I'm even more... humbled...that I inspired you that way."

"Okay, good."

Her gaze dropped to his mouth and Caleb's body tightened.

But before they went there, he had something else he wanted to talk about. "Can we talk about the zoo for a second?" he asked.

Her gaze dropped to the front of his shirt at that. "I'm not going to apologize for what I said to Jenna."

"Good."

Lexi's eyes came back to his. "Yeah?"

"Of course. If you feel the need to defend one of the kids or what we're doing or how you're feeling or...anything...you should say something." He ran his hand from her ankle up her calf and back down. "Anytime you have something to say, you should."

She wet her lips. "Really?"

"Yes."

"To you, too?"

"Definitely." He paused. "Especially."

She swallowed. "Okay."

He ran his hand up and down her calf again. "Do you have something to say to me, Lexi?"

Caleb really did want to hear whatever it was. But he'd be lying if he said he didn't hope that she was going to say something that involved her being naked.

She swallowed. "I've been thinking about what you said when we were leaving for the zoo. About the...kitchen counter...and stuff."

Yes. Fuck yes. He squeezed her leg. "Yeah."

"I think I should tell you..." She took a breath and blew it out. "I don't think I'm going to be able to...go there."

Oh. Shit. Not what he'd been expecting. "Lex—"

"And I'm kind of having a hard time adjusting to *you* saying that stuff to *me*."

He frowned slightly. "Oh?"

She laughed a little at that. "I *shouldn't* be surprised to hear those words from you?"

"You don't like them?" He didn't move his hand now. He had to make sure she was comfortable with all of this. But he was surprised to hear that she might not be. He didn't think that made him an asshole. For two years it had been a fairly well-known fact that Lexi had a thing for him.

She swallowed. "I didn't say that." She blew out a breath. "But it's very *different* for us."

He nodded. "I guess it's all been in my head before this, but saying it out loud is different, yeah."

She looked surprised again. "See, even hearing you say that you've *thought* those things is different. All this time I've been thinking this was one-sided...on *my* side. I don't know what to do with it."

"You handled it last night." He didn't even have to try to drop his voice on that one. His voice was naturally husky when talking about last night.

"I'd had schnapps last night."

Yeah, fuck, he knew that.

"But," she added. "I will admit that the schnapps probably made me more likely to say—and do—what I really felt."

Relief arrowed through him. "Do you want me to stop?"

"It's just sudden. Out of the blue. You've been treating me like a little sister and now this."

He'd already told her that he did *not* think about her as a sister. "Do you want me to stop?" he asked again. It occurred to him, possibly belatedly, that Lexi might be one of those girls who wanted a lot of romance and needed to be wooed. It also occurred to him that he should have known that about her and it kind of pissed him off that he didn't know it.

He'd never gone out with a woman like that before and he knew fuck-all about it. He'd screwed around with tourists in town for a wild, good-time weekend in the Big Easy up until he'd become a pseudo-dad. Since then, he'd only had hookups with women who knew the score and didn't want anything more from him than a few laughs and a few orgasms. But maybe talking about putting Lexi up on the kitchen counter and going down on her wasn't the way to take this thing between them from platonic to more.

No, that wasn't true. That was *definitely* one way to do that. But maybe not the way with *Lexi.*

In his head, the only difference between what they'd been doing and a more-serious-actual-relationship was that they weren't having sex. He'd figured that would be the easiest thing to fix, considering that she'd supposedly wanted him for so long.

But it was possible he had no idea what he was talking about.

"It's just like a switch got turned on and suddenly you're...hot and intense and dirty." Lexi's voice dropped to a near whisper on the last word.

"Lexi," Caleb said firmly. "Do you want me to stop? I don't want to make you uncomfortable. I don't want you to think I'm disrespecting you. I just want to move forward. And I guess, with you, I feel like we've been working up to this for two years. I want to go fast and I was just...talking."

He sat with his hand on her leg, but not moving it. He waited for her to answer. If she said she wanted him to stop talking to her like that, he could do that. He could stop coming on to her altogether, if that's what she really wanted. But it might kill him.

"And those are just the things that come out when you talk to me about this stuff?"

He gave a soft laugh. "Yeah."

"You don't talk to other women like that?"

Oh, okay. He wasn't going to lie to her. "I'm not saying I never talk..."

"Dirty," she supplied when he trailed off.

"Okay. Yeah. I'm not saying I never do that." Why couldn't he say the word "dirty" to her? He'd said more graphic words than that.

But that had been in the heat of the moment. Before he realized that Lexi might be a romantic. Before he realized that he didn't know her as well as he'd thought. Or even more, he'd realized he hadn't given her as much thought as he'd assumed. She was on his mind a lot, but...damn, not the right stuff. Clearly.

"But it's different with you," he said.

"Why?"

"Because it's you." He didn't have a better explanation for her. Or for himself.

Thankfully, she nodded. "Yeah."

"And you don't think you can say that stuff back to me?"

"I don't know."

"Damn."

The corner of her mouth quirked at that. "Damn?"

He nodded. "I'd *really* like to hear a few of those things from those lips."

She smiled and her cheeks got a little pink. But then her smile dropped. "So...maybe we can't be...more."

No. "We can absolutely be more, Lex."

She shook her head. "I'm not sure. I can't initiate this, Caleb. And I don't think you can...do what I need."

Romance. She needed romance. Okay, he could figure this out. Gabe Trahan was a very romantic guy. Corey, another guy in their support group, too. They'd give him some lessons if needed. "I didn't say that I *couldn't*. I just haven't done it before."

She took a deep breath, pulled her foot away from him, and swung her feet to the floor. "I don't know."

"Just tell me what you want."

She shook her head. "I can't."

Caleb scowled. "You can say anything to me." He paused. "Lexi, look at me."

She pulled in another deep breath, then turned her head.

"Listen, I know I'm coming on kind of strong. I'm sorry," he said. "We can take it slow. We can...go on a date." Yeah, they should do that. They could do more talking that way. He could help her relax. He could bring her flowers and take her to a romantic movie and...something else that he'd find out about from the support group. He could help her see that while he really wanted to put her up on his kitchen counter, he also wanted more. "We can go on a hundred dates. I don't want you to look at this as something where I was kind of your boss, or I'm someone who you somehow *owe*. I want—"

He was interrupted by her laugh.

He looked at her curiously. "What?"

"If I had to give you blow jobs in exchange for everything you've done for me over the past two years, my jaw would be *very, very* sore."

There was a long, completely silent pause.

Caleb stared at her. Lexi Scott had just said *blow jobs* to him. And his entire body liked that *very, very* much.

"I, um..." Yeah, he wasn't sure where he was going with that. Or where he *should* go with that.

"But, I guess, if you tell me that I need to get down on my knees and start working on it, I'm game."

All of the oxygen left his lungs. All the blood in his body routed to his cock. And Caleb had no idea what to do.

Lexi turned to face him more squarely. "So, is that what you're saying, Caleb?" she asked. "Are you saying that you want some repayment for everything you've done for me?"

He shook his head. "No. Of course not."

She blew out a breath. "Damn."

Caleb's eyebrows rose. "Damn?" What the hell did that mean?

"Yeah. I'd *really* love for you to say something like that."

He ran a hand through his hair. What the hell was going on? How had he missed that demanding blow jobs was romantic? He was totally on board with that. He just hadn't known. "Well, I think I'm gonna need to hear what *this* is all about."

"You sure?"

He'd never been more sure of anything in his life. "I told you that you have to initiate things between us. So...initiate it." The last word came out as more of a command than he'd meant it to be. But judging by the way her lips parted and her breathing got faster, she didn't mind.

"That's just it," she said. "I don't want to initiate it. I want *you* to take over. To order me around." She took a breath. "I want you to tie me up and blindfold me and say filthy things to me and tell me what to do and spank me."

Her words came out in a rush and Caleb felt the room shifting. Or maybe it was his perspective on the woman in front of him that was shifting. Like when she'd told him to back off at the zoo. When she'd more or less told Jenna to back off as well. When he'd realized that she only ducked her head around him, and only when they were talking about things she was unsure of or looking for his approval on. Her work, for instance. But not Shay. Not their kids. Not their co-parenting.

It wasn't meekness he was seeing in her.

It was submissiveness.

That idea rocked through him and his lungs squeezed.

She wanted to please him. She was easily influenced by him. She deferred to his authority on everything. Well, almost everything. Not their kids. That, she was confident in. But everything else...yeah. He'd pointed all of that out to her earlier as a reason why she had to initiate sex.

But, if his authority turned her on, if she truly wanted to

please him, then that could mean that she wouldn't want to initiate sex.

When he didn't say anything, reeling from all the revelations, as well as a knee-buckling wave of lust, Lexi leaned over and pulled something out of her bag, which she'd dropped beside the couch when he'd brought her over to talk.

She held it up. Or rather *them*. Handcuffs. The handcuffs Santa had given her at the Christmas party last year. Caleb remembered seeing her unwrap them and being stunned. For one, because he'd given Logan gift ideas for her to get from "Santa" and handcuffs had definitely not been on the list. And two, seeing Lexi with those cuffs dangling from her fingers had been one of the hottest things he'd ever seen. It had been the image in his mind when he'd jerked off later that night, as a matter of fact.

"I want you to cuff me to your bed," she said. She put the handcuffs on the couch between them. "I also want you to be my boss and absolutely insist that I start repaying all the car repairs you've done for me. Or you can be my boss and I'm your secretary and part of my job requirements is helping you relax after a really hard day of high-pressure business deals. Or, in this case only, I can do the babysitter thing—you can be the single dad who hired me to babysit but you've decided to pay me in orgasms instead of money." She took a deep breath and finished with, "My safe words are red for stop and yellow for slow down."

Caleb focused. Or tried to. So many images were going through his mind that he was having a hard time coming up with those things she was expecting...what were they called...oh, yeah, *words*.

Lexi waited for nearly two solid minutes. Then she nodded and stood up. "Yeah, that's what I thought." She let out a breath. "I get it, Caleb. I really do. You take care of me. You see me as this...*girl*...who doesn't quite know what she's doing. To tie me up, you have to accept that I totally trust you, but you also have to trust *me* to know what I want and what I don't and that I'll tell you to stop if need be. That's the only way we can both really let go. And I don't think you trust me to know myself that well. And that's partly on me. That's our relationship. I know that tying me up and—" she cleared her throat, "—dominating me, would be hard for you."

Caleb shifted on the couch, his cock pressing against his fly, insisting that it would be *hard*, but not difficult. At all.

His brain wasn't as convinced. The things she said were true. He knew she trusted him, but yeah, the trusting her to know her needs and limitations was different.

"And you've been so good to me," she went on. "And there is nothing about our situation that I would change. So, we just can't...go there. Go here. Do this." She stopped as she evidently realized she was stumbling over her words. She breathed in through her nose and then let it out. "And that's okay. I want you to know that. We're still friends. I'm still here for Shay. Always. And Jack still needs you in his life. So this is how it is. And it's fine. But now you know...everything. And why I can't initiate things." She grabbed the handcuffs, stuffed them back into her bag, and pulled it up onto her shoulder. "Good night, Caleb."

Lexi stepped around the end of the couch and started for the stairs.

And Caleb wondered if his heart was ever going to beat normally again.

———

Caleb stalked into Trahan's Tavern thirty minutes later. He headed straight for the bar. Josh was working tonight so there was a chance that Owen was here, too.

He took a seat next to James, his best friend from Engine 29, and slapped his hand down on the bar. "I need a beer and Owen."

Josh, the bartender who helped Gabe and Logan now that

they were family men, continued drying the glass in his hand. "Well, hey, Caleb. I'm great. Thanks for asking."

"Josh," Caleb said with a sigh. "You look good. How's the swamp?"

Josh was a quarter owner in the Boys of the Bayou swamp boat tour and fishing company. Along with his brother, Sawyer, their friend Tommy, and their cousin, Owen. The guys from the tiny bayou town of Autre made regular trips to New Orleans and Trahan's in particular.

"Wet and profitable," Josh said, grinning. "The usual."

"Wonderful. Lovely to hear," Caleb said dryly.

"Thanks. So how can I help you?" Josh asked.

"I need to talk to Owen."

Josh frowned. "You were serious about that?"

"Yep."

If there was anyone in Caleb's group of guy friends who knew his way around handcuffs, sex toys, and spanking, it would be Owen.

"Why do you need *Owen*?" James asked.

"I...need some advice."

Josh coughed and James laughed. Then looked at Caleb and realized he was serious. "You need advice from *Owen*?" Josh asked.

"Yeah."

"Wow. I have to hear this," James said.

"Specifically, I need some advice on Lexi," Caleb said.

"Marry her," James said.

"Make her move out," Josh said.

Caleb sighed. "So Owen's not here?"

"Sorry, man," Josh said, not looking all that sorry.

"Who's Lexi?"

Caleb leaned in and peered at the man on the other side of James. He was a big guy and looked vaguely familiar.

"Lexi is Caleb's roommate and babysitter," James said, lifting his beer.

"She babysits Caleb?" the guy asked.

James laughed. "Kind of. But no, she babysits Caleb's niece, Shay."

"She's not my babysitter," Caleb said with a scowl. But he shifted on the barstool as images went through his mind. Him coming home after work, her studying on the couch with her glasses on, the kids fed and bathed and put to bed. Like a good babysitter would do...

He coughed and focused as Josh said, "Lexi is hot, in love with him, and sleeping just down the hall."

In love with him? Caleb thought about that. Before when his friends teased about Lexi's feelings, it had always seemed like a hero-worship-crush-type thing. Now though...it felt like more than that. She knew him. She was a part of his life. She was more sure of herself and what she was doing than he'd given her credit for. She might want to be submissive in sex, but she handled stuff. Life stuff. Kid stuff. ER stuff. He didn't need to *worry* about her.

But he still wanted to take care of her.

Which meant giving her orgasms in whatever way she wanted them.

He just needed to figure out what exactly that meant.

"So what's the problem? Sounds like you just need to move her into a new bedroom," the big guy said.

"Who are you?" Caleb asked. And maybe he needed objective input from a guy who didn't know him or Lexi.

"This is my brother, Sawyer," Josh said.

Ah, the infamous head of the Boys of the Bayou swamp boat tour company. Sawyer didn't come up to New Orleans very often, so Caleb hadn't met him before. But he'd heard about him.

"Hey," Caleb greeted. "Stella's told me all about you," he added with a chuckle.

Gabe had just returned to the bar from delivering food to the dining room. He rolled his eyes at Caleb's comment.

Sawyer grinned at Gabe. "Yeah, that's why I'm here. Working out the details of the dowry with Gabe." He pulled a piece of notebook paper from his back pocket and spread it out on the top of the bar.

I love your boats. I want to be an airboat captan. I think we should get marryed. Friends forever, Stella Ann Trahan.

It was written in green crayon. And had an alligator drawn at the bottom.

"Makes sense to me," Josh said, nodding. "You've got that pretty girl from the Department of Wildlife wrapped around your finger and you already know where Big Mac hangs out. That would save Stella the time of figuring that all out for herself. And runnin' us out of business."

Sawyer nodded. "All good points. And she's bossy. She told Owen that he hadn't done a good job hosing off the dock the other day. We could use someone like her."

"Hilarious," Gabe told them all dryly. "Really."

Stella was Gabe's seven-year-old daughter. While dating her mom, Gabe had won Stella over by taking her on a swamp boat tour with Sawyer. Now it was a regular thing. And Stella was enamored. More with the alligators than with Sawyer, but apparently she'd figured out a plan for getting her hands on one of those airboats.

"Who's Big Mac?" Caleb had to ask.

"The biggest, oldest alligator in our part of the bayou," Sawyer said with a grin. "We try to show him off since the tourists get a kick out of how huge he is. But he's pretty lazy. We feed him too well."

"Did I hear you say something about needing advice about Lexi?" Gabe asked, interrupting talk of the bayou and his daughter as a swamp boat captain. "Because, I'm here for you. Clearly these jackasses don't know anything."

Caleb wasn't sure that was true if he needed advice about tying a woman up for sex. Josh was one of the most popular bartenders in the quarter and not because of his Pimm's cups. And James had plenty of female company. Caleb didn't know about Sawyer, and he wasn't sure he wanted a lot of details about Gabe's sex life since Caleb also knew his wife, Addison. Then again, Addison was a very happy woman.

"Any of your girls read erotic romance?" Caleb asked the group.

"Never get to the point of discussing reading habits," Sawyer said, lifting his beer.

Gabe shook his head. "Working mom of three? No, sorry. But she does know every word to *If You Give a Mouse A Cookie*. Guessing that's not helpful?"

Caleb lifted a brow. "Please, I know that one *and If You Give A Pig A Pancake* by heart," he said.

Gabe laughed. "I like *If You Give A Moose A Muffin*, personally."

Caleb looked at Josh. Of the group at the bar, Josh probably had the best chance of knowing something about fuzzy handcuffs. "How about you?"

"I have no idea if the girls I hang out with can read anything other than a drink menu," Josh said with a grin.

Caleb blew out a breath. He wanted to read some of these books to see where Lexi's ideas were coming from. He could surf the web, of course. Even if he'd never spanked a woman, he *did* know that the internet would have a plethora of, um, information. Some of which could be *way* off. He was, frankly, chicken to just Google "spanking and handcuffs."

"Yep."

Caleb focused on James. "Yep? What's yep?"

"I know a girl who reads erotic romance."

"You do?"

"My neighbor." James gave him a big grin.

"Your neighbor?" Caleb asked. "You mean Professor Broussard?"

Caleb had met James's neighbor...and tenant, since James owned the building. They were the only two apartments on the top floor and they ran into each other a lot, it seemed. Harper Broussard was way too classy for Caleb's buddy, which he suspected was part of James's attraction.

"I do mean Professor Broussard," James said.

"Who's Professor Broussard?" Josh wanted to know, leaning in with eyebrows up.

"The classy linguistics professor who's about ten years older than James and shares the third floor," Caleb said. "And who *doesn't* think he's funny and charming."

"Oh, she does," James said. "She just doesn't admit it."

"She hides it very well," Caleb agreed.

"An older woman, huh?" Josh asked. "Nice."

"She's like four or five years older," James said. "Not that much."

"I was talking in terms of maturity compared to you," Caleb told him.

"Oh," James said. "In that case she's more like twenty years older."

They all laughed and Sawyer asked, "How do you know she reads erotic romance?"

"I saw the books on her table."

"When did you see her *table*?" Josh asked, wiggling his eyebrows up and down.

"When I went over to take Ami to the park."

"Who's Ami?" Sawyer asked.

"The dog." James grinned. "I call him Fred."

"Why do you call him Fred?" Sawyer asked.

"Because it bugs her."

"But the dog's name is Ami?" Josh asked.

"Yeah. It means *friend* in French. But she doesn't know I know French," James explained.

Josh looked confused. "But you do?"

James lifted a shoulder. "Yeah, my grandmother speaks French about ninety percent of the time."

"And you don't want the professor to know that you know French?" Gabe asked.

"It's fun to mess with her," James said. "She swears in French. It's adorable."

Caleb lifted an eyebrow. "You find her adorable?"

"Very," James said, without hesitation.

"And she reads erotic romance—" Caleb started.

But Sawyer butted in. "Why were you taking her dog to the park?"

"He's *our* dog," James said.

"Is he?" Caleb asked. "Or did she come over and take the dog away from you because she thought you couldn't take care of it when you were working twenty-four hours at a time? And not all that capable of taking care of *yourself*?"

James was a good-looking firefighter who lived in the French Quarter of New Orleans. He was surrounded by bars, music, and women. And he took advantage of all of it. He was also a jazz musician. A pianist, to be exact. He'd been playing since he was a kid, taught by the same grandmother who'd taught him French, and he spent a lot of his free time on Frenchman's Street, one of the best jazz locales in the entire country. He was damned good, too. Caleb had caught a few shows and had been shocked, and impressed.

James was definitely letting the good times roll.

But putting him in charge of another living being on a long-term basis was probably not a great move. Clearly Dr. Harper Broussard agreed. She'd come over to get the dog from James within two days of him adopting the mutt that had been hanging around the fire station.

"We set up a joint-custody thing," James said. "I get him in the afternoons when I'm off and he sleeps at my place at least once a week."

Caleb shook his head. "Until the good professor finds out that you're going through her stuff when you're over there."

"The books were just sitting out on her coffee table. She didn't care that I saw them. And it gave her the chance to give me a twenty-minute lecture on the difference between romance, erotic romance, and erotica." James rolled his eyes. "But what she reads *is* erotic romance. Though if you want some erotica, she can probably point you in the right direction."

"Erotic romance. A few books. Just the basics."

"Okay, what's the question?" James asked.

"Lexi reads it. And wants to do...some stuff. I just want to know how this is all spelled out in the books."

"Some stuff?" Josh asked. "Do go on."

Caleb had known it would get around to this, of course, but he was now regretting asking the question. "She wants me to tie her up in bed. And spank her. And role-play. So—" He cleared his throat. "Thought I needed to see firsthand where these ideas are coming from."

"Why not ask her what *she* reads?" Sawyer asked.

Okay, that was a good question. And Caleb had an answer. It just wasn't a particularly noble answer. He loved just knowing the shit Lexi needed him to know.

"I've got a rep here," he said lightly. "She's used to me knowing what I'm doing. You think I just naturally knew how to rewire a ceiling fan? I looked that up. Figure this can be the same."

"You don't want to do this stuff?" Sawyer asked.

"Sure. I mean, she wants it, so I'm game."

"But you're afraid of doing it wrong," James said.

Caleb scowled at him. "No."

"Yes. You do everything right."

Not everything. Caleb couldn't avoid the thought.

Was he beating himself up over the situation with Shay? Yep. In the midst of the chaos Shay's diagnosis had caused, moving Lexi and Jack in with him had felt like a *solution* to *their* situation, something he could influence and fix. He'd done something positive for one of the two girls who depended on him the most.

And then he'd found out that Lexi still had needs that she wanted him to meet that he wasn't.

Both of his girls now needed stuff from him that was out of his wheelhouse and that, yes, he was afraid of *not* being able to fix.

He'd tried to be proactive with Shay's situation and had done as much reading about her injury as he could take. But he'd realized that he had to have a lot more information about her specific diagnosis before he went on. There was a huge variation in types of brain injuries and their consequences.

So now he was going to focus on Lexi and meeting a need that he should be able to handle.

Still, there were countless kinks out there and a spectrum of ways to explore and indulge each of them. He wanted to start learning about role-playing and the rest the same way Lexi had. That seemed the most logical approach.

"I'm not always right," Caleb answered James. "But I can do my damnedest to get as close as possible."

"Okay, I've got you." James had his phone out on the bar and he'd already dialed.

"James? What's wrong?" a feminine voice answered.

"Hey, Professor. Nothing's wrong." James was grinning at the phone even though it was not a video call.

"Then why are you calling me?"

"I have a question."

"Okay." Now Harper sounded suspicious.

"If a guy ties a girl up in bed—"

"Oh my God, James. Does she have a safe word?"

He frowned. "Who?"

"The girl you're tying up," Harper said. "You're *sure* she wanted you to do that? You have to *talk* about this stuff." James opened his mouth to reply, but Harper was still going. There was a bang and a rustle on her end of the phone. "I'm coming over."

"You'd come over if I have a girl tied up in bed?" He looked stunned and amused at the same time.

"Do I need to bring scissors?" Harper asked. There was another bang on her end that could have very well been the sound of a drawer slamming shut.

"You think I tied her up and can't get it undone?" James asked. He was clearly trying to be offended but he was grinning. He lifted his eyes to Caleb.

Caleb had to admit this was...interesting.

"*Zut!* I don't know where my scissors are," Harper said. "I have a knife. That will work. But tell her not to freak out when I come in."

"Not to freak out that you're carrying a *knife* when you come storming into my apartment where she's tied to the bed and can't get undone?" James shook his head. "Wow, Professor. Take it down a notch."

"Open the door, James," Harper said.

"I'm not home."

"Where are you? I need to drive this knife over to you?"

James looked around at the men surrounding him, all of whom were staring at the phone as if it was the most interesting thing they'd ever seen. "Put the knife down, Harper," James said firmly. "I'm not home. I don't have a woman tied up. I was asking...for a friend."

"Did she know it would be *two* of you?" Harper said. "You *really* have to talk this stuff out ahead of time. Avocado makes a good safe word."

Now her voice sounded completely normal.

James blew out a breath. "You aren't standing outside my door, are you?"

"No."

"You're also not holding a knife, are you?"

"I'm not even at my apartment," she said. "But I'll have you know that I know exactly where my scissors are."

His eyes narrowed, though a grin was teasing his mouth. "You think you're pretty smart, don't you?"

"If you called to tell me that you had a woman tied up in your apartment and couldn't get the knots undone, I'd call 9-1-1," Harper said.

"Because you couldn't stand the thought of seeing another woman in my bed?" James asked.

"Because all of your firefighter and cop buddies would show up and would torture you over it forever," she said.

The grin on his face broke free and he picked up the phone. "I'm taking this outside," he told Caleb, Sawyer, Josh and Gabe.

They watched him go.

Josh gave a low whistle. "That woman might just be able to handle him."

Caleb laughed. "I'm guessing she's too smart to even try."

Gabe moved down the bar to wait on a new arrival, and Josh pushed another beer at Sawyer.

They sat drinking without talking for a few minutes.

Then Sawyer said, "So, obviously, you're crazy about this girl."

Caleb looked at him. Crazy about Lexi? Yeah, he was. He hadn't really thought of it in those terms before. He was protective of her. He was attracted to her. He was impressed by her. But yeah, he was crazy about her. She made everything better. When she wasn't with him, he didn't feel right. And when she was with him...yeah, definitely crazy.

"I am. She's...special."

"So you need to be sure she sees you reading those books," Sawyer said.

"The romances?"

"Yeah. I mean, she needs to know what you're willing to do to make her happy."

Caleb thought about that. He shook his head. "I don't know, I kind of like the idea of her thinking I just know what I'm doing."

Sawyer chuckled. "Yeah, but if you're in love with her, you need to let her see the real you, right? The one who doesn't *always* know what he's doing."

Hell, no was Caleb's instinctual reaction to that.

"She needs for me to know that I always know what I'm doing," he said absently as *in love with her* bounced around in his mind. Was he in love with Lexi?

But the answer was clear. If he wasn't in love with her, he was a dumbass.

"Harper is texting me a list of authors for you to check out." James rejoined them at the bar.

Caleb gave him a look. "She's...a lot."

"That's funny, she thinks *I'm* a lot."

"You are."

James grinned. "Yep." He picked up his beer again. "She's cute, though, huh?"

"She was more than cute when I met her," Caleb said. "I go so far as to say beautiful."

James frowned. "You thought she was beautiful?"

"If you're into that studious, smart, classy type." Which Caleb was becoming more and more sure James was.

"Not really," James said, suddenly less grin-y.

Well, maybe he hadn't been up until now, but Caleb thought that had changed. About the time Harper Broussard moved in across the hall.

The dings of a series of incoming texts on James's phone drew their attention.

And suddenly Caleb had a list of twenty authors to try. All

cross-referenced by the type of "lesson" he could learn. There were restraints, spanking, toys, and yes, role-playing.

"Where are we starting?" Sawyer asked, looking over the list with appreciation.

Caleb looked at the other man. "We?"

Sawyer shrugged. "Hey, if a woman ever asks me to tie her up in bed, I don't want to have to make the drive clear up here and talk to you guys about it first. I just want to go right in."

Fair enough.

Caleb blew out a breath. "Role-playing."

"Yeah?" James asked.

Caleb shrugged. "She gets off on the guy-in-power thing. Boss-employee. Professor-student. Pirate-slave girl. Single dad-babysitter." He gave a little shudder on the last one.

Josh laughed. "Hot."

"A little close to home."

"Okay, well you know what's equally hot and kind of like babysitter but not?" Josh asked.

"Cheerleader," Sawyer and James answered at the same time.

Caleb and Josh looked at them in surprise. He looked back. "Am I wrong?"

"That was exactly what I was going to say," Josh admitted.

Cheerleader. Huh. Maybe he could be the football coach...

Five minutes later, Caleb had downloaded four books with hot role-playing scenes in them onto his phone. Ten minutes later, Josh had read three short passages from two of the books out loud. And twelve minutes later the guys had set up a time for a weekly erotic romance book club.

9

Caleb left for a twenty-four-hour shift at six a.m. Sunday morning. Then he had to swing by Bea's to pick the kids up on Monday because Lexi had already gone in to work twelve hours at the ER. Bea always kept the kids when their schedules overlapped. Sometimes it was just for an hour or so, and sometimes it was a few hours if Caleb needed to go home and sleep. As was the case on Sunday.

When Lexi got home that night a little after eight, the kids were in bed and Caleb encouraged her to sit on the couch with him for an hour, just talking. Not about sex. Not about the book he'd started reading at the fire station between calls. Just talking.

She acted a little suspicious, jumpy even, at first. He held her hand, stroking his thumb over the back of her knuckles. But after about twenty minutes, she started to relax. There were plenty of moments where her gaze would drop to his lips or when his hand would pause on her knuckles and his palm would literally itch to move up her arm—and further. But neither of them did anything other than talk. It was as if they were each waiting for the other to make the move. And then, slowly, they both relaxed into the conversation, and it seemed as if neither of them wanted to stop talking.

Lexi told him about her shift and the woman who had delivered one of her twins in the ER's waiting area and the other twin two minutes after getting into one of the exam rooms. Caleb told her about pulling a car out of the river and the two guys who'd both gone into cardiac arrest while arguing over a game of checkers in the park.

Then, when it got too late to stay up any longer, they went to bed. Separately. Across the hall from one another.

Caleb was off the next two days after that and Lexi worked.

They talked on the couch both nights. And did nothing else.

He'd gotten through two of the books entirely and had skipped to the sex scenes in the others. He had a pretty good idea of where she was coming from at this point. But he was now building the anticipation.

And enjoying their talks. They shared about work, but also stories about their families, favorite holidays, movie preferences, and more.

The talking, just like the spanking, was something new that he hoped to do a lot of.

They were both off on Thursday and they hung out with the kids all day and then went to the support group meeting together. Friday, Lexi worked and Caleb and the kids went to the zoo.

Then to Shay's first PT appointment.

Now he was sitting on the couch waiting for Lexi to get home, resisting the urge to pace. And swear.

To say that Shay's first PT appointment hadn't gone well would be possibly the biggest understatement of his life.

She hadn't wanted to go to the appointment in the first place. The appointment time fell right in the middle of *Bubbles and Bingo*, one of her favorite TV shows. Then he'd made her brush her hair. Which was, obviously, the meanest thing an uncle could do to his niece. And then the therapist had made her do a bunch of activities that Shay wanted no part of.

It had started out fine. They'd had new-to-her toys and they'd played some games. They'd included Caleb and Jack in the games as well, and Shay had gotten caught up in the novelty of it all. But when they'd needed to assess certain specific performance areas, Shay had slowly gotten more and more frustrated until she'd finally announced that she wanted to go home *right now* as loud as she could. That had upset Jack, and within seconds Caleb had a four- and a two-year-old both crying and begging to leave.

It had been hard enough watching Shay pushed to do things she didn't want to—and couldn't—do. It had been hard enough hearing the therapist say, *we want to restore as many normal patterns as we can so that her function is as full and efficient as possible.* That, of course, emphasized the fact that there were *abnormal* patterns and that her function wasn't—and wouldn't ever be—full.

But making Shay stay and continue working with the therapists, telling Jack that Shay had to keep doing the stuff she didn't like and upsetting *him*, and dealing with the reality that this was all going to be a regular part of their routine for the foreseeable future had been the icing on the crap-tastic cake of a day he'd had.

The cherry on top was when the therapist had said the word "brace."

As in, they thought a brace for Shay's left ankle and foot would help with her tripping and stumbling. It would provide the support that her muscles weren't and would improve her balance and walking.

But a brace...that was an outward sign that there was a problem. And that it wouldn't get better. That she would always need external support because her body wasn't able to do the things she needed it to do.

Caleb knew that Shay's safety and function was the most important thing, but he couldn't help thinking about her having to explain it, possibly being made fun of, or judged because of it, that people might make assumptions about her abilities because of it. He knew it shouldn't matter, but that it would.

She was a little girl. A *little* girl. Who knew what she might want to do someday. What if she wanted to try gymnastics or wear high heels or go hiking? How did all of this impact those things? Would she be able to do any of it? What if she couldn't? And was he going to have to be the one telling her she couldn't do things she wanted to?

Of course, she might accept all of it with grace and humor. She could be one of those people who used it as an opportunity to educate others and become an advocate for people with brain injuries. She could find ways to do the things she wanted to, leg brace be damned, and be an inspiration to others.

But she might not.

She was *four*. He would do everything he could to support her. To help her find the grace in the situation. To encourage her to educate and advocate. *He* could become an educator and advocate.

But she was *four*. He didn't know what she'd want, how she'd handle it. If she'd just accept it as a part of her life—probably more likely at her young age—or if she'd resent it.

Shay, of course, had her own personality. She was her own little person. But she had a lot of learning and growing to do and experiences to go through. Good and bad. He didn't know how all of this was going to look in ten years, in twenty years, even next month. And he fucking hated that.

One thing about being a controlling guy who had become a guardian to an eighteen-month-old was that she hadn't had her own ideas and beliefs yet. He'd been able to tell her where to go and when, how things were going to be, how she should view the world around her.

That would not always be true.

And she was going to have a physical disability that was going to color and influence that world around her and those ideas and beliefs.

He didn't know what to do with that.

He'd realized halfway through Shay's appointment that he'd been hoping to hear that he'd been making too much of the little bit of information he'd been given. That he'd been thinking of the worst-case scenario. That his limited knowledge in this area had made him jump to conclusions that were not real.

That wasn't the case.

Shay was going to have permanent disabilities.

Period.

There were always going to be some things that Shay couldn't do as well as the other kids her age. There were always going to be some things that she couldn't do at all without assistance.

You will see some progress, Mr. Moreau. She will gain strength and confidence. But the weakness in her left leg, particularly around the ankle, is not going to go away.

So, wound tight, his thoughts scattered, his emotions in knots, he'd thought of Lexi. And how she had given him the chance to give her something she wanted and something that would give her absolute pleasure. And he got to be completely in control of how it went.

It was amazing that she'd given him that without even knowing just how much he'd need it. Lexi, of course, knew that he liked to be in charge, but she didn't know how much, in the midst of all of this with Shay, he would need that control.

He might not have a clue about how to help the little girl who depended on him to navigate her new reality, but he could give *Lexi* what she needed.

"Hi."

She came through the door and Caleb felt the tension in his shoulders and neck ease slightly.

"Hey."

He heard her drop her bag and kick off her shoes, then pad into the room. He looked over his shoulder. "How was work?"

"Good." She took her place on the end of the couch where she'd spent the last week talking to him. "Quieter than usual. Kid came in with a big, angry appendix. Guy came in with a stab wound but he'd accidently stabbed *himself*. Another kid needed stitches. But overall pretty good."

She leaned her head on her hand and gave him a soft, happy smile.

He loved that smile. She was content. With him.

At least he was getting *this* right.

"Anybody tell you that you smelled good tonight?" he asked.

"As a matter of fact, all three of those who I just mentioned."

Caleb chuckled softly, already feeling better. "Why *do* you always smell like bubblegum?"

She grinned. "One time I stayed and forgot shampoo so I used Shay's. Later Jack told me he liked it when I smelled like your house."

"My house? The whole thing doesn't smell like bubblegum."

She shrugged. "To him it does. The smell makes him feel good so I started using it all the time. And I've been amazed by how it calms him—and people in the ER." She paused. "It's like when I was reciting the kids' books to that guy in a coma. It's something that's familiar and happy. I guess it's hard to be scared or sad when smelling bubblegum."

Caleb felt what could only be described as affection rock through him.

She kept talking, telling him about the argument between two of the surgeons and that the hospital was starting a fundraising drive to raise money for a new sleep study lab.

He knew that. He'd seen the posters around the hospital when he'd been up there for Shay's PT appointment.

He worked to keep his expression from giving that away,

though. He wasn't ready to tell her all about Shay. Mostly because he didn't have all the answers he wanted to have, and he really didn't want to tell her about the spectacular failure today's appointment had been.

But also because he had a much better way to spend their time tonight.

"Okay, I'm going to head up to bed," she finally said, and Caleb realized she'd been telling him stories for nearly an hour. She got up from the couch. "I'll see you Sunday when you get home." She hesitated for a moment, as if she was going to say something more.

Caleb braced himself. Maybe she was going to initiate things after all. Maybe the anticipation was slowly killing her, too. Maybe the past week of nightly talks had made her feel like they were in a new place and it was time to take the next step.

Maybe that's how it should be.

But a larger part knew that it wasn't just for Lexi's sake that he needed to take charge here. It was for him, too. In the wake of today's...events...*he* might need him to take control even more than *she* needed him to.

"Good night, Caleb." She started for the staircase.

"'Night."

He thought about letting her go. They'd talked. She was happy. Hell, *he* was happy.

But...they could have more. He could give her more.

"Lexi."

His low, deep, firm voice stopped her. He didn't even have to look over his shoulder to know.

There was a long pause, but finally she asked, "Yeah?"

"Come back here." Another low, firm command.

He gripped the arm of the couch tightly, willing himself to stay put. To do this. For her. Could he spank her? Fuck if he knew. He'd never spanked a woman before. And yeah, laying his hands on Lexi like that seemed wrong. Or maybe just weird. Could he tie her up? Maybe. His fantasies had no trouble putting her in handcuffs. Could he blindfold her? Probably. He'd never done either of those things but he was willing to try. Sex was good. It was hot. He talked dirty and he loved different positions and he'd been known to push things pretty far in public. But restraints and stuff? He hadn't needed those.

But hell, he could try all of it. None of that seemed crazy. What was hanging him up was the role-playing. She *wanted* him to be her boss and demand sex from her? Or even role-play with her as the babysitter? Was that okay? Could he really get into that? And what if he really could get into it? Was *that* okay?

Lexi came to stand in front of him, and as he took in the way she was breathing faster than she should be, he realized that he had to at least try.

But where to even start?

"Yes?" she finally asked.

Okay, she wanted him to take over in the bedroom, get bossy, get a little rough, fulfill some fantasies. But he flashed back to that morning in the kitchen when she wouldn't let him take care of her cut finger. And then he remembered that she'd pulled a metal skewer out of a guy's face. And then he remembered that she'd moved into an apartment over a bar rather than beg to sleep on someone's couch. And *then* he remembered a time, almost nine months ago, before Nate had proposed to Ashley, when he'd shown up at the support group meeting and started arguing with Ashley. Lexi had gotten in between them, pushed Nate back, even though he was ten inches taller than her and easily outweighed her by a hundred pounds or more. She'd told him that she'd just learned about all of the common household products that, when ingested, could cause severe abdominal and intestinal distress. "And if you think that I couldn't sneak some of the shit into your food without you ever knowing it and make you *very, very* miserable, you're an even bigger idiot than I thought," she'd told Nate. Loudly, in front of witnesses.

Sure, she'd threatened the guy. But she knew there wasn't a single person in that support group who wouldn't have her—and Ashley's—back. And that had probably scared Nate just as much as her direct threat.

Especially when Corey said, "I've got shovels."

And Austin said, "I've got twenty acres."

This woman was not meek. She just wanted to submit sexually. To him.

Fuck yeah, he was going to give this his best shot.

"Take your clothes off." His command was firm and his cock swelled.

Well, that hadn't been difficult.

But instead of panting and stripping, she put a hand on her hip. "What?"

He fought a smile. "Take your clothes off."

"Now? What's going on?"

He met her gaze directly and cocked an eyebrow. "Take. Your. Clothes. Off."

She frowned. "No."

He reached up and hooked his finger in the front of her scrub pants and pulled her to stand between his knees.

"Hey," she protested. Though without any heat. "I said no."

"No is not your safe word." He stroked his finger back and forth along the waistband of her pants over the hot, silky skin of her stomach.

The muscles tensed slightly, but she said, "So you *were* listening," instead of, *Oh, Caleb, take me now.*

He nodded. "Heard it all. Handcuffs, you doing anything I want—the dirtier the better—and licking you from head to toe."

He also heard the hitch in her breathing.

"I didn't say the licking part," she said.

"Then it's a good thing you have a safe word." He leaned in and put his mouth against her skin right above his finger. "So... take your clothes off."

She slid her hand up his arm to his shoulder and into his hair. Her fingers against his scalp felt amazing and he groaned.

"Caleb?"

"Yeah?"

"Why now?"

"It's time," he told her simply.

"And you plan to do this right here? On this couch?"

"Oh, yeah." He kissed her stomach again. *Finally*, he had his mouth against her skin.

She took a quick breath and then said, "Red."

Caleb froze. He looked up. "Excuse me?"

Lexi nodded. "Red."

"No licking?" He wasn't sure he was okay with that, but a safe word was a safe word.

"Just not here." She stepped back. "The kids could come down."

Bullshit. He narrowed his eyes. "There's a baby gate at the top of the stairs and you know it. They'll call down to us if they do get up. Which you also know is a very slim possibility." Their kids both slept like rocks once they were asleep. Shay was notorious for being up several times before finally going under, but once she started to snore softly, she was generally down for the night.

But as Caleb looked up at Lexi and inched his finger up further under her top to the soft, and apparently slightly ticklish, skin over her ribs, he realized that he liked that she'd used the word to stop him and talk about the situation. He needed to know that she would. And for a second, he wondered if that was the reason she'd said it, rather than because of a true concern about the kids.

Yeah. He was *in* on this dirty-submissive-fantasy-role-play thing.

"I'm not handcuffing you to my bed tonight," he said.

"No?"

She looked a little disappointed and he loved that.

"No. No matter how much you beg." Oh, he definitely wanted to hear Lexi begging him. "Because no matter how many times I've jerked off to thoughts of you in my bed," he went on, gratified to see her lips part at his words. "I've just as often thought about stripping you down and fucking you right here on this couch. Like every time I came home and you were here studying." The cushion beside him was the one closest to the lamp on the end table, and she was often propped up against the arm of the couch with the light shining over her shoulder onto her book. And she was always wearing those glasses that made her look cute and nerdy.

Maybe they could role-play professor and naughty student, too.

Caleb was surprised, but pleased, by the stray thought. Maybe he could get into this role-playing thing after all.

"And I wanted to put you on your knees and make you suck me off every time I came home and you were asleep right here." He shifted on the cushions, spreading his knees, leaning back, and propping his arms along the back of the couch. "And every time I was here, waiting for you, seeing you come through my front door looking gorgeous and tired, but happy after a day of making the world a better place, I wanted to bend you over the back of the couch and lick you 'til you screamed."

She was standing in front of him, breathing hard, her eyes wide. And he didn't think she'd ever looked more beautiful.

"So, yeah, the first time I make you come is going to be right here." He paused, then said firmly, "Take your clothes off, Lex."

Her hands were shaking slightly as she reached for the tie on the front of her pants and damn if that didn't make him even harder. He definitely liked having an effect on her. This dominating thing might not be all bad. Or not even a little bad.

The top of her pants loosened and she pushed them to the floor and stepped out of them.

"Take your hair down."

She reached up and pulled the ponytail holder from her hair, tossing it toward him. It fell to the floor by his foot. She ran her hands through her hair, loosening it and letting it cascade down her back.

"Take your socks off, but turn around so I can see your ass when you bend over."

She did exactly what he told her to and Caleb felt a surge of *fuck yeah*. Bossing her around was working for him so far. Not to mention that she had an amazing ass and he could see the damp spot on her silky purple panties when she bent over. She straightened after tossing her socks to the side. And waited.

Caleb had to shift to ease some of the pressure against his cock. "Turn around."

She did.

"Shirt off."

She pulled her top off. Her gorgeous breasts were cupped in a matching purple bra. The plum color looked amazing against her skin, and Caleb's mouth was already watering thinking of getting his tongue against all of it.

And then he realized exactly what he had to do. He wasn't going to fuck her tonight. He was going to tease her, test this whole him-in-charge-completely thing out, and he was going to make *her* come—hard—but he needed to be totally in charge. In charge of his own reactions and actions. He wanted to play with her. He wanted to push her. That thought shocked him a little, but yeah, this was sinking in quickly. He wanted to see how much she'd really let him do, how much she'd really let him be in control, and if she liked it as much as she seemed to think she would. He was in charge, but he could still make this all about her and that sent a thrill through him that was startling in its intensity.

He'd never really thought about tying someone up as being about them. But of course it was. If that was what got them off. *He* didn't need it. He supposed for some men that played into their fantasies, too. Not his. But if it was Lexi's, then it became a way for him to take care of her.

"Let me see your gorgeous tits."

Lexi reached behind her and unhooked her bra, letting it fall down her arms and then drop to the floor.

Her nipples were hard and she was breathing fast, her breasts lifting and falling. Caleb could picture her with nipple clamps on those amazing tips, a pretty chain hanging between them, swaying against her stomach, and then swinging as he fucked her from behind.

He wiped his palms on the thighs of his jeans. Damn, he was adjusting quickly, it seemed.

"Play with your nipples."

She lifted her hands and cupped her breasts, then ran her thumbs over the stiff points. She breathed in and out, her eyes sliding shut as she rolled her nipples between her thumbs and fingers.

"Eyes on me, Lex."

Lexi opened her eyes and met his gaze, plucking and squeezing her nipples harder now.

Fuck yes.

"Okay, let's see that pretty pussy," he told her gruffly. His fingers were digging into his thighs as this scene played out in his mind.

She obediently—and yeah, he loved that word, too—slipped her panties down her legs and stepped out of them.

And Caleb's mouth went dry.

Holy damn, she was gorgeous. She stood before him proudly, completely bare, her curves on full display. Full, magnificent breasts, tight centers. Hips that curved out to complete the hourglass. Her hair hanging loose. And her gaze hot, her lips parted, her hands at her sides, waiting for his next command.

He was so hard it hurt, and his cock was already protesting the whole "just play with her tonight" thing. He unbuttoned his jeans and unzipped, to ease the pressure, but didn't open them or push them off.

"Come sit on my lap."

She took a deep breath and came forward. Completely naked, she straddled his thighs and lowered her ass to his lap. Her breasts were right there, her legs were spread so he could see everything, and yet, he couldn't look away from her face.

She was completely turned on. On edge. Her body humming with the desire that was coursing between them.

He wasn't going to handcuff her tonight. Or spank her. Or blindfold her. That could all happen eventually, if she wanted it. But right now, this was just about the two of them. No toys, no props, nothing but their feelings for each other and the chemistry that had been there from the start. Chemistry that had only grown over the past two years as they became an integral part of the other's lives.

Caleb shifted forward slightly and she jumped a little. He let a slow smile spread his lips. "What's your safe word?"

He had no intention of doing anything that would require a safe word, but there was something undeniably hot about the *idea* of it. Of reminding her that she could stop this. And having her *not* stop it.

"Red," she said breathlessly.

"Good girl."

Her pupils dilated at that and Caleb felt one of his eyebrows rise. She liked that. Duly noted.

He lifted a hand and ran it down the length of her hair from the crown of her head to the tips that hung against the curve of her lower back. It was warm and silky and he had no choice but to wrap it around his hand and tug.

She gasped softly as her head tipped back. The position exposed her throat and arched her back, bringing her nipples closer. There was no way he could deny that her being exposed, in a vulnerable position like this, didn't fire his blood. He'd always felt protective of her, but now it felt a lot more like possessive.

"How many guys have spanked your ass?" he asked roughly.

She shook her head but couldn't move as much as usual because of how he held her hair. "None," she said, her voice husky.

None. That was the perfect answer. "You wouldn't lie to me about that, would you, Lex?" He reached up and ran a single finger from her belly button up between her breasts.

Her nipples tightened and goose bumps danced over her body.

"No," she said. "I would never lie to you. No one has spanked me."

"How about tied you up?" His gut clenched with the idea that another man might have made her vulnerable like that. But, more, that she would have trusted someone that way. Yeah, he got it. This was all about trust, and this was already feeding a part of him that he hadn't even realized he had before Shay and Lexi and Jack. He *needed* to be trusted. Fully.

"No one," she said again.

The wave of satisfaction at her answer didn't surprise him a bit. He reached down and pinched one of her nipples, tugging on it and making her whimper. "Then how do you know you want that?" he asked.

She wet her lips and didn't answer immediately. He squeezed her nipple harder. She moaned and wiggled on his lap. She liked that, too. Also noted. "Answer me, Lexi."

"Being with you—around you—has made me see that I like the power you have over me. It turns me on. So, I, um...started reading."

"Reading about bosses who fuck their employees?" he asked, tugging on her nipple again.

She nodded. "Kind of. Romances. Started with boss-employee books. But that led into...more."

"About guys who tie women up and spank them?"

"Yes."

He ran his hand down her side to her ass and squeezed. "What else?"

"Erotic romance. BDSM," she said. "And some websites."

"Porn?"

"Some. But also just sites that talk about BDSM and..."

She swallowed and his focus was drawn to her neck. He leaned in and kissed her throat. Then licked. Then bit down softly. She wiggled again.

"And?" he asked against her skin.

"Toys," she said on a breath out. "And stuff I don't want to do."

"But you do want to do toys?"

She nodded. "Well, maybe not plugs."

He choked on a soft laugh. "We'll have to cover all of this. But for now..." He kissed her neck again as he squeezed her ass. "It's all my mouth and fingers."

Her eyes flew open. "But what about—"

"Who's in charge?" he interrupted. He loved that she wanted him to fuck her. Which meant it would be fun not to. She thought she wanted to give up all control to him? Well, she was going to find out if she really meant it.

"You," she finally said softly. Submissively.

Possessiveness and lust flooded through him. He pulled back to look at her directly. "And when I want to fill your pussy with my fingers, or my tongue, or a dildo, or my cock, I will. And you'll love it and you'll say thank you."

She swallowed hard, lust swimming in her eyes as well. She nodded. "Yes."

Hot damn.

"Hands behind your back."

She moved her hands and linked them right above her ass. He clamped one hand around her wrists, holding her in place.

"So you want me to hold your hands like this and say things like suck my cock?"

Her eyes got wide. "Yes."

"And you want me to put you over my knee and pink up your ass?" As he looked at the little pink spot on her neck where he'd nipped her, he was thinking that he could be okay with that. Marking her. Not permanently. Though if she wanted to tattoo *Caleb's*—and yes with an apostrophe *s*—on her stomach right above her pussy, he'd be okay with that. A mark to show her trust in him, and that he could go right up to her limit and not beyond would be hotter than hell. Control. That was his thing. Knowing he could do what the people who depended on him needed him to do.

She swallowed. "Yes." Her nipples got tighter and she squirmed on his lap.

"God," he groaned. "I can *see* that that turns you on."

"It does. But...you have to want it, too. I know that for some people it's uncomfortable and if you don't—"

"Lexi."

"Yeah?"

"Do you want me to do it?"

"Yes."

"That's what will give you the most pleasure? And you want it to be *me*?"

"Yes." She wet her lips. "Only you."

Those two words were the perfect two words to get *him* to submit to whatever *she* wanted. "Then I'm going to do it."

"But you don't have to—"

"Yes, I do. If that's what you want, then yes I do. I would do *anything* you wanted me to do."

There was a long pause as she just stared at him. "Damn," she finally said. "I really hope you're good at this. Because that was really *hot*."

He let out a soft, surprised laugh. "You don't think I'll be good at it?"

She moved as if to lift her hand, but he was holding onto her. She blew out a breath. "I have *very* high hopes."

He chuckled again. "I gotta say, if all I have to do to get you bare-assed naked and spread open on my lap is to tell you that I'm happy to tie you to my bed, I would have said it a long time ago." Yeah, the tying-her-up thing was definitely sinking in.

She wiggled again. "But none of that tonight?"

He looked her up and down, from the pretty pink between her legs to the deep brown of her eyes. "I want you right here like this."

"Okay."

Fuck yeah, it was okay. He stroked his hand up and down her side, loving how she shivered under his touch. The adrenaline was coursing and he wanted to take her right to the edge. And right over.

He lifted his hand to her right breast, cupping it and thumbing her nipple. "Goddamn, you're so fucking gorgeous."

She shivered again and arched into his touch as much as she could with him holding her wrists together.

"I love your tits." He leaned in and licked the tip. "I've been obsessed with your tits since I first met you. Even when I was trying my damnedest not to be."

She wiggled. "You never look at them."

"Not true. That first night your nipples were hard, pressing against the light-yellow T-shirt that cupped these gorgeous things perfectly." He lifted her breast, loving the weight of it. He couldn't wait to have her on her hands and knees and these glorious mounds swaying.

"They weren't hard until you came over to talk to me."

"Fuck, Lex." Heat coursed through him and he leaned in, taking the nipple in his mouth. He flicked his tongue over it, then sucked.

"Yes," she breathed.

He sucked harder.

"Bite me, Caleb."

Jesus. He closed his teeth around the hard point, scraping them over the sensitive tip as he pulled back.

"Oh my God, yes," she moaned.

Yeah, this was going to be fun. He pinched the same nipple, watching her face. Her cheeks were flushed and her pupils wide. "I want to drag ice cubes over your nipples," he told her. "I want to put them in clamps. And I want to slide my cock between these gorgeous tits and then come all over them."

Her breathing hitched and she had moved to panting.

"Anything you want," she said.

"Damn right." He leaned in and sucked on her again, making her hips circle on his thighs. He grasped her ass, making her stop. "You feeling needy, Lex? You wet and achy?"

"Yes. So much," she moaned.

"Okay, I'm going to let go of one of your hands. But you can *only* touch your pussy. Not your nipples, not your clit, not me. Just slide your fingers in and fuck yourself a little."

She nodded and he loosened his grip on her wrists. Her right hand came forward and she slid a finger into her wet, heat. He didn't miss the fact that she rubbed over her clit on the way, but he didn't call her on it. Every bit of his attention was on her hand moving between her legs. She moved them deep and fast. He could tell she was getting close to an orgasm and when she was on the edge of it, he grabbed her wrist, stopping the motion.

That, of course, brought his hand near the sweet, wet heat that he was craving.

He pulled her fingers free and lifted them to his mouth. Her eyes widened as he slid them into his mouth, licking and sucking her fingers clean.

"Play with your nipple," he said, putting her hand on her breast. "I want to feel what that does to your pussy."

Then he slid his finger into her.

Her moan was everything.

Then he added a second and her next moan was louder. Fuck, she was tight. And wet. And so damned hot.

"Pinch your nipple." She did and he felt the resultant tightening around his fingers. "Fuck yeah. Damn, girl. When I suck on your nipples while you're riding me, I'm gonna feel that same squeeze, aren't I?"

He felt her squeeze him in response to that, too. But she nodded.

"I love having my nipples played with."

"So you will let me clamp them?"

"God, yes."

He was ordering clamps tomorrow. "I think I'll put a nice, thick dildo on that order form, too," he told her. "You're so damned tight. I don't know if I can get in."

She shuddered, her pelvic muscles tightening hard. "*Caleb.*"

She was still pinching her nipple and her hips rocked against his hand.

"Get one with a vibrator, too," she said. "I come so hard with a vibrator on my clit."

Now *he* shuddered. "You don't have a vibrator?"

She bit her bottom lip but nodded.

"You do?"

"Yes."

"You think of me when you use it?"

"Every time."

He fucking loved that. He rubbed his thumb over her clit. "You imagine me sucking on you right here?"

"Yes."

"How about my fingers?" He was still circling the sweet bud, and she was tightening around his fingers as they moved in and out.

"*Yes.*"

"I want to see that sometime. I want to watch you getting yourself off with that vibrator."

She whimpered.

"Maybe I'll tie your legs to my bed. Nice and wide."

He felt her pussy clench his fingers as she moaned.

"Or maybe I'll use the vibrator on you and then lick you clean after you come."

Again, she tightened hard on him.

"Right now, I want to feel you come on my fingers, though." He leaned in and sucked hard on one nipple as he pumped his fingers deep, curling against her G-spot and pressing on her clit.

She ground against his hand and after three deep strokes, she cried out, clamping down on his fingers.

"Fuck. Lex, need you."

"Yes."

He knew she thought he meant he wanted her on his cock, but he had another idea. He grabbed her hips, swung around to lie on the cushions, pulling her up and over him. Then moving her up to his mouth. He squeezed her ass as he licked and sucked, the sweetness between her legs the best thing he'd ever had on his tongue. He thrust his tongue deep, lapping it up, then sucking her clit hard. She came again, gasping his name, the hottest, best sound he'd ever heard.

He held her there as the ripples went through her body, then he let her slide down until her head was resting on his chest.

Her body was spent, pliant against his, as he stroked his hand up and down her back. She was hot, smelled like sex and bubblegum, and so soft and silky. He wanted to take her over and over again. He wanted to make her cry out like that. He wanted to give her pleasure. He wanted to wring her out.

This submission thing was going to work out very, very well.

10

H e hadn't even taken his shirt off.
The thought occurred to Lexi, dimly, in the back of her mind. The very tiny corner that wasn't currently firing all synapses at *holy-shit-that-was-amazing* level.

It was kind of hot that he hadn't gotten undressed. That he'd made her strip and done all of those delicious things to her. Not *with* her. *To* her.

Yes, she wanted to be his partner. She wanted him to need her, too. But this embodied that. It might not seem like it on one level, but she'd led this. He'd done all of this *for* her.

And he'd done it so, so well.

As her breathing returned to normal, she wiggled against him. That had all been amazing. And there was so much left to come—he seemed on board with tying her up and lots of other fun. But she *really* wanted him naked and moving under—or over—her.

The next thing she felt was his hands clamped on her ass, holding her still. "Not tonight, Lex." His deep voice rumbled in her ear.

She lifted her head. "Why not?"

One of his eyebrows rose. "Because I said so."

"But—"

He swatted her. The sharp contact making her gasp. And squirm.

"If you want to do this, you have to go along with what I say," he told her. "I decide what fills your pussy up. And when."

God, his dirty talk was perfect. She felt a deep, needy ache start again. She licked her lips. He was testing her. How much did she *really* want this? Did she really know what she wanted? Yes, she definitely did. "Okay."

His hand rubbed over the spot where he'd spanked her. "That's my girl."

That made that ache intensify. But she loved it. And she'd known it—Caleb was really good at this.

"Now, go to bed."

She pushed herself up off of him. She looked at him, sprawled out on the couch, looking big and gorgeous and hot and in charge. His gaze tracked over her naked body and she soaked up the heat of it.

"Sleep naked," he told her.

She felt the corner of her mouth quirk, and she thought about sassing him with "are you going to come in and check?" but she just nodded. She noted the pleased look he gave her and hid her smile until she'd turned to retrieve her clothes. She bent over, giving him a full look at her and heard the soft growl behind her. Clutching her clothes to her chest, she grabbed her purse and faced him again. "Good night."

"'Night, Lex."

Her name always sounded affectionate when he said it, she realized, but now it sounded affectionate and sexy as hell.

She started for the stairs.

"And, Lex?" he asked.

She turned back. "Yeah?"

"No using your vibrator."

Surprised she said, "I already had two orgasms. Why would I?"

"Because you're going to go upstairs and replay all of this and get worked up again."

Yeah, he was right. "How about my fingers?"

"How about you remember that that pussy is now *mine* and I decide when you get to come and when you don't."

Holy. Crap. She swallowed hard and nodded. Then realized that he wasn't even looking at her. He just expected her to do what he said. That was hot. "Okay."

"Okay."

She made it upstairs and slumped against her door, breathing deeply in and out. She'd started this. And he was everything she'd hoped he'd be.

———

L exi and the kids were still in bed when Caleb left for work the next morning.

A huge fire broke out on the docks, requiring Caleb to work an additional six hours. Lexi was at work by the time he picked the kids up from Bea. Then the ER got slammed just before seven, and Lexi ended up working another two and a half hours.

And that was how it went for the next four days. They both worked long hours and came home exhausted. They talked, but only briefly in the foyer, rather than on the couch. They were back to where they'd been before. Talking only in passing, discussing the kids and their work schedules only.

It occurred to Lexi that it was everything she'd been happy with up until she'd moved in with him.

And now it wasn't enough.

Her body flushed and hummed every time she walked past the couch. She fell asleep thinking of Caleb every night. She thought about him during her shifts at work, keeping track of little details that she wanted to be sure to tell Caleb about. She missed and craved the talking as much as his touch.

Wednesday night she climbed the front steps at the normal time. Finally.

She felt her heart pounding. She didn't know if Caleb would be awake. She knew he'd had several long days and wouldn't blame him for being in bed already.

But she hoped he'd be awake. She missed him. That was crazy, of course. They saw each other all the time. They slept just down the hall from one another every night. But she wanted to talk to him.

And kiss him.

So tonight, even if he was in bed, she was going to go to his room. And kiss him. At least.

She opened the door and locked it behind her. Then she took a deep breath. Could she seduce Caleb?

She glanced toward the couch. Oh, yes, she definitely could.

But then something caught her eye.

There was something draped over the back of the couch. It looked like a dress. Kind of.

She kicked her shoes off and moved into the living room. Closer to the couch. And the...cheerleading uniform.

There was a note pinned to the front of it.

Miss Scott, Get undressed. Put this on. Wait to be called into my office. Coach Moreau.

A shiver of excitement and heat went through her.

Caleb wasn't in bed.

She dropped her bag and unpinned the note. Her body was covered in goose bumps as she stripped out of her scrubs, bra, and panties and it wasn't because the house was cool. It was the heat of Caleb being willing to play with her.

And a cheerleader, huh? She hadn't thought of that one. This might be a fun way of finding out some of *his* fantasies, too.

She pulled the skirt on and then the fitted top. It fit like a glove and she wondered briefly how he'd known her size. With her curves it was sometimes hard to find things that fit at the waist and on top. Then she moved her arms and realized that the top probably didn't pull up this high on girls with smaller breasts —there was *a lot* of bare midriff here—and the skirt probably hung lower on their thighs.

Lexi grinned and she slipped the white tennis shoes on. She hoped she wasn't going to have any of it on for very long so it didn't really matter how it fit.

She licked her lips and looked around. No bra, no panties, not even socks. Okay, so she'd followed the directions. She took a seat on the sofa and waited.

By the time she heard the door to Caleb's office open, she was jumpy, her body humming with anticipation and desire.

"Miss Scott, I'm ready for you."

His deep voice and the "Miss Scott" thing sent tingles racing through her body. Lexi stood, smoothed the front of her skirt, pulled the top down as far as it would go, wet her lips, and turned.

Caleb stood in the doorway across the foyer, his hands on his hips, watching her with a hard-to-read expression. As she stepped around the edge of the couch, her heart hammering in her chest, he looked her up and down. But he didn't give any indication about what he was feeling about seeing her in this uniform. He stepped back. "This way, please."

The office had been his brother-in-law's office and she wasn't even sure what Stephen had done for a living. She'd never seen Caleb use it, but it held a huge oak desk with a high-backed leather chair, a set of big, floor-to-ceiling bookcases, and file cabinets. She'd only been in the room a couple of times to get a copy of Shay's current immunizations and the warranty on the washing machine out of the file cabinet.

But it wasn't the wood-and-leather office that was causing her stomach to tighten and her core to ache. It was Caleb. He was dressed in slacks and a button-down dress shirt, complete with a tie.

She had seen him dress up like this only twice before. Once for a funeral for a fellow firefighter, and once for a luncheon with the mayor.

He was pulling off the tie look. Times a thousand. She loved him in jeans, and seeing him in his uniform got her about halfway to an orgasm just from looking, but there was something about this that really fired her blood. And it wasn't the tie— though that was very nice. It was that this was unusual. It was not what he was comfortable in. And he was doing it for her.

"Have a seat."

His voice was low and commanding and Lexi responded immediately with a flood of heat in her bloodstream and her feet moving her directly for the chair that was positioned in front of the wide desk. That was not usually there. He'd set this up for their role-playing.

The chair was wooden with a padded leather seat, but the seat was very firm. And cold. The cool leather on the backs of her thighs and butt made her suck in a little breath. Especially since she didn't have panties on.

Lexi was aware she was breathing fast and she worked to take deep breaths and relax.

Caleb moved around to the other side of the desk and sat.

"Do you know why you're here, Miss Scott?" he asked. He pretended to sort through some of the papers on his desk.

She fought a little smile. "No, Sir," she said softly.

His head came up at that and he pinned her with an intense look.

So he liked Sir, huh? Noted.

"It's come to my attention that you're a bit of a distraction in Mr. Jenkins' class."

She ducked her head. Damn, this was good. He was doing this for her. This was so not something she would have expected

Caleb to ever be into, but he was making this happen for her. *That* was the hottest thing of all.

She toyed with the hem of her cheerleading skirt. Then smiled. Okay, so he was maybe a little into this. The cheerleading uniform was all his idea.

"I don't mean to be," she answered.

"Don't you?" he asked. "Look at me, Miss Scott."

She looked up.

"I think that perhaps you're distracting Mr. Jenkins on purpose."

"Why would I do that?" she asked.

"Because you can." He leaned in, bracing his forearms on the desk. "I think that you're very aware that you're incredibly beautiful. I think that you know that you can't walk into a room without the men tuning into every move you make. I think you *expect* to have men eating out of your hand. I also think that Mr. Jenkins is trying to do his job and he's ignoring you and you simply can't stand that."

Lexi felt her body growing even warmer. Something in Caleb's expression told her that he was talking about himself. He was tuned into every move she made. He thought she was incredibly beautiful. She had *him* eating out of her hand.

All of this was proof, wasn't it? Role-playing was not something Caleb did. Except with her.

She swallowed. Then scooted back in the chair and crossed her legs, assuming a more bored, I'm-not-nervous-at-all attitude. "I don't know what you're talking about." She put a little haughtiness into her voice now. She needed to play her role, too, and she'd decided that instead of the sweet, shy, straight-A student, she was going to be the bratty, mean-girl, prom queen who did, indeed, know how she affected men. Who'd gone through all of the *boys* in her class, and now that she'd turned eighteen was now moving on to the men around her.

"I think you do," he said. "I think you're very aware that every single male in our school wants to fuck you."

She sucked in a little breath. "I know that a couple of the guys on your football team have a crush on me," she said. "But I'm not interested. Are they the ones who told you I was distracting in class?"

"They are," he said. "But it's not just a couple, is it, Miss Scott? And you're not flashing your pretty bare pussy just at them, are you?"

Lexi swallowed hard. And uncrossed her legs. She didn't part her knees, much, but it was enough to draw Caleb's attention to her thighs. "Well, it's not my fault Mr. Jenkins is looking where he shouldn't be."

Caleb lifted a brow. "You'd be pretty upset if he *didn't* look, wouldn't you?"

She shrugged and shifted so her skirt rose a little higher. "Why do *you* care about what's distracting Mr. Jenkins?"

"Because of the big test you're all taking on Friday."

"Oh, right, the test."

"Two of my players are already almost failing the class, and if they fail that test they can't play in the big championship game. But Mr. Jenkins hadn't been going over the material adequately to prepare them. Because he can't concentrate."

Lexi fought a smile. That was a little bit of a reach as far as reasons went, but she didn't care at all. This was really working for her.

"So you want me to drop that class?" she asked. "That's not really fair, is it?"

"I want you to cover your pussy and wear a bra in that class," he snapped.

Lexi's eyes widened at the tone that sounded very real. He was getting into this. "I'm not really comfortable in panties and bras," she said. "They're very *restraining*."

He just looked at her for a long moment. Long enough to

make her squirm for real. Then he nodded. "I thought maybe you'd say that. But I have a solution."

"Okay."

"We're going to get all of this out of your system."

Her eyebrows rose. "All of *this*?"

"This need to flaunt your gorgeous body in front of older men."

She gripped the arms of the chair. *Yes, please make me strip.* "How are we going to do that?" she asked mildly.

"You're going to be reviewing for the test with me. So that Mr. Jenkins can review the material with the rest of the class."

"Oh, you're going to...*tutor*...me?" she asked, clearly indicating that she had a different idea about what tutoring meant.

"Yes. I'm going to review the material with you for the test. One on one. Privately."

She rolled her eyes like a good bitchy teenage girl would. "Fine. Whatever."

"We're going to start right now."

"Whatever."

"Show me."

She lifted a brow. "Show you what?"

He leaned back in his chair, propping one ankle on his opposite knee. "Show me how you sit in Mr. Jenkins' class."

Ah. She wet her lips again, her pulse pounding. Then she opened her knees and lifted her skirt far enough that he could see everything.

He just looked. Took it all in. Her nipples beaded and pressed against the front of her top and she had to work not to start panting.

"Name the two lower leg bones."

She blinked at him. Lower leg bones. So Mr. Jenkins must teach anatomy. Lexi grinned for a second before she hid it again. Caleb had picked anatomy because they would both know the answers, at least the basics. "The tibia and the fibula," she said.

"Very good. So you have paid some attention."

She nodded. "I'm good at multitasking."

"Are you? Not easily distracted yourself?"

She shook her head. "No, Sir."

Caleb's eyes flared. "Well, let's see. Pull your top up."

"Off?" she asked, sitting a little straighter.

"Did I say off, Miss Scott?" he asked.

Her nipples tingled at his displeased tone. "No."

"Do what I say."

She pulled the top up, exposing her breasts.

There was definite heat in his gaze, but he otherwise didn't react. "I want you to play with your nipples."

She lifted a hand, eager to ease some of the ache in her breasts. She cupped them, then rolled the nipples, the sensation shooting to her clit.

"What is the tip of the sternum called?" he asked.

Lexi wet her lips. "Um, the xyphoid process."

"Very good." His gaze zeroed in on her nipples as she played with them. "Name three other bones in the upper body, not including the sternum or xyphoid process."

Damn, she was actually going to have to *think* here? "The, um, clavicle, scapula—"

"Don't stop pinching your nipples."

She realized she'd done just that. She pinched one and her clit throbbed.

"Go on."

"The ribs."

He nodded. "Nicely done. I see that your gorgeous tits aren't enough to distract you. Play with your clit."

She sucked in a breath. Then she slid a hand down over her stomach and between her legs. She glided her middle finger over her clit and shivered.

"Name three of the bones of the foot." His eyes were glued on her hand.

Dammit, the foot bones were hard. There were twenty-six bones in the foot and ankle. She wasn't going to do as well here. No matter how she was being distracted.

"The talus is all I can think of, Sir," she said.

He nodded and sighed as if she'd disappointed him greatly. "Come here."

Yes.

She stood, her skirt falling down, but her top staying bunched over her breasts. Caleb pushed his chair back from the desk and swiveled to face her as she came around to the back of the desk.

"Yes, Sir?"

"Have I adequately proven that it's harder to perform well in class when you're distracted?" he asked.

She put a hand on her hip and tipped her head, as if she wasn't standing in front of him with her breasts exposed and her nipples begging for his mouth. "Well, I'm not the one who needs to pass that test," she said. "Maybe your players would be better at football, too, if they learned to concentrate better."

There was the tiniest curl to the edge of his mouth with that, but he gave her a scowl and said, "I see our lesson isn't finished."

"What's the objective here, if I may ask?"

"Why, Miss Scott, is that not obvious?" he asked.

She shook her head.

"To punish you for your behavior, of course."

She shivered. For real. Her body actually shook a little at that and goose bumps erupted all over. Holy shit, *yes.*

"So it's *not* to teach me anatomy?" she asked.

Now he did give her a sly smile. One that made him look incredibly hot and even a little sinister. "Oh, I'm going to give you a very *deep* appreciation of anatomy."

Lexi almost couldn't contain her grin this time.

"Put your hands on my desk."

She did. Eagerly. Palms flat down on the cool wood right next to where he was sitting.

"First important anatomical landmark," he said, reaching out and running his hand up the back of her thigh to her butt, then pushing her skirt up to her lower back, baring her backside. "Is this gorgeous ass."

He rubbed over both cheeks and Lexi closed her eyes, absorbing the feel.

Then he swatted her.

It wasn't enough to really hurt, but it surprised her and she jumped.

"Fuck, that makes your breasts bounce," Caleb said huskily. "That's another very important area we need to spend time on."

He swatted her again. She was ready for it that time, kind of, but she still jerked. He rubbed his hand over her ass, soothing the slight sting. Then he reached under her with his other hand and flicked one of her nipples.

Lexi gasped, then moaned.

"Did you know that the nerve endings in the buttocks connect to the genitals?" he asked, almost absently as he tugged on the same nipple. "That's why there can be such pleasure from spanking." He flicked her nipple again and then gave her a swat.

Lexi pressed back into his hand as he massaged the spot.

"And when you're in pain, endorphins are released in the brain to block the pain. But it can also give you a feeling of euphoria. The same thing that happens with a runner's high. Or an orgasm." He slid his hand from her butt cheek, down between her legs and over her clit.

Lexi felt already on the verge of an orgasm. Her fingers curled, trying to grip the desktop as he slid a finger into her.

"Damn, you're wet," he muttered.

She didn't know if it was Caleb or Coach Moreau talking now, and she didn't care. She pressed back onto his finger.

He removed his hand and gave her another stinging swat, this one a little harder. "We'll get to your sweet pussy," he said. "But this lesson isn't over yet."

She almost whimpered. She'd never been this turned on in her life.

"I don't know if I'd ever use a paddle or flogger on you," he mused as he massaged over her ass, giving little swats here and there, making her moan. "I love the feel of my hand on your hot, silky skin." He spanked her harder this time. "And I love the look of my hand print on your ass."

He reached up and tweaked her nipple, this time playing longer, tugging and squeezing until she was wiggling, the ache between her legs intensifying.

"But I definitely want to clamp these sometime," he said. "You're so sensitive." Suddenly he shifted back in his chair. "I want you over my knee, Miss Scott."

Breathing hard, she straightened and faced him. Her whole body was tingling, her ass was warm, and Caleb had never been this hot before.

She positioned herself over his lap without his help.

He groaned softly as she settled into place, reaching for her breasts and cupping them, rubbing the nipples, then pulling gently.

She finally felt his hand run up the back of her thighs to her butt.

"I can see why Mr. Jenkins can't get anything done," he said, huskily. "You're far too tempting. But you're going to get the poor man fired when he's lecturing about the body and accidentally says 'pussy.'"

Lexi squirmed on his lap. "I'm sorry, Coach Moreau."

He brought his hand down against her ass, making her jump, then moan. "I prefer Sir, Miss Scott."

"Yes, Sir."

He smacked her again.

"I called you Sir," she said breathlessly. "Why are you still spanking me?"

"Because it makes you wet." He slid his hand between her legs and circled her clit, then slipped two fingers into her. "And you need to be very wet for when I fuck you."

"Oh, yes, Sir," she gasped.

He slid his fingers in and out, slowly, maddeningly. But Lexi still felt her orgasm tightening her lower belly. He played with her, one hand between her legs, one hand on her nipples, for several long minutes. She never got too close to the edge, but her body was humming, tight, anticipating. She felt his cock against her hip and wiggled against it, hoping to spur him on.

"That's right," he said, lazily, drawing circles around her clit. "We haven't covered *male* anatomy yet, have we?"

"No, Sir."

He gave her a final swat and said, "On your knees, Miss Scott."

Lexi scrambled off his lap. She hadn't seen, touched, or tasted Caleb yet, but she'd been fantasizing about him for months. Years. She was eager and excited as she knelt between his knees.

She reached for his fly, but he caught her wrists. "No touching until I tell you to."

She was disappointed and he clearly saw it before she covered it.

He *tsked* and shook his head. "I don't trust that you won't forget who's in charge," he told her. "You've been very naughty in class. And you like being spanked. What am I going to do to be sure that you follow my commands?"

He reached for his tie and Lexi felt her pelvic muscles clench.

Caleb slowly undid the knot and pulled the blue silk from his collar. Then he leaned forward. He put his mouth against her ear. "Hands behind your back, Miss Scott."

The roughness in his voice danced down her neck to her nipples then deep in her core.

Caleb Moreau was perfect.

Lexi put her hands behind her back. Caleb spent a moment playing with her nipples again as they were thrust forward. He kissed her neck, just below her ear, dragging his beard over her skin, making her nipples bead even tighter, then pinching and plucking at them until she was squirming again. "I love your nipples," he said, gruffly. "I could play here all night."

But he didn't. He finally slid his hands to hers, looping his tie around her wrists. He tightened it, tying the ends. Lexi tested the tension. If she pulled really hard she could get loose, but it was tight enough to give her the thrill of being restrained.

"That's better," he said, sitting back.

Then his hands went to his fly. He pulled his belt loose, tossing it onto the desk, then unbuttoned and unzipped his pants, watching her the entire time.

"Have you ever seen a grown man's cock, Miss Scott?" he asked.

She pressed her lips together and tightened her inner thighs. She shook her head. "No, Sir."

He opened his pants and pulled his cock from his boxers.

Lexi, in real life, gasped. He was huge. And hard. For her. She affected him like this. She couldn't deny that was a thrill. She knew Caleb wanted her. She'd seen proof against his pants before, felt it even. But seeing him grasp his length and stroke up and down and say, "You look like you can't wait for this", was heady.

"I want you," she said, honestly, meeting his gaze. "So much. I'll do anything."

His pupils dilated and he squeezed his cock. "Then put those pretty lips around me," he told her.

Yes, please and thank you. She leaned forward. He held his cock for her and she licked over his tip. His breath hissed out at the first touch, and again she was hit by the fact that even though she was the one restrained, she had a lot of power here.

She slid further down, taking him deeper, licking, then sucking.

Caleb's hand tangled in her hair, gripping and tugging slightly. That sent heat rolling through her and she took him even deeper. She bobbed her head, taking him over and over, for a few minutes. Caleb's hips lifted closer to her and his hand gripped her hair tighter and tighter, until finally he pulled her off of him, breathing hard.

"We'll come back to this lesson," he told her. Then he stood, pulled her up, and set her on the desk. He unbound her wrists and then put a hand on her chest, urging her to lie back. "Now for your quiz," he said. "Besides fingers and cocks, what else can fill up a pretty, wet pussy?"

Oh, she knew this one. "Tongues."

"A-plus." He took a thigh in each hand, spreading her wide and bending to lick her.

He licked and sucked at her clit and Lexi cried out. Then he thrust his tongue into her, lapping at her, winding her tighter and tighter. He returned to her clit, sucking hard, and she came apart without warning.

"Caleb!" she cried out, gripping the edge of the desk.

He didn't say anything, didn't correct her to Sir or even Coach Moreau. He straightened, sheathed himself with a condom, and pulled her ass to the edge of the desk. Then he slid home. Slowly, but surely.

"Lexi," he said, gruffly. "Damn. Fuck. You feel amazing."

She certainly did. Caleb was still completely taking over. She was lying back, with very little leverage, as he pulled out and thrust again. And she loved it. Her body took him completely. She was tight and he was huge, but she was wet, and hot, and had never wanted anything more in her life. Watching him grit his teeth as he watched himself fucking her reignited the burn of an orgasm, and Lexi felt herself tightening.

"Yes. You feel so good," she told him, her voice husky.

He looked up at her and increased the pace. The thrusts made her breasts bounce and it was clear he loved that view as well. He reached up and tugged on a nipple.

"Damn," he said as he felt how that made her core muscles tighten around him.

"More. Harder," she urged.

Heat flared in his expression and he thrust deeper. "Like that? You like that?"

"So much."

His thrusts got faster, but she was sliding on the desk, even as she tried to cling to the edge.

"Come here," he finally said, pulling out and grabbing her hips.

She didn't really do any of the work, but she found herself leaning over the desk, her feet on the floor, breasts pressed against the hard wood.

Caleb wrapped her hair around his hand, grasped her hip with the other, and then thrust deep.

"*Yes.*" That was so much deeper and the angle was perfect.

He did it again and again, filling her, setting her nerve endings on fire. She was on tiptoe, pressing back against him, when he reached around and found her clit. He pressed, circled, then pressed again. He tipped her head back by tugging on her hair. "You are so fucking amazing," he said against her ear. "I want you. Every part of you. I want to fill you up every night. I want to hear you cry out my name. I want to hear you laugh. I want to hold you when you cry. I want to hear every single story you've got to tell. I want to be able to come home to you over and over again. I want to tell you how much I love you every single day."

And that was what sent her hurtling over the edge.

She grabbed his wrist, gripping it tightly as she came hard, crying out his name just like he wanted.

———

C aleb came hard, pumping into Lexi with an orgasm unlike any he'd ever had before. It went on and on. Finally, completely spent, he braced his arms on the desk on either side of her hips. After a few deep breaths, he dealt with the condom in the trash can under the desk, then leaned back over her, kissing her softly.

It was as if that woke her and she lifted up to meet his mouth, wound her arms around his neck and wrapped her legs around his hips, clinging to him.

He hugged her close and stepped back. He sat down in the desk chair with her in his lap. She snuggled into him, not saying anything, her breathing still a little ragged.

"You okay, Lex?" he asked huskily, running a hand over her hair.

She looked up at him. Then she shifted, moving to straddle his lap, and looked into his eyes. "Thank you."

"Thank you?" He squeezed her hips. "Are you kidding? You just blew my head off. Thank *you*."

"But the whole...thing. The uniform and the setup. You did that for me."

He nodded, wanting to make light of it, but not quite able to joke. "I would do anything for you."

She gazed up at him with that familiar you-are-my-hero look and Caleb felt his heart expand. That look. He would do anything for that look. It fed something inside of him that he hadn't even been aware of until Lexi and Shay had come into his life. He *needed* her to look at him like that. Like he was everything she wanted.

Lexi gave a happy, contented little sigh. "That was so nice."

He laughed. "It was *nice*? I dressed you up, paddled your ass, and fucked you on my desk."

A shiver went through her and her smile grew. "I *know*."

He shook his head and ran a hand from her hip to her ass. "So, I didn't hurt you?"

"Just enough."

He blew out a breath with another soft laugh. This was going to take some getting used to. But it had felt good to be able to just let go. To get dirty. To hike her desire and pleasure up to those levels.

"Did you like it?" she asked.

"You couldn't tell?"

She tipped her head. "Of course. I mean, the physical pleasure was obvious. But did you...enjoy any of it?"

Okay, he could be honest here. They'd just had sex for the first time. They'd just been *very* intimate. Being able to admit a fantasy, something that might make people judge you, took a level of trust. Actually *indulging* that fantasy, letting yourself really get into it, was another level. He'd never thought about how getting really dirty with someone could take trust and letting them close, but it did. And he loved that they'd gone there.

He also loved that he could just get into it. He knew she would stop him if needed. But he also loved being able to read her, being able to tell when she needed more of something, when his actions were affecting her and giving her pleasure.

Giving Lexi pleasure was one of his main goals in *life*. And this scene, or whatever it had been, had helped him feel closer to that than a lot of the other things he did. Fixing her car helped her. Taking care of Jack helped her. Their friendship, making this home together—those things made her happy. But pleasure—true, primal, base-instinct *pleasure*—that was something he hadn't been able to give her until now.

And he was officially addicted to it already.

"I loved doing this with you," he told her, running his hand over her bare hip and butt cheek. "It was amazing to be able to do that to you, for you. And yeah, letting go, getting into it, knowing that we were both right there, together, was intense and amazing."

She gave a happy sigh and shifted to sit across his lap, curling into him again. "That all made me feel really...close to you. Free. Hot. And..." She trailed off.

He *had* to know what else she'd felt. "And?" he prompted, squeezing her ass.

"Loved," she said softly. Almost embarrassed.

He reached down and tipped her head up. "You are. And I can't tell you how fucking amazing it makes me feel that you know that. And that this is one way I can show you."

She gave him a smile that was unlike anything he'd seen before. It was so much more than the you-walk-on-water smiles she gave him. This one was...pure happiness. And he'd made her feel *that*.

This was all so good. So, so good.

"I'm in love with you, Caleb," she told him. "And that you would do this all for me—when I know it's out of your comfort zone, when I know that you would rather pamper me and take care of me and treat me like a princess...to know that you will trust me and do this for me, it's really truly..." She sighed. "Everything."

His heart squeezed in his chest. And he squeezed her tightly to him.

"I shouldn't have told you that I love you in the midst of sex, right?" he asked. He knew that, but he'd been unable to hold it back.

She grinned up at him. "Telling me that when we were doing what we were doing? You completely letting go and trusting me and realizing I completely trust you and that you can meet every one of my needs? That was the perfect time."

God, how did she know just what to say and do? She had no way of knowing how much that meant to him. She didn't know how much he'd needed to hear that he was fulfilling her needs, that he *was* taking care of her in a very intimate way, and that he was making her happy.

"I was thinking that we could use this room for other role-playing," he said, absently, absorbed in everything about this that seemed absolutely perfect. He'd orchestrated it all and carried it out successfully. He'd given her orgasms, and he'd showed her she was loved.

"Yeah?" She looked up at him.

He focused on her. "Yeah. We could get a couch in here. We can keep handcuffs and nipples clamps and toys in the drawers. Get some more costumes. This could be the professor's office where you have to come and beg for an A." He squeezed her butt as she wiggled in response to his words. "Or this could be where the billionaire conducts that first interview with his new secretary."

Lexi wiggled again, but gave a soft laugh. "How do you know about billionaires and secretaries?"

"I've been reading," he said smugly.

"Reading?" She looked up at him. "What do you mean?"

"I got some erotic romance recommendations from Harper, James's neighbor. I think I'm getting a *feel* for all of this."

He gave her a slow grin. But she didn't smile back. She looked...shocked.

"You've been reading erotic romance?"

Right. He hadn't intended on telling her that. He wanted her to just think he was good at this naturally. But... "Yeah. I figured it would be good to figure out where some of this was coming from."

Her eyes widened and suddenly she was straddling him again and kissing him deeply.

"That's amazing," she said, pulling back after several long delicious moments. "Wow."

"Yeah?" He really did fucking love that look in her eyes.

"Yeah." She looked around the room. "And you're going to make us a playroom? Just wow."

He laughed. "And here I almost brought you flowers to show you how I feel."

She focused on him again. "This is so much better. It will last *far* longer than flowers. And it's good for *both* of us."

It really was. "You letting me take that control, make all of this happen for you, is good for both of us," he told her. He hadn't understood that before, but now he got it. Completely. "I love being able to push you like that, to make your fantasy come true, to have the hottest sex of my life with you, and to know that you are with me the whole way."

"So you totally trust me here?" she asked. "You know that you can really let go, right?"

"I do." He rubbed her hip. "Thank you for that."

She cupped his face between her hands. "Of course. As much as you love giving me pleasure? I feel the same way about you. And I know that what gives you the *most* pleasure is being in charge and being *everything* I need. And you are that, Caleb," she added softly. "You really are."

That grabbed his heart and squeezed hard. He needed to tell her about Shay.

The brace fitting today had changed everything. It had finally broken through the last of his *maybe this will all be okay*. It *would be* okay. The brace didn't change the amazing little girl Shay was, nor did it affect his pride in her or his love for her one iota. But it truly was the symbol that this was a permanent thing and he was going to have to face it. Literally. They made a mold today and the brace would be in soon. He was going to, obviously, have to tell Lexi. He couldn't fix it first and then tell her. This wasn't completely fixable and he was going to have to admit that.

He opened his mouth, still not sure exactly *what* he was going to say, when Lexi's phone started ringing in her purse where she'd dropped it in the foyer.

She sighed. "I should get that. I asked work to call me about the lady who came in at the end of the shift."

"Want to tell me about it?" He wanted to hear. He wanted to know all of her stories.

She smiled as she climbed off his lap and pulled the uniform down over her breasts and smoothed the skirt. "I do, actually."

"Great. Are you hungry? I have leftovers." He started putting himself back together as she headed for her bag. And it hit him. This was completely normal. They'd just acted out a very hot and intense sexual fantasy and now they were going to talk about work and eat leftover chicken.

He smiled to himself as he got to his feet. This was...how it should be. This is how he wanted it to be. Always.

11

"Hi, Bea," Caleb heard Lexi say into the phone as he crossed the foyer to her.

That pulled his attention away from the way the tiny skirt barely covered her luscious ass.

"Of course," she told Bea, opening the office door and heading out to the living room.

Caleb followed her and watched as she shrugged out of the skirt, with one hand, which left her bare from the bottom of the uniform top. He was completely distracted at that point, of course. He wanted her again.

But he wanted her in his bed. Just bare naked, in his sheets, under him, on top of him. He wanted to make love to her. Strangely, at least until it had happened, he wouldn't have believed that fucking a woman in a cheerleader costume after spanking her could be making love, but it had been. And now he wanted her without the props and pretending. Just them.

Lexi was struggling to get the top off while staying on the phone. She'd somehow managed to get her panties and scrub pants pulled up, but she couldn't tie them one-handed and they were hanging very loose around her hips.

He didn't know what was going on, but she was getting dressed. He stepped forward and pulled her pants up, tying them in front. She smiled at him gratefully. Then he pulled the phone away from her ear and stripped the cheerleading top up and over her head.

Again, he got a little sidetracked by her bare breasts and nipples. In fact, he almost leaned in and took one in his mouth. But she pointed at her bra and scrub top.

"Yes, I know," she told Bea. "That's fine. It's not a problem at all."

Caleb grabbed the garments and held the bra up. She put one arm through, switched the phone to her other ear, and stuck the other arm through the strap. Then she turned and he hooked it behind her. He helped her into the top as well. He much preferred *undressing* her, of course, but there was something really nice and normal and intimate about helping her dress. That and leftover chicken. It was these little things that brought one word to mind over and over. *Forever.*

"I'll see you soon."

Lexi pulled her hair out of the back of the scrub top as she turned to face Caleb and disconnected with Bea.

"Everything okay?" he asked.

She shook her head. "I need to go help Bea. She's not feeling well and she's at Commander's Palace for Taylor's birthday dinner."

Taylor was Bea's granddaughter and she was turning sixteen. Caleb frowned. "I'll come with you."

"You need to stay with the kids." She grabbed her purse.

"But—"

"It's nothing serious. This happens sometimes. I'm just going to get them home and settled." She pulled her bag up onto her shoulder. "She doesn't want to make a big deal out of it with the kids. I'm going to just show up, have dessert with them, and then drive everyone home."

"What are the kids going to think about you driving them home when Bea drove them there?"

Lexi shrugged. "We're going to get her drunk. Or so they'll think."

"She can't tell the kids she's not feeling well?" he asked. He didn't like this.

"She doesn't want to scare them."

"Why would they be scared of her having a headache or a stomach bug?" Caleb pressed.

Lexi blew out a breath. "It's a little more than that. I'll fill you in later, okay? I need to go."

"This has happened before, though?" he asked, his frown deepening. Bea was another person in his life that he cared a lot about.

"It has," Lexi amended. "But don't worry, I've got this." She pulled the door open and looked up at him.

He was nearly on top of her and grabbed the edge of the door over her head. He didn't want her to leave. He wanted to know what was going on with Bea. "Call me if it's a bigger deal than you think? Or if you need me?"

"Of course."

"Call anyway," he added as she stepped through the door. "Just let me know how things are."

"Okay. If I have a chance. This really might just be a quick stop over there and I'll be right back."

"Okay."

He watched her until her car had pulled out of the driveway and driven off down the street. When he shut the door, he felt stupidly frustrated. In what way was Bea not feeling well? Was she stressed out about one of her grandkids? They were teens and she often shared in class how hard it was on them to have their mom in jail. It was hard on Bea, too, of course.

But Lexi had said Bea wasn't feeling well. Maybe it was something physical. Bea was in her late sixties. She didn't have health issues that Caleb was aware of, but then, why would he be aware?

Even as he pulled his phone out and dialed the number, he knew he shouldn't. He should just leave it alone. But he was worried. And, fuck, his day had been a roller coaster. Shay's appointment on top of pulling the fantasy scene off with Lexi, telling her he loved her, and now Bea?

"Hey, Logan, is Dana around?" Caleb asked when his friend answered. It was possible the women of the support group had shared information they hadn't let the whole group in on.

Lexi was there for Bea, but Bea could be stubborn as hell. It wasn't impossible to think that Lexi might need some backup.

"Caleb?" Dana asked a moment later. "What's up?"

"Bea and her grandkids are at Commander's Palace and Bea isn't feeling well. Lexi just headed over there. Just wondering if it was something we should be concerned about?"

"She actually wasn't feeling well last Thursday, either," Dana said. "She said she was just tired, but I know she and Lexi talked for a little bit during the break. Neither said anything to me, though."

Damn. "Lexi didn't mention it to me, either," Caleb said.

"You're going to head over?" Dana asked.

"I'm...not sure," he said honestly.

"Bea can be stubborn as hell," Dana said, echoing his earlier thought. "If this has been going on for a few days, it's something she should get looked at, right?"

"Lexi will be able to tell her that," Caleb said. She was, after all, a nurse, and it seemed that Bea had already confided in her.

Dana laughed. "Sure, Lexi can *tell* her that. But getting Bea to actually do it is something else. Do you think she called Lexi over to stay with the kids so Bea can go to the ER?"

The ER. For some reason that word made Caleb's chest tighten. He dealt with the ER all the time but sending a friend there was something else. Still, if something was going on at this time of night, that was where Bea would need to go.

"Maybe," he said. "Or to drive her? The kids are old enough to stay alone for a while." Bea's oldest granddaughter, Kendall, was seventeen and often helped sit for kids of other parents in the support group.

"True," Dana said slowly. "Bea doesn't ask for help easily. If she needs someone to drive her, that concerns me."

Him, too. "It's more likely that she thinks she can get over whatever it is with some crackers and tea and having Lexi check her blood pressure or something," Caleb said.

"Even if she needs more than that," Dana agreed. "If she's hoping Lexi can do something for her and save her a trip to the ER, Lexi might have a hard time convincing her she needs to head in."

Damn, he really fucking hated when people he cared about had stuff going on he didn't know about. He realized it was ridiculous to think that every one of his friends would always tell him everything, but he still hated not knowing.

"I can send Logan over to hang with your kids if you want to go check things out," Dana said.

"Yeah, maybe I should go make sure Bea's being a good patient."

"Lexi could probably use another adult there whether it's talking Bea into going to the ER or taking a couple of ibuprofen. Bea's so used to taking care of everyone else that I can't see her being a good patient."

"Yeah, I'll head over if Logan doesn't mind coming here."

"No, that's great. Bea's way more likely to listen to you than Logan. Or me," Dana said. "It makes sense for you and Lexi to be the ones checking on a health concern. And you've got all those firemen carries so you can *take* Bea to the ER if you have to."

He chuckled. "Well, there is that." He was already heading

upstairs to get dressed. "Tell Logan the kids are asleep and they shouldn't be any trouble."

"No, problem. He just headed out to his truck."

It hit Caleb how amazing it was to have all of these people in his life. And Lexi's. And Shay and Jack's. Lexi and Caleb might not have their parents right here and both were only children now, but they had a family that they could depend on.

———

"I don't know why I can't get this right."

Lexi gave Bea a smile and squeezed her hand. They were sitting at the table at one of the Garden District's best restaurants. Commander's Palace had been a landmark in New Orleans since the late 1800s. The blue and white exterior with the striped awnings were iconic, and ornate interior with the gorgeous chandeliers and white tablecloths made it the perfect spot for special occasions.

"It's a big adjustment. It takes time," Lexi said.

Bea was still trying to figure out how to manage her new diagnosis of type II diabetes.

"I guess." Bea sighed. "Things are just supposed to stay the same. Steady."

Lexi shook her head. "Come on. You know better than anyone that doesn't happen. You mean you want things with *you* to stay the same. Because everyone around is changing all the time."

Bea nodded. "I like being the one who takes care of everyone else. I bail them out. I clean up after them. I tell *them* that they're being dumbasses. I don't like being the dumbass."

"You're not a dumbass," Lexi said firmly. "You take care of everyone else and you're just not used to taking care of *yourself*. It's not because you're dumb. But," she added. "You have to. This is important. And if you get sick, then what are all the people who depend on you going to do?"

Bea scowled, clearly frustrated and a little angry. "That's what I'm saying. I don't have time for this shit. And I can't be feeling crappy. I've got stuff to do."

Lexi had declined the waitress's offer of dessert for Bea's sake, though turning down the Bananas Foster and the bread pudding soufflé was not only difficult, it was nearly a sin. She did, however, order coffee. They'd sent Bea's grandkids a few blocks down to La Boulangerie, a bakery where Taylor could have cake or pastries for her birthday, to get them out of the way so Lexi and Bea could talk about how she was feeling and what they needed to do next.

She'd had a low blood sugar episode that had scared her badly. Sweaty and dizzy, she'd called Lexi. Even though she was surrounded by food at the restaurant, it wasn't the fast-acting simple sugar she needed, and she didn't know what to ask for. Lexi had coached her to ask for some honey and by the time Lexi got there, she'd eaten it and was feeling a little better.

"Then you need to take your meds on time and watch what you're eating," Lexi said firmly, but gently.

She understood that Bea was frustrated. She wasn't used to having any weaknesses. She kept things together for her four grandchildren, for her husband, for the members of the group, and indirectly for her daughter. She truly didn't have time to be sick. But she was quite capable of figuring out what she needed to do to handle this new diagnosis, and if she did it right, she'd be fine. Completely capable of handling everything she normally handled.

Bea hated needing help, and the fact that she'd confided to Lexi after she'd been diagnosed with type II diabetes, and then called Lexi for help, meant a lot. She loved that she finally felt like she had something to give to the people who had been supporting her for the past two years. And if Bea needed Lexi to hold her hand through learning all about managing her condition, Lexi would be here every time the other woman called.

"And you know I'm always here," Lexi said. "I love being here when you need me."

The older woman smiled and squeezed her hand, the frustration in her face replaced by affection. "I know you do, sweetie. I'm so proud of you. You're so good at all of this." She paused. "Caleb and I are a lot alike, aren't we?"

Lexi lifted a brow. "Yes. Definitely."

"So you know that even when he's prickly and doesn't *want* to need you, he still appreciates you and loves you?"

Lexi felt her heart flip over. "You don't think he wants to need me?"

"Of course not," Bea said matter-of-factly. "Some of us are just used to being in charge, it actually feels like a failure to need someone for something."

"But you know that the people who love you *want* to help you. It needs to be a two-way street. A partnership."

Bea shrugged. "That's not how it feels to us. My husband was gone for days at a time when our kids were little. Now he and my daughter are gone and I've got these kids. And I bitch about it, but it's how I like it. I know best." She gave Lexi a little smile. "At least I can tell myself that when no one else is around who has ideas or opinions."

"Well, now *I'm* here with ideas and opinions about your diabetes," Lexi told her dryly.

"Exactly. And you're at Caleb's. With ideas and opinions about pretty much everything, right?"

Lexi thought about that. Yes, of course. And that wasn't new. But now that they were living together, spending time together during their time off, sleeping together, it wasn't a matter of her implementing her opinions and ideas when she was there alone and him doing the same when she wasn't there. They needed to do it all together. Partners. Equals. Even with the sex. Though he was in charge and she got off on submitting to him, it was still something they'd decided to do *together*. She'd *put* him in charge. She'd *chosen* to submit.

She nodded. "Yes, I do. And it's working. We're figuring things out."

Bea smiled. "Good. I understand Caleb. I get where he's coming from. Being in charge, being the go-to person, being the one who figures things out, can be exhausting. And it's really hard to ask for help. Just keep that in mind."

"I get it," she said. "And *you* need to keep in mind that when you ask for my help, I love it. Since I started nursing, I'm feeling that I can be valuable for the first time in my life. I'm not the dependent one. The one who people need to worry about. I can help people, I'm respected, and *I* can worry about people." She gave Bea a smile. "And I think for the first time, I've realized I *do* worry about people. Which sounds strange. But when you're always the one people are bailing out and supporting, it's hard to focus on meeting *their* needs. Now I can really look outside of myself and see that I can be a part of something."

"I'm so glad," Bea said sincerely. "You've grown up so much—"

Suddenly there was a commotion at the front door of the restaurant. Bea straightened and Lexi pivoted. And her mouth dropped open.

Caleb was coming toward them. Followed by Gabe and Addison and Lindsey and Corey.

And Lexi realized she should have expected this.

"What are you all doing here?" Bea demanded of the group as they came to the table.

Gabe, Addison, Corey, and Lindsey took the three remaining chairs at the table. Caleb stayed standing.

Lexi just lifted an eyebrow at Caleb. His gaze had come straight to her and she felt a stab of irritation. She'd told him she would call him when and if she needed him. What was he doing?

"Logan texted to say he was heading to Caleb's because he

and Lexi were here with you," Gabe said to Bea. "Our kids are at my mom's, so we thought we'd head over and see if you needed anything."

"Caleb wasn't here," Bea said, frowning at Caleb over Lexi's head.

"Yeah, we met up on the sidewalk out front," Addison said.

"And you guys?" Lexi asked of Lindsey and Corey.

"I called Dana to see if she still wanted to borrow my mixer," Lindsey said. "And she told me she couldn't come over because Logan was at Caleb's because Caleb and Lexi were here. So I took the mixer and the boys to Dana and thought I'd see if everything was all right."

"I stopped at Caleb's to ask if he could help me with my garage roof next weekend," Corey said. "And Logan told me where you all were."

"I'm here because I was worried." This came from Caleb and he didn't sound nearly as lighthearted or apologetic as the others had managed to. Probably because he wasn't apologetic.

"I called *Lexi*," Bea said. "No need for you to worry. Or come over. My house isn't burning down."

"Well, I know how stubborn you can be and how sweet Lex can be," Caleb said. "Thought she might need backup if you weren't being a good listener."

Lexi scowled at him. She was sweet. When she needed to be. But she could be tough. He knew that. Didn't he?

"I needed a little bit of sweet tonight," Bea said. "I've been yelling at myself enough, I didn't need anyone else doing it. Lexi knows what she's doing, but she's calm and straightforward and kind about it."

"You didn't think I'd be kind?" Caleb asked.

"No, I didn't," Bea said. "You don't have quite the bedside manner Lexi does."

Caleb frowned at her. "Some patients need someone to be a little more take charge."

Lexi felt her eyes widen. He was frowning at Bea, and he wasn't wrong about Bea being stubborn and a know-it-all and a difficult patient, but Lexi *had* taken care of the situation.

"I'm fine," Bea informed him. "I don't need all of you traipsing in here and embarrassing me. Lexi and I have this under control."

Lexi looked around. Obviously their group had attracted attention.

Caleb clearly didn't care. He crossed his arms, looking big and imposing and annoyed.

Lexi knew how he felt. Annoyed was definitely what she was feeling at the moment. And hurt.

"*What* is under control?" Caleb demanded. "What is going on? You, of all people, don't go around calling people at night and asking for help. You can see why we would be concerned."

"You shouldn't be concerned if you knew Lexi was here," Bea pointed out.

And Lexi wanted to hug her.

Caleb glanced at Lexi. It took him a second to answer and Lexi felt her heart drop. He didn't say, *You're right* or *That's true* or *I definitely overreacted* or *I just felt left out because everyone always comes to me for everything and I don't know how to step aside and let the girl I've been taking care of for the past two years actually be in charge once in a while.* All of which would have been dead accurate.

"I did feel better knowing Lexi was here," he finally said. "I just wanted to check in on both of you."

"You thought Lexi would need checking on?" Bea asked.

"I thought she might need some help dragging your stubborn butt out to the car to head to the ER," Caleb said.

"We're not going to the ER," Bea said with another glare.

"Well, I didn't know—"

Lexi shot up out of her chair. "You didn't know that I could easily assess if she needed to be at the ER? You didn't know that I was resourceful enough and knowledgeable enough and that Bea would *trust* me enough to get her to the ER if that's what was required?"

Caleb looked mildly surprised. "I didn't know *anything* about what was going on."

"Excuse me, is everything all right here?" The restaurant manager approached cautiously.

"And you don't *have* to know anything about what's going on," Lexi exclaimed, completely ignoring the manager. "Not everything that happens to every single person you know is your responsibility or even your business, Caleb."

His mild surprise went to outright baffled. "I'm just here to help."

"We don't need your help."

Everyone else was totally quiet.

Lexi took a deep breath. "I know you're concerned. But you have to trust me when I say *I've got this*. You have to be okay with not being a part of every single thing every single second."

She swallowed hard. She was spilling all of this in front of everyone—and okay, the other patrons in the restaurant, too—but this was their support group. These were the people they shared the good, bad, and holy-crap-I'm-screwing-everything-up parts of their lives with. Yes, it was mostly about parenting, but there was nothing in their lives that their parenting didn't touch and influence. They all knew a lot about each other's lives, period.

"Can we possibly move your party to—"

"I don't think you would have rushed over here if you knew Gabe was here," Lexi said over the top of the restaurant manager. "Or if you knew Lindsey was here. Or anyone else. You came over because you were worried about *me*."

"I want to be there for you, Lex," he started.

But she shook her head. "You were worried about me being in over my head. Like I was after mom left. And in this case, that also worried you for Bea. You thought I couldn't handle this."

He shook his head. But she wasn't done.

"And I'm starting to think that might not go away. You can't just immediately assume that I'm not able to handle the tough stuff. You have to trust me. To know my limits, to know when I need to tap out, to recognize when I *can't* handle something that's happening and to tell you." She could tell from his expression that he realized she was using the sexual fantasies and her safe word as an analogy. "We're both going to be a lot happier if you acknowledge that I know myself and trust that I will let you know what I need from you."

The entire restaurant was completely silent for several long moments.

Then Lexi said simply, "You need to go home, Caleb." She said it firmly. The only other time she'd used that tone with him was when he'd been trying to bandage her damned finger that morning in his kitchen.

What the *hell* was with this guy not thinking she knew what she was doing?

He studied her face. Lexi just held her breath and kept her gaze steady.

This was her saying, "Red" in this situation. Would he understand that?

There was a long pause. Then he said simply, "Okay." Then he turned and left the restaurant without looking back.

She blew out a breath as she watched the door shut behind him.

"Okay, so—" Gabe looked around and then back to Bea and Lexi. "You're all okay?"

Lexi wasn't so sure about that. Caleb had just left. Without fixing anything. Because she'd asked him to. That was...new.

"I've got Lexi," Bea said. "I'm fine."

Lexi smiled at her and then nodded. "We're fine."

Gabe nodded. "Then we'll head out."

Everyone got up and filed out. The manager sighed. He didn't look particularly placated, but he moved off toward the kitchen.

Lexi watched everyone go. Then she took a deep breath, sat back down, and looked at Bea. "What are we going to do with all of them?"

Bea smiled. "Love them."

Lexi took a deep breath. "Well, not loving them isn't even an option."

Bea nodded. "I know you love that boy in particular," she said.

Lexi knew she was talking about Caleb. "I do. But...I'm really mad at him right now." She wasn't sure why she'd confessed that. "I don't think I've ever been mad at him before." It was a really strange feeling to acknowledge that Caleb Moreau had fucked up. With *her*.

Bea didn't say anything right away, but after a moment she leaned in. "He's not going to change, Lexi. At least not much."

Lexi sighed.

"We're a lot a like—me and Caleb," Bea continued. "We kind of got dumped into the parenting thing. At least, I did this time around. Everyone else in our group is the parent of kids they chose to raise."

Lexi thought about that. She hadn't really realized that before, but Bea was right.

"I know Dana didn't *choose* to lose her husband," Bea went on. "Corey didn't choose to lose his wife. Austin didn't plan on getting divorced. You and Ashley didn't plan on getting pregnant. But still, everyone else was more involved in the choice to become parents than Caleb and I were. Caleb was shocked to find out his sister made him Shay's guardian. I was, obviously, shocked when my daughter had to go to prison. But, in some ways, that makes us even more aware of the things we're doing. Or not doing. Because we're taking care of someone else's kid. For them. Because they trusted us over everyone else they knew. We want to do it right."

Lexi blew out a breath.

Bea went on. "And then *you* trusted him, not just with Jack, but with *you*," she said, squeezing Lexi's hand. "There's no way he's going to shut off that need to make sure you're always okay."

"So you're saying that I need to get used to being mad and frustrated with him?" Lexi asked. She loved that Caleb wanted to take care of her, but why couldn't he see that she could take care of people, too? Even take care of *him* once in a while?

"Yeah, there are going to be those moments for sure," Bea said with a little laugh. "You just need to understand that when he *does* ask you for help or defers to you, it matters even more than if it was coming from someone else. That won't ever be his instinct or natural inclination. It will take a conscious effort. But I want you to know, it means even more then."

Lexi realized this applied to Bea calling her tonight when she wasn't feeling well. She hadn't wanted to. She'd wanted to take care of it on her own. But the fact that she'd realized she should let someone in, and that she'd chosen that someone to be Lexi, *did* matter.

"I think I get it," Lexi said.

"People like Caleb and I need someone who will keep coming over and helping us even when we've been stubborn, hardheaded assholes."

Lexi looked at the two empty packets of honey that Bea had used tonight. "You're not an asshole, Bea. You're just learning that it's okay to not *always* be the strong one and the right one. And," Lexi continued, "I will come any time and every time you need me. I understand that it's hard for you—and people like you," she added with a smile, "to ask for help. But *I* personally find it very easy—because it means I have a *family* to lean on. You need to look at it that way."

Bea nodded. "You're probably right." She gave Lexi a final squeeze. "And when you need a reminder about how to deal with people like me...you just give me a call."

"*When?*" Lexi asked with a laugh. "You think Caleb's going to be a stubborn, hardheaded asshole sometimes?"

Bea nodded. "Inevitably."

———

L exi let herself into the house an hour later. It was quiet, all the lights downstairs off except for the tiny lamp on the table in the foyer.

She kicked off her shoes, dropped her purse, and turned to lock the door.

She loved being able to lock the door behind her. It was a little thing, but it meant that she was staying and she wasn't used to that yet. Or how good it felt.

It was something that families took for granted every day, she was sure. Being home, all together, cozy and secure together under one roof.

Of course, she didn't know how cozy and secure things were at the moment. Caleb was upset and she was mad at him.

"Hey."

She turned at the sound of Caleb's voice. He was on the couch in the living room.

"Hey," she said wearily, coming around the end of the sofa. She didn't know where they stood at the moment. They'd never really had an argument. She'd never pushed him away like she had at the restaurant.

He leaned to shut the TV off and took a deep breath. Resting his forearms on his thighs he said, "We need to talk."

She nodded. "Yeah. Okay." She let her bag drop by the couch and took a seat on the cushion next to him. Her cushion. Where she always sat when they talked.

"There's something going on with Shay you should know about," he said. "Something big."

Lexi felt a jolt of surprise. This wasn't about Bea and what had happened at the restaurant? But then she frowned, concern overriding her surprise. "What's going on?"

"She has a brain injury."

Lexi stared at him as he blew out a breath, as if relieved.

"*What?*"

He shook his head. "It's not new. It happened in the car accident when her parents died." Caleb looked down at his hands clasped between his knees. "I didn't really notice anything until recently, but when I brought up her stumbling and stuff with the doctor, he did some testing." Again he blew out a breath. "They've done all the tests. CT scans and everything. The damage is affecting her left side, causing...everything we've always noticed. The stuff you were working on with her."

He looked over at her. His expression was sad but he gave her a smile.

That tugged at Lexi's heart. She wanted to hug him. But she couldn't move.

This all made sense. It wasn't at all hard to accept that the car accident had caused a brain injury and that that was affecting Shay now as she grew and developed.

Caleb went on. "In addition to the weakness and foot drop, she also has some learning deficits." His voice got scratchy and he cleared his throat. "She's going to need PT, OT, speech and some learning intervention. Once she starts school, there are going to be special learning plans for her so that she keeps up as well as she can."

Lexi just nodded. She didn't really know what else to do. She hadn't been expecting any of this and now he was giving her so much information at once, she was having a hard time processing it.

"But she'll never...quite keep up. She's always going to have issues." He swallowed hard. "And there's nothing I can do to fix it."

"You just found this out?" she finally asked. "Today?"

She couldn't put her finger on it exactly, but it seemed like he knew more, or that there was more going on, than could have all been discovered just today.

Caleb shook his head and said, "She started therapy on Friday. Her doctor's appointment was the Thursday before. That's when they did the scans and stuff."

"The Thursday before last? The day we moved in here?" Lexi frowned.

Caleb nodded. "Yeah."

Lexi thought about that. Something about it felt...wrong. Weird. "So on Friday, when we were talking about the exercises I do with her and the memory games, you knew then?" she asked, piecing it together.

He looked at her and she realized that he knew where her mind was going with all of this.

"Yes."

"And you didn't say anything?"

He shook his head.

"Why not?" But she knew why. Because Caleb didn't think she could handle it.

"I didn't know anything yet," he said. "Not really. The scans showed there was something going on but they didn't have any specifics. That's what the therapy assessments were for. To see where she was currently and to talk about where they thought she could go. And how to get there."

Lexi nodded, feeling a cold ball of emotion settle in her stomach. It was a combination of anger and confusion and hurt and... a realization that she almost didn't want to look at too closely.

But she had to.

"I wanted to have as many answers as I could before I started talking about it," he said. "I wanted to have a plan."

That sounded like Caleb. He was a problem solver. Especially in her life. And Shay's, obviously. "You had to know that it would take a long time to actually have those answers and a plan."

"I didn't really know anything," he said. But then he admitted,

"But yeah, I knew it was going to be a process."

"So you weren't actually planning to tell me about this tonight, were you?" she asked.

He took a deep breath. And shook his head.

"So why are you telling me now?" she asked. "What changed?"

"They want to put a brace on her left foot," he said. "They think it will help her walking and running. Make her safer. And they did the mold for it today."

"And I would obviously have noticed that," she said.

"Right."

So he'd let her in on this because he didn't have a choice.

Well...fuck.

"It's no coincidence that the same day you moved Jack and me in here was the day you saw the doctor, is it?" she asked quietly.

Caleb looked at her with a frown. "What do you mean?"

"You overreacted about me and Jack living in Trahan's apartment because you were upset about Shay," she said, her thoughts forming as she spoke. "You were feeling confused and guilty and...helpless. So you did something that would make you feel in control again."

He didn't immediately reject that idea. He took a breath. "I would have wanted you and Jack out of that apartment no matter *when* I'd found out about it."

She knew that. She nodded. "I know. But if it wasn't for what had happened with Shay, you would have given us a place to stay for a few days while you helped me look for a new apartment. You probably would have even paid the deposit or first month for me. You wouldn't have immediately insisted on us living here permanently." She sucked in a breath as another thought occurred to her. "And you wouldn't have rushed right into changing things between us."

Her stomach sank. Caleb had been feeling out of control with Shay's situation so he'd turned his energy and attention on the other person in his life that needed him most—*her*. And he'd changed things, deepened things, done exactly what he knew she wanted him to do—make them into a family—because he was feeling helpless to do what Shay needed him to. He couldn't fix Shay's brain, so he fixed Lexi's need for a family. Her need for *him*.

Her face flushed with heat as she realized that he really had known how she felt about him, and it was what he'd used to feel important and in charge again.

She started to stand but, almost as if he'd sensed her intention before she moved, Caleb reached out and clamped a hand around her wrist. "Lex, I love you. I want *all* of this."

Lexi looked at him, feeling her eyes stinging. "You moved me in here so you'd have something you had control over. Then, I told you about my...kink...and that made it even better for you. I basically *begged* you to take that control." Her throat felt tight and she stood.

This time he let her.

"With what's going on with Shay, you have to face that you won't—can't—always be the one who does it all. For any of us. You have to accept that sometimes other people are better at taking care of things that you are. Until you do that, you won't be a *partner* to anyone. To me." She lifted her chin. "And I deserve someone who sees me as a partner. Someone who needs me, too. You can't control everything and you have to stop trying to."

C aleb thought that he couldn't feel worse than he had when he'd heard that Shay had a brain injury and he'd missed the signs.

He'd been wrong.

Looking at the hurt on Lexi's face now was way worse.

Because he was the cause of this.

He'd never hurt Lexi before. He'd very purposefully and consciously never hurt her. Making sure she was protected and happy had been one of his main focuses for two years.

Yes, he'd missed the indications that something was going on with Shay. No, he hadn't known the milestones she should be hitting, and wasn't. But her injury was not his fault.

Lexi's hurt was his fault.

He got to his feet, facing her, determined to make this right.

He reached out and she let him take her hand. "I'm *very* sorry, Lex. I was going to tell you. I just didn't know how, really. I wanted to reassure you. Maybe I shouldn't have, but that's my instinct. And I know this is all a shock. And there are a lot of questions about Shay and her future. And I don't have all the answers. But I can tell you that I'm trying. I'm reading. I'm—"

"Stop it." Her voice was quiet. And it sounded rough.

He realized her eyes were shimmering with tears.

He tugged her forward. "It will be ok—"

Lexi stiffened in his arms and put a hand on his chest, preventing him from hugging her. "*Stop*, Caleb."

He frowned. "Stop what?"

"Stop trying to make me feel better about Shay."

"But I want—"

"Making me feel better is not always your job." She narrowed her eyes. "And sometimes you can't do it. No matter how much you want to."

Caleb scowled. "I've always been able to before." God, he hoped that was true. That needed to be true.

She nodded. The rush of relief was ridiculously strong.

"But that's not always going to be the case. You need to come to terms with that."

The relief dried up instantly.

"Lex—"

She held up her hand, stopping him. "I'm not upset about Shay. Because she is exactly the same person she was yesterday, and last month, and when I met her. We already knew she had some trouble on that side. We already knew that she wasn't the most graceful child in the world. We already knew that she probably wasn't going to be a professional ballerina. Now we know why. But it doesn't really change anything. Except, because we know what's going on, we can also find things that might help her."

He stared at her. His heart was pounding and he felt a surge of hope warm his chest. "I guess that's true."

"And you can't focus on making *me* feel better because making me happy makes *you* happy. You have to let me...not be happy all the time. And you need to let yourself not always be the guy with the answers."

Caleb blinked at her. Lexi was disappointed in him. That thought wasn't exactly a revelation but it was something new. There had been very few times, if any really, when he could remember that being the case. He was a problem solver in her life. She looked up to him. But she thought he was handling this badly.

And she was probably right.

Had he moved her in here so he'd feel in charge of something? Yeah, kind of. He was thrilled she and Jack were here but yes, he'd overreacted that first night because of Shay. Had he pushed their relationship to the next level because he was entirely focused on making her happy and fulfilled because he *needed* someone to be happy and fulfilled because of him? Yeah, maybe.

It didn't change how he felt now. How great they were. How much he loved everything about their situation. How much he wanted it to keep going. Forever.

But maybe it hadn't started for the right reasons. He had a tendency to overreact when it came to his girls. He didn't regret it. But he could acknowledge it.

"I'm sorry, Lex," he finally said huskily. "I should have done it all differently."

"You said you trusted me to know what I could and couldn't handle. And to tell you if I got to that limit," she finally said. "I trusted *you* for that, too. You have to be able to tell me when you can't handle something."

"I've been in mourning, okay?" he finally snapped. He drew in a breath and shoved a hand through his hair. "I was dealing with the...loss." He blew out a breath. "I know that sounds horrible. But it was like when I heard"—he lowered his voice—"'brain injury', it was suddenly *for sure*, it was confirmed. She's going to have issues, Lex," he said, his voice raspy. "She's going to have trouble keeping up with the other kids, physically and in the classroom. And—" his chest was aching, "—I just want things to be easy for her. I just want things to be happy and good and perfect, and it seems like every time I go in to talk about answers and solutions, they tell me about a bunch more problems."

Lexi's expression didn't soften. "Your idea of happy and good and perfect isn't the only one, Caleb."

Suddenly he felt a jolt of anger. Dammit. He'd been trying to do right. He'd been dealing with something unlike anything he'd been through before. And Lexi clearly had no sympathy for that.

"So, I'm an asshole because I wish things were better for her? Because I'm sad about the things that she'll have to give up and struggle with?"

"This isn't about *you*," Lexi informed him. "You're feeling bad because someone else *is* working to fix this. The therapists, the doctors. There *is* a plan now but it's someone else's plan, not yours. You're going to need to trust that. Trust *them*. You're not in the driver's seat now. You now need to let someone else help her in a way that you can't."

In the back of his mind, Caleb recognized that not only was Lexi right, it was probably a good moment for growth of character for him, or some damned thing. But in the *front* of his mind was an instinct to resist all of it and insist he still knew best.

Which he very clearly did not.

"You hated therapy today because someone else was not only in charge, but because their plan included things that upset Shay. All of that goes against your view of the world where you are in charge and everything is nice and easy for her. But," Lexi added, her voice getting firmer, "she needs this. So you can handle it. You were able to handle doing things to me that went against your worldview, too. Because you realized it was good for me. That I needed it. This will be the same."

In the midst of her anger and hurt, she was still encouraging him.

The thought hit him square between the eyes. He loved her so fucking much.

"You're comparing her therapy with your kinks?" he asked.

"I'm comparing how *you're* handling those things," she said, refusing to let him lighten the tone. "Just because it's not something you came up with, doesn't mean that you can't be a big part of it. You can adjust how you think about what's good for Shay. And me."

He took a deep breath. And nodded. "I love you, Lex."

She gave him a look and said, "I love you, too. But I don't like you right now."

He deserved that. But his relief at her *I love* you was immense. He knew that arguments and disagreements and even hurting the other person's feelings didn't cancel love out. But he still loved hearing it. "We're okay then?"

She paused, then shook her head. "Not completely."

Caleb braced himself.

"We have to figure this out. For now, we need to go back to how things were before—our work schedules and sharing chores and stuff. And I'm going to start looking for an apartment."

"No."

"Yes."

He sucked in a breath. "I get to vet all apartments. If I don't like it, you don't move into it."

"And you think you're going to just say no on everything."

"Maybe."

"This isn't the way to convince me that you're serious about being partners and not always in charge."

He knew she loved him, but her being upset and disappointed in him was new. And he realized he could lose her.

"Lexi," he said, his voice low.

"Yes?"

"Take your clothes off."

She rolled her eyes.

He lifted a brow. "I have nipple clamps."

She gave him a look. "Caleb?"

"Yes?"

"Red."

Dammit.

He sat silently, watching as she moved toward the staircase. But at the bottom step she paused.

She looked over at him. "Did you know that Greg is a mechanic?"

Caleb frowned. "Your step-dad is a mechanic?"

She nodded. "Worked for a friend here and now has his own garage in Shreveport."

Caleb hadn't known that and he wasn't sure why she was telling him this now.

"When you first started fixing my car it was because I needed you to. I didn't have another option. But after Mom met Greg, he could have done it. I still kept asking you. Not because I needed it to be you, but because I wanted it to be you."

Caleb watched her ascend the stairs then, without waiting for him to respond.

Which was probably a good thing, considering he couldn't even take a deep breath after that.

12

"Well, you look like shit," Josh informed Caleb when he took a seat on one of the barstools at Trahan's.

"Don't Gabe and Logan *ever* work anymore?" Caleb groused.

Josh pushed a beer across the bar and grinned. "They've got hot girls at home to keep happy."

"I thought *you* had a hot girl at home to keep happy," Sawyer said.

Oh, great, this was just what he needed—to talk about all the ways he was *not* keeping Lexi happy.

He didn't want to talk about it. He was here only because he'd needed to get out of the house once Lexi went upstairs and got into the bathtub. At this very moment she was probably using the bubblegum shampoo that made him crazy. And she had specifically *not* invited him in to join her. But maybe these guys would have some advice.

She'd safe-worded him, for fuck's sake.

Dammit. He'd messed this all up so badly.

And yet, nothing was really messed up. Lexi was fine. She loved him. She was asking for a partnership, not a breakup. And Shay would be fine, too. Because she had a whole team of specialists working on a plan for her. A plan that he could be a part of and trust. With some help from Lexi.

He blew out a breath and took a drink of beer. "What are you doing here again?" he asked Sawyer.

Sawyer was nowhere near the regular that Owen was at Trahan's, but Caleb suspected that Sawyer got the same beer discount from Josh.

"Came to find out who told Stella that we hunt alligators."

Caleb's eyebrows rose and he swiveled toward the other man. "What?"

Sawyer nodded and pulled a new piece of paper out of his pocket. It was a hand-drawn picture of an alligator. A very angry-looking alligator. At the bottom was written *I don't want to marry you. Sincerely, Stella Ann Trahan.*

Caleb looked back up at Sawyer. "Sincerely, huh? Damn, you're in trouble."

Sawyer sighed. "Yep."

"Well, probably for the best. What with the whole twenty-four-year age difference and all."

"Not to mention that she really only wanted you for your airboat," Josh added.

Sawyer rolled his eyes. "Yeah."

Caleb narrowed his eyes at the other man. "But you're actually a little upset?"

Sawyer took a draw of his beer, then looked at Caleb. "There's just something about having a fan, you know? Kind of hurts falling off that pedestal."

Caleb felt a job in his chest. Damn. That was a little close to home. "Yeah, man, I get it."

"I know it's silly, but I feel like shit thinking that Stella is mad or disappointed in me." He tucked the note from Stella back in his pocket.

"For what it's worth, Gabe didn't tell her about the hunting trips," Josh told his brother. "Stella found it on our website. Gabe was talking about it yesterday. She was really upset."

Sawyer blew out a breath and lifted his beer again.

"What are you gonna do about it?" Caleb asked. What was a guy supposed to do when a girl had found out the guy wasn't as amazing as she's believed?

"Well, I don't have a lot of choices here," Sawyer said. "I *have* hunted alligators and I'm going to keep taking people out on hunting trips. I guess either Stella accepts me for who I am, or I accept that someone else is going to have to be Stella's hero."

Well, no one else was going to be Lexi's hero, Caleb thought immediately. But then he blew out a breath. What if Lexi couldn't accept him the way he was? Every overprotective, over-reactive, always-had-to-be-the-fixer inch of him?

He looked over at Sawyer. "I think there's another option."

"Yeah?"

"Yeah," Caleb said. "Compromise. *Try* to do what she needs you to do. At least some of the time." He wasn't going to be able to shut all of his protective instincts down. He would always want to do everything he could to keep Shay and Lexi and Jack safe and happy. But he could let Lexi in more often. And not always insist on doing things his way. She'd made up the bridge game. She'd come up with the memory exercises. He really should let her be a part of things. All the things.

Sawyer lifted a brow. "Uh, yeah. Okay. I could *try* to compromise to make Stella happy. Or," he added, with a shrug, "I could also remember that she's *seven* and not actually my fiancée. Or my boss."

"Yet, anyway," Josh added.

Sawyer lifted his glass in agreement. "Yet."

Okay, so Stella was seven and Sawyer didn't really owe her anything.

But Caleb owed Lexi...everything.

He set his beer down and looked at Sawyer. "Thanks, man."

"Glad I could help," Sawyer said dryly.

"And take pictures for me, okay?" Caleb asked, tossing a few bills on the bar for Josh.

"Pictures of what?"

"Stella protesting at Boys of the Bayou. I can already imagine her with her signs, marching up and down your dock."

Sawyer opened his mouth, but then closed it. Nodded. And sighed.

13

L exi glanced at her phone screen as she pulled a piece of jelly toast from Jack's pocket. The nice thing about bread was that it got harder the longer it was in his pocket, unlike so many other things he stuffed in there—like the raspberries from the other day.

She shuddered remembering it and wiped her hands on the bottom of one of Jack's T-shirts that was going in the laundry, too. She pushed the button to answer the call from Caleb.

He and Shay were out buying new shoes. Apparently she needed ones that were a little wider and laced up to accommodate the brace.

"Caleb? What's up?"

Things had been tense between them over the past couple of days, but he'd worked a twenty-four-hour shift yesterday, which had given them some space from one another.

If she moved into a new apartment, they would have space, of course, but she had yet to even open the newspaper to the apartment listings.

"Lex, I need you."

She immediately straightened. "What? Okay, what's going on?"

She heard him blow out a breath.

"I just...I can't do this. I need you here. Shay needs you."

"You can't buy shoes?" But she knew that wasn't what he was talking about. Somehow.

"The therapy. I can't make her do it."

"I'm on my way." She was already scooping Jack up from the playroom and was halfway across the living room, on her way to get *his* shoes. And she was going to ignore the fact that Jack's left pocket was squishing.

Fifteen minutes later, she was striding down the hallway of St. Michael's hospital toward the rehab department. Her heart was hammering and she was fighting the urge to run.

Caleb and Shay were here. They were unhappy. And she needed to get to them so she could fix it.

Was this how he'd felt when he'd found out that she'd moved out of her mom's and into the apartment? Because she got it now. She hated the idea that one or both of them weren't happy.

And Jack's right pocket was now crunching, she realized as she shifted him from her hip and set him on the floor. Good lord, had the kid found chips or crackers in the backseat of the car or something? But she couldn't worry about that right now.

As she approached the wide doorway at the end of the hallway, she could hear a little girl crying. And her heart stopped. Was that Shay? Lexi had never heard her cry like that. She sounded heartbroken.

Lexi felt protectiveness swell in her chest.

"Cab!" Jack crowed.

Lexi swung around. Caleb and Shay were walking toward them from the other direction.

Shay wasn't crying. She was carrying a juice box in one hand, her other securely in Caleb's.

Lexi made herself breathe. She and Jack met them halfway down the hall.

Jack squirmed in her arms. "Cab!"

"Lexi!" Shay exclaimed, noticing them for the first time.

"Hi, Shay-Shay."

"Why are you here?"

"Because I wanted to play with you," Lexi said.

Shay frowned. "I'm not playing."

Lexi focused on Caleb. He looked tired. But he also looked hopeful.

"Hi," he said.

"Hi. I thought you were in therapy."

"I pulled her out."

Lexi sighed. "You can't do that, Caleb. She needs this."

"I know." He paused. "I didn't want you to think I was just asking you to come to make up for everything else. I needed you to know that...I really needed you."

She gave him a smile that she knew was full of love and exasperation. "I do know that. I know therapy is hard on you. I wanted to bust in and take over way before this, but I needed you to... initiate this."

His eyes flickered with understanding when she used the word they'd used discussing the balance of power in their sex life. "Please," he said. "Please take this over."

"Okay. What's your safe word?"

His eyebrows went up. "I need a safe word?"

"For when I'm going too far, pushing too hard to be in charge, not letting you in, making you uncomfortable with any of this."

The corner of his mouth curled up. "Red has been working well for us. And, not everything has to be green or red between us. Sometimes it can be yellow, right? Proceed with caution? Things are still okay, but we could get to a point where we have to talk about things and adjust."

She smiled. He was getting it. He might not totally change,

but, like Bea, he was figuring out when he needed to make a phone call to someone else. "Absolutely things can be yellow between us sometimes."

"I'm relieved you're here. I'm not going to lie. If I had to, I could do this, but I love that I don't have to." He paused. "Thank you for that."

She nodded. "I was just waiting for this phone call."

He took a big, almost contented breath, and Lexi felt a surge of happiness knowing that she was making him feel better. This had to be how he felt when he fixed things for her. Yeah, she could understand how this could be addictive. "And now," she said, turning her attention on the little girl that needed her. "We have a play date."

"Okay!" Shay took Lexi's offered hand and they started toward the therapy department.

But as they neared the door, Shay started to resist. "No, I don't want to do therapy."

Lexi stopped and crouched so she was even with Shay. "I know. But I'm going to make it better. I *promise*."

Shay looked at her with a worried, sad expression.

"Shay, do you trust me?" Lexi asked.

"Yes," Shay finally said.

Lexi felt her breath whoosh out. Damn, that really was powerful. "Okay, then come with me. Let me show you that this can be okay."

She wasn't sure how she was going to do that yet, but she would. She had to.

"No." Shay shook her head emphatically. "It's not fun."

"I'm sorry, sweetie," Lexi said honestly. "How about we just talk for a little bit?"

"Okay."

She lifted Shay and headed into the therapy department. One of the therapists saw them and started in their direction.

"Hi, Lexi. Hi, Shay."

"Can we try it again?" Lexi asked. "We're...adjusting. But we want this to work." She looked at Shay. "Right?"

Shay nodded. But she didn't look convinced.

Lexi glanced back at Caleb. He and Jack were nowhere to be found.

She shook her head with a smile. She was glad he'd taken the opportunity to get a break. She could totally handle this and she loved that he knew that.

Lexi, Shay and Beth sat down on a squishy pink mat on the floor. And talked. Beth reviewed a lot of what Lexi had gotten from Caleb and assumed from her own knowledge. But Beth filled in gaps. Like which part of Shay's brain was affected and to what degree. The things she *could* do as well as the challenges. Lexi hadn't known that Shay was supposed to be able to balance on one leg for five seconds and should be able to walk toe-to-toe.

Bottom line was that Shay hated the brace. It felt funny and it didn't let her ankle move freely and it made it harder for her to walk. For now. But it was hard to reason with a four-year-old on a good day, and today was clearly not a good day.

"So her walking won't get completely better without the brace, right?" Lexi asked.

"Not entirely, no. The weakness and foot drop will still be an issue even with strengthening and practice. The brace will be really important for her safety."

Lexi pulled in a long breath. Okay, well, if Shay needed a brace, she needed a brace. If it kept her from falling and prevented some sore knees, then they needed to get her into it sooner versus later.

"Hey, Shay, tell me about this." Lexi picked up the brace and looked it over. It was a piece of thick plastic that was shaped like an L. There was a hinge between the long piece and the shorter piece. Lexi assumed the long piece went behind Shay's calf and the shorter fit under her foot, keeping it up and preventing her from tripping.

Shay scowled at it. "No."

"What's it for?" Lexi asked.

Shay shrugged.

"It's supposed to make you walk better, right?"

"I don't like it."

Lexi nodded. "Okay. Tell me why."

"It doesn't feel good."

"Huh." Lexi slid her shoe off and fit the brace against her own foot. It was too small and she was holding it upside down on purpose. "Yeah," she agreed. "That's not comfortable at all." Shay made no move to help Lexi put the brace on correctly.

Beth smiled. "We can pad it and we can get it in fun colors."

"What colors?" Lexi asked.

Shay looked at Beth for the first time since they'd sat down.

"Any color. Or we can do a whole rainbow of colors. Stripes maybe?" Beth said. "Or a zebra print."

"Wow." Lex was actually impressed. "Well, that would help, wouldn't it, Shay?"

"This is just the practice one," Beth said. "We're getting it adjusted correctly and getting Shay used to it. She's supposed to take it home and work with it."

"Okay." Lexi leaned and looked down at Shay. "You know, I get why this isn't fun."

Shay sniffed and nodded.

Lexi lifted Shay out of her lap and turned her so they were eye to eye. "I don't like it, either. I wish you didn't have to have this. But I also don't like it when you fall down. It makes me sad when you hit your knees and makes me worry that you're going to get hurt."

Shay's bottom lip protruded.

"You know what else I don't like?" Lexi asked. "When I have to wear my glasses to read my books." She gave Shay a smile. "But I *really* like to read. So, even if I don't like the glasses, I would be way sadder if I had to give up stories, so I'm going to keep wearing them."

Shay didn't react, but she was listening.

"I also have to take medicine before I go on a long trip because my stomach gets upset. I don't like the way the trips make me feel, but I love going to new places."

Shay frowned. "Your tummy hurts on trips?"

"Yep."

"Do you know that I love to play volleyball?" Beth asked. "But I have to wear a brace or my shoulder really hurts."

Lexi gave her a surprised—and grateful—smile.

Shay twisted to look at the therapist. "Really?"

"Really."

"See, sometimes to do fun stuff, we have to use things that help us do them safely or even better than we can do them without glasses and medicine and braces," Lexi said.

Shay seemed to be thinking about all of that. Lexi and Beth just let her process it all.

"Can I have kitties?" she finally asked.

Beth looked at Lexi. "Kitties?"

"You want a kitty?" Lexi asked. Of course she did.

"On the brace," Shay said.

Lexi grinned, a little relieved. She figured at some point they would have cats, but it would be great if the kids were a little older first. "Oh, for sure."

"Um, we don't have any with cats on them," Beth said apologetically.

"We can paint them on," Lexi said, running her fingers over the plastic of the brace. "I'm sure craft paint would work on these." She looked up at Shay. "Maybe Lauren would paint them for us," she said as the thought occurred.

"Lauren could paint my braces?" Shay asked with wide eyes.

Lexi didn't even mind that the idea of having Lauren involved clearly made the braces a much better option. She loved this idea.

"That way you can *keep* those kitty pictures. You always have to wash the face paint off, but this way you could have them always."

"Okay."

It was the closest Shay had been to enthusiastic all day.

"What color do you want? Maybe black? Lauren can paint a white kitty face then?" She certainly hoped Lauren would be up for this. But she had seen the other woman interacting with Shay and Jack. It was clear they were special to her, and Lexi was sure she'd help Shay out this way.

That warmed her heart as she thought about it. No one would love Jack and Shay as much as Lexi and Caleb did, but it was amazing to think about all of the people who cared about them.

"White," Shay said. "I want a black kitty and a brown one and an orange one and a gray one. And a tiger. And a cougar."

Lexi laughed. "Well, of course."

"Can I keep this one?" Shay asked Beth. She reached for the brace in Lexi's hand and started to put it against her leg.

"Sure," Beth said. "You can keep that one *and* we'll get the permanent one."

"Perfect," Lexi told her. "Then Jack can have this one once your official one comes." No doubt Jack would want to have a brace of his own. "Jack is going to think this is really cool."

Shay was already trying to strap the brace to her leg. Beth leaned over and helped her, showing her how to slide the strap through the metal square and how to tighten it. They got her shoe on and got her on her feet.

Shay still didn't like it, but it was less obvious. She kept it on. For about ten minutes. Then she sat down, pulled it off and said, "I'm done."

Beth nodded. "Okay. That was a good start."

"That was enough?" Lexi asked.

"Definitely. We work up to longer wear times. And eventually she'll see it really is easier to do some of the things she loves with the brace on."

"Wonderful."

They discussed the physical therapy schedule. And the occupational therapy schedule. And the speech therapy schedule. As well as the things they could and should work on at home.

It was a lot. Lexi felt more than a little overwhelmed. She really just wanted to take Shay home and snuggle with her on the couch and watch cartoons and eat fruit snacks and pretend that everything was exactly the way it had been two weeks ago.

But she realized that the way it had been two weeks ago was really only in her mind. All of this had been there then, too. They just hadn't known it. And knowing it now might add some appointments and a brace to Shay's life, but the cuddles and cartoons and snacks would be the same.

She also realized that not only was Caleb feeling overwhelmed, she knew he was feeling guilty that Shay was struggling and that he couldn't snap his fingers and fix it. She knew him. She knew this was killing him.

She wanted to go and hold him.

She also wanted to punch him in the face for not asking her to come sooner.

She supposed that pretty much summed up what being in love was all about.

———

Caleb and Jack had hung out in the hospital for a few minutes after Lexi arrived.

But he'd already been feeling claustrophobic and restless. That didn't improve much when Lexi showed up. So he'd headed out.

He'd texted her, *we'll see you at home.* And then he and Jack had gone for ice cream.

Because he didn't need to be at the hospital. Lexi was there with Shay. And she was a hell of a lot better at all of that than he was.

He was going to beg her to continue being the therapy parent. If begging didn't work, he would tie her to his bed and tease her with almost-orgasms until she agreed.

He really hoped that his initial begging wouldn't work.

By the time Lexi and Shay came through the front door, Caleb had spaghetti sauce simmering and was in the middle of salad prep.

"Hi."

He braced his hands on the countertop and looked Lexi over, feeling a combination of love, relief, hope, and bone-deep happiness course through him. "Hi."

She looked gorgeous. And a little tired. The kind of tired that he could completely relate to. The tired that came from putting Shay through her paces in therapy. It was harrowing to watch her struggle. But at the same time, there was that glow. That glow that he saw in her when she'd come home from a shift in the ER.

"I'm going to keep doing the therapy thing," she said.

"That is the best thing you could have said to me," he told her honestly.

"And in exchange…"

His body hardened thinking about all of the ways he'd be happy to pay this back.

"You get to figure out a way to keep Jack from putting food in his pockets."

Oh. Yeah, that wasn't nearly as fun.

"I could come up with some *other* ways to—"

"Partners," she said. "Partners in parenting. Equal."

"Of course. But I could—"

"Not in the bedroom."

He felt his eyebrows go up. "No?"

"Nope. In there, you're totally in charge."

"I'm completely okay with that," he told her honestly.

"But nowhere else."

He nodded. "Okay."

"So I want to talk about leasing a new apartment."

No. But he didn't say it out loud. If she still thought she should move out so they could figure out the partner stuff, then she'd move out. He'd move Jack's bed into the new place himself. And then he'd work like hell to prove to her that *this* was where she belonged.

He waited. She pulled the newspaper out of her purse and slid her glasses onto her nose.

Caleb felt his cock harden. Damn, he really liked that nerdy hot look.

"There are simply no other apartments available with all the things I need." She looked up through her glasses. "Can you believe that *none* of them come with a sweet little girl, a stash of coconut crunch donuts, or a hot, dirty-talking firefighter? I mean, where do they expect a girl like me to live, anyway?"

"That's definitely a problem," he said with a nod.

"So I'm thinking that maybe I just need to stay here."

"Huh. Interesting." He moved around the kitchen island. "Is now a good time to tell you that the rent is going up here?"

She made her eyes round. "Oh, no. How will I afford it?"

"Your dirty building manager will discuss payment plans with you tomorrow night."

"Tomorrow? Not tonight?"

He took her glasses from her fingers. "Tonight, your favorite professor is going to give you a chance at a very special extra credit assignment."

"Oh? You like these glasses?"

He moved in, nearly on top of her and said roughly, "When you wear those glasses it makes me want to bend you over my desk and spank you with a ruler before making you write *I love big cock* one hundred times while I eat your pussy. Of course, you have to finish the assignment before I let you come."

She was breathing fast as she took the glasses from him, put them on and pushed them up her nose. She looked up at him. "Duly noted, Professor Moreau."

"Detention starts at nine," he nearly growled, his entire body hard. "Don't be late."

"Of course not. I just hope I have time to find my plaid skirt and Mary Janes."

"Put your hair in a ponytail, too."

"Yes, Sir." She gave him a sassy smile, then turned and called, "Kids! Dinner time!"

A date for hot role-playing sex after dinner and story time with their kids.

He loved his life.

———

Six months later

T he music swelled and Caleb turned to face the doorway in the community center where Lexi would be entering.

The place looked nothing like the room where the support group met every week.

There were white flowers and tall candelabras everywhere. Rows of chairs draped in white and tied with big white bows filled the room and held every person that he loved in the world. His parents were in the front row with Amber and Greg. The rest of the chairs were filled with the members of the support group and all of the firefighters from Engine 29 as well as all of the St. Michael's ER staff that could get off work. A white silk runner led from the main doors to the wooden arch where Caleb stood, in a tuxedo, with James at his side.

Ashley, their maid of honor, was at the back of the room, whispering to Shay and Jack.

Caleb felt his chest swell with pride and love as they started down the makeshift aisle.

"Is Jack *growling*?" James asked him after they'd taken a few steps.

Caleb chuckled. "Yep."

"Because?"

"He's the ring bear."

James thought about that and then grinned. "Of course he is."

Jack stopped next to Logan and not only growled but also curled his paw and swiped his claws at Logan. Logan recoiled in mock terror and Jack grinned before continuing up the aisle, looking entirely too pleased about his role in the wedding. He went to sit next to his grandfather until they needed the ring. Caleb gave him a big thumbs-up. Then he focused on Shay.

Shay was walking down the aisle with her brace on her left foot. She was doing great. Her gait pattern—according to Lexi, who said it was according to the therapists—was much improved.

But, just as he thought everything was going to go off without a glitch, Shay stopped. And sat down.

She tugged her shoe off, unstrapped her brace, and took it off. "I'm done," she announced.

Caleb blew out a breath. He didn't care, of course. The room was full of people who loved Shay no matter if she was wearing a brace. Or not. But he'd kind of hoped this would be the first time Shay wore the thing as long as she was supposed to.

He started to take a step toward Shay, but before he'd even shifted his weight fully, Lexi appeared at the back of the room.

She headed down the aisle in front of her maid of honor and was already to Shay before Caleb was even able to recover from seeing her in her wedding dress.

She was stunning. Her shoulders were bare and the bodice of the gown clung to her breasts—his favorite of her curves, though he really loved them all—showing a lot of delicious cleavage. The skirt flared just below her hips and Ashley rushed to pick up her train as it dragged behind her.

Unconcerned about her dress, Lexi knelt next to Shay, talking softly. Shay handed her the brace and Lexi stood, picking Shay up in her arms.

And that was how his bride approached him. Love shining in her eyes and his niece in her arms.

"Well, we almost made it," he said, kissing Shay's head, then taking her from Lexi and setting her down.

"Sometimes we all need to be carried part of the way, right?" Lexi asked him.

Love welled up inside him and he grabbed her hand, pulling her close.

"Hang on there," the minister said, clearly reading Caleb's intentions. "We've got some vows to say first."

Caleb gave a little growl, his eyes never leaving Lexi. "Okay, but let's get going."

Everyone laughed and Caleb and Lexi turned to face the man who would make their marriage official.

They went through everything they'd rehearsed and then it was time for the rings.

"You're up, buddy," Caleb said to Jack.

The little boy hopped up from his chair and came forward, digging in his pocket for the rings.

He produced them a moment later.

Covered in peanut butter.

Lexi and Caleb looked from the rings in Jack's palm to one another and burst out laughing.

"The snack holes are a work in progress," Caleb said with a half smile.

Lexi watched him take an offered tissue from his mother and

wipe the rings clean. Or as clean as they could get them at the moment.

As he slid the sticky diamond onto her finger, she looked up at him. "Life will always be a work in progress. But it's *our* work in progress. For better or worse, in sickness and in health, with leg braces or peanut butter, for as long as we both shall live."

Caleb cupped the back of her head and leaned in, but with his lips still a few centimeters from hers he said, "Come on, say it, Padre."

The minister sighed. "You may now kiss your bride."

And he did. Nice and slow and easy.

Thank you so much for reading Caleb and Lexi's story! I hope you loved Nice and Easy!

There is so much more coming from the
Boys of the Big Easy!

Up next is James and Harper's story,
Getting Off Easy!

New Orleans firefighter, James Reynaud's true love is hanging out in the jazz clubs on Frenchmen Street and playing piano with some of the best musicians in the city. But driving his cute, bookworm neighbor Harper Broussard crazy is right up there on his list of favorite things.

The buttoned-up linguistics professor is a little older, a lot smarter, and way too good for him. And she knows it. But wow is she beautiful when she blushes.

She's equally gorgeous when she's saving his ass. Because now things just got serious. A baby has been, literally, dropped off on his doorstep and to say he's in over his head is an understatement. Not that Harper knows anything about babies either. But at least they now have something in common.

————

And don't miss the **FREE series prequel novella, Easy Going!**

————

Read on for an excerpt from
Easy Going, the free series prequel!

EASY GOING

A sexy, New Orleans bartender.
A little jazz. A few beignets.
And ONE very hot weekend.

Just one.

Supposedly.

———

Excerpt

"What can I get you?" Then he glanced at Addison. "And please don't say a hurricane." He gave her a wink.

She smiled. "You don't know how to make a hurricane?"

He chuckled. "You can't get your liquor license in New Orleans without proving you know how to make a hurricane." The drink had been invented at one of the most famous bars in the Quarter,

Pat O'Brien's, and they served them by the gallons over there. But they didn't make the best ones. Several places served them and a few even did it pretty well. Pierre Maspero's, for instance. But no one could touch the recipe Ellie Landry used at her tiny dive bar just outside the bayou town of Autre, Louisiana.

So Gabe didn't even try.

"If you want a hurricane, I'll take you to the best place for them in Louisiana," he said. Though why he'd said "take you" instead of "send you," he wasn't sure. "Just like if you want gumbo, I won't serve it to you, because if you're gonna eat gumbo, you're gonna do it right and that means havin' my grandma's. Now," he said, taking out a glass and filling it part-way with lemonade. "If you want a Pimm's cup that will make you wonder how you ever drank anything else, or seafood pot pie that you'll dream about, or brown butter pecan pie that you'll want to roll around in, then you've come to the right place."

Addison looked at Elena with wide eyes. "Brown butter pecan pie?"

Elena laughed. "Yeah. And it's that good. It's how Gabe and Logan get all the ladies."

Addison looked back at Gabe. She lifted a brow. "Which one are you?"

"Gabe." He pointed behind her. "That's my brother Logan."

Addison glanced over to where Logan was setting plates of food down in front of customers. She looked back. "You both need pie to get ladies?"

"No one said *need*," he told her with a grin.

"What do you know about pralines?"

"I can make you a praline milkshake that will make you want to propose to me," he told her honestly.

"Huh. What's in that?"

Playful. That was exactly his impression of her from the texts, and he couldn't begin to describe how amazing it was to find out she was the same in person. "Whiskey, caramel, ice cream and—"

"Say no more," she said. "I want that."

"You got a ring in your pocket?" he asked.

She laughed. "Maybe we New York girls are harder to impress than the girls you've been feeding whiskey to."

Grab Easy Going right now!

ABOUT THE AUTHOR

Erin Nicholas is the New York Times and USA Today bestselling author of over thirty sexy contemporary romances. Her stories have been described as toe-curling, enchanting, steamy and fun. She loves to write about reluctant heroes, imperfect heroines and happily ever afters. She lives in the Midwest with her husband who only wants to read the sex scenes in her books, her kids who will never read the sex scenes in her books, and family and friends who say they're shocked by the sex scenes in her books (yeah, right!).

Find her and all her books at
www.ErinNicholas.com

And find her on Facebook, BookBub, and Instagram!

BOYS OF THE BIG EASY